A FORGIVING HEART

A Forgiving Heart

KASEY STOCKTON

GOLDEN OWL PRESS

For those who've felt the comfort of forgiveness

KATE

*T*he sun shone on nine-year-old Kate's pale skin and warmed her soul as thoroughly as it did her body. The empty basket swung from her fingertips as she strolled along the open country lane, relishing the solitary freedom and keeping an eye out for the split tree she had overheard Uncle's servants talk about.

She needed to hurry. If Uncle knew she was outside unaccompanied and not locked in that wretched schoolroom upstairs with nasty Mrs. Herman, he would take a switch to her backside in a heartbeat. She'd learned that the hard way when she first came to Split Tree Manor six weeks ago.

Six weeks. Longer than a month since she'd felt the sun on her skin or breathed crisp, clean air outside. For a child so used to playing out of doors when the chores were finished, Uncle's strict rules forbidding Kate to leave the house were nearly tortuous. And this momentary reprieve, her clean escape after Mrs. Herman fell asleep in the middle of the afternoon, was a balm. She drew in a deep breath. Whatever punishment awaited her return was worth this gulp of fresh air.

A stilted bird call sounded in the distance and wind rustled through the tall grass, but all thoughts of wildlife and scenery left Kate when the infamous split tree came into sight. There, off to the right of the lane was the glorious tree, with not one but *two* trunks shooting out of the base in a slight "v" forma- tion. Kate gawked up at the biological marvel. She hadn't seen anything quite so amazing in all of her nine years.

Removing the small, blank book from her apron pocket, Kate sketched a rough picture of the tree before including the rolling hills behind it and the country lane beside. She added in the plump blackberry bushes on the opposite side of the road before closing her book and tucking her lead pencil into her hair.

Scooping up the empty basket, Kate skipped over to the blackberry bushes and gathered as many berries as she could without staining her dress. She was faintly aware of the sun moving along the sky, but the berries were so ripe and juicy, more of them were making their way into her mouth than into the basket. Glancing over her shoulder, she drew in a quick breath, noticing how low the sun had fallen.

She needed to return to Split Tree Manor, and fast. Uncle never allowed her to leave the house, and if he noticed she was missing, she would certainly regret it.

Turning back for the lane, Kate heard the same bird call she'd heard before followed by a chorus of laughter. It sounded like boys, but could it be children? Perhaps there was another girl her own age who lived nearby.

Was there time to investigate? Her gaze dragged from the lane which led back to Split Tree Manor to the woods just beyond the hedge of blackberry bushes. The thick copse of trees beckoned her with their intrigue, dim and deep.

Curiosity ever her downfall, Kate tucked the basket neatly under the bushes before tiptoeing into the dense forest. She could be quick about it. The bird call sounded again, followed by more laughter, and Kate took careful, soft steps toward the noises.

The less muffled the sounds became, the quieter Kate made herself. Two boys appeared on the bank of a small creek, a few years her senior, at least. Crouching behind a green bush littered with small, purple berries, Kate peeked through the leaves to watch them. She swallowed hard at the sight of the boys, quite savage with their shirts stripped off and cases of arrows slung over their bare shoulders. They took turns shooting at a birch tree and missing by a large margin.

Pulling back on his arrow, one of the boys tilted it higher, shooting it to the uppermost branches. Losing the arrow among the branches, he scowled, and Kate squinted to see better through the bush.

A faint bird call floated through the air, followed by tiny baby bird chirps. Mocking calls made by one of the savage boys met her ears and she shivered. They docked more arrows and aimed them at the nest.

What animals!

Kate stood to intercede, indignation coursing through her, when something fell on the top of her head. She rubbed her skull, lifting the piece of tree bark that had fallen on her and tossing it aside.

The larger of the two golden-haired savages was aiming his arrow once again. How could he purposefully hurt a nest of baby birds? She opened her mouth to call to him when she was pelted with multiple pieces of tree bark.

That was no accident.

Kate looked up this time, sweeping her gaze over the tree. She saw nothing but a canopy of tree leaves and branches. Shaking her head to loosen any remaining bark, she took a step away from the bush and collapsed when something hard hit her square between the shoulders. *Ouch.* That was certainly too hard to be tree bark.

Sprawled on her hands and knees, she scrambled to her feet and cringed at the mud smeared across her pinafore. There would be no hiding this mess from Uncle. She searched the branches above her, shielding her eyes from more falling debris. They appeared empty.

Another horrid attempt at a bird call pulled her attention toward the savage boys. She had to do something.

A quiet whistle reached her, and she whipped her head up again. A small hand waved from within the branches nearly at the top of the tree. She couldn't quite make out anything beyond the waving hand at first, but her eyes focused, and she narrowed her gaze on brown breeches and a shoeless foot dangling from a high branch.

A boy hid, perched in the branches, his thin face angled toward her, eyes wide with fright. Was he afraid of the savages, or afraid *for* Kate? Regardless, the magnitude of his fear was warning enough for her, and she crouched down behind the bush once again, watching helplessly as the two older boys shot arrow after arrow at the poor defenseless bird and her chicks.

Time stretched slowly, dragging on before the boys ran out of arrows. Instead of gathering what they had shot, they discarded their weapons, pulled shirts over their heads and turned to walk away from the scene—and directly toward Kate.

She looked up to the branches. The shoeless boy put a single finger up to his lips, and she nodded. It would be a mistake to call out, but she desperately wanted to ask why he was hiding. Would the boys hurt him if they found him? Would they hurt *her*?

Crouching lower into the bush, she squeezed her eyes shut as the sound of boots crunching twigs grew steadily louder in her ears.

"Charles, take a look," a voice said directly beside her.

Her shoulders jerked in surprise, startled to hear the refined accent of the upper class on so savage a boy. But a peek at the blond boys' clothing revealed quality fabric and well cared for boots. Though, the credit for the shine to the boots likely went to their servants.

Kate shuddered before peeking into the face of the one called Charles and immediately wished she hadn't. His expression was a display of mild curiosity, but within his eyes was a gleam which she recognized from Uncle.

Hate.

"I see," Charles said in an uncomfortably tranquil tone. "Looks like we've found a lost little girl in need of a helping hand. Shall we help her?"

"I'm not lost," Kate said belligerently before snapping her mouth closed. If Uncle's switch had taught her anything, it was that talking back only made things worse.

The savages looked at one another in silent conversation before narrowing in on her once again.

Charles, obviously the leader, said, "You're on our land. Do you know what the penalty is for trespassing, little girl?"

Kate tried not to cringe as Charles's breath washed over her face. He had evidently eaten fish and had chosen to skip cleaning his teeth afterward. She edged back into the bush as far as she could but immediately saw the mistake of boxing herself in. Quick thinking had always been Kate's saving attribute, and she glanced around to see what she had at her disposal. Her small fingers felt behind her until they closed around a shoe.

It took all of her self-control not to glance up at the boy in the branches and his stockinged foot. This must be his shoe; it was too random, otherwise. She wanted to commend his quick thinking, for he must have tossed the shoe at Kate when the bark hadn't done the trick.

Taking a quick glance behind the boys, she routed her escape, and with an arm quick as lightning, she flung the shoe into Charles's face and took off in the direction of the blackberry bushes.

Footsteps thundered behind her, and Kate hiked up her skirt

to run faster, zigzagging a path through the woods. She glanced over her shoulder to gauge her attackers' distance and before she knew it, her foot snagged on a root, the ground rushing up and colliding with the side of her head.

Pushing up from the dirt forest floor, she groaned. Her ears rang, and the entire left side of her face throbbed where dirt and small rocks had scraped it raw. Something warm and wet dripped into her eye, but she wiped it with her sleeve and tried not to panic at the sight of blood.

The pounding grew louder as she pushed herself into a seated position.

"Grab her!" Charles yelled as his minion crashed toward her. The other boy came behind and grabbed both of her arms, yanking her to stand and pinning her hands behind her back.

She winced when Charles stepped up to her, holding the shoe she'd thrown in his face. Looking Charles in the eye, she swallowed a smile. A faint blue bruise was already beginning between his nose and right eye, and Kate imagined it would only grow with time.

"Where is he?" Charles asked through his teeth, his face distorted in anger.

Kate swallowed. She glanced at the empty forest on either side of Charles before trying to look over her shoulder at the boy who held her back.

"Not my brother, you nitwit," Charles said in exasperation. He held up the shoe and spoke again, enunciating each word laced with anger. "Where is *he*?"

Realization dawned. He was asking about the little boy hiding in the tree. Kate lifted her chin. "I have no idea what you're talking about."

Charles's minion tightened his hold on her arms, and she cried out.

"Tell me where the little brat is!" Charles shouted.

Kate dropped her head to protect herself in what little way

she could. She wasn't quick enough, for Charles pelted the shoe at her stomach and she let out a cry that reverberated among the trees.

Kate felt the slightest slack of the minion's hold on her arms. "Charles, maybe we should—" His voice just behind her ear was softer than she'd expected. She wanted to turn around and look in his eyes, to see if they held the same hate as his brother's.

"No," Charles cut him off, his voice steel. "I will find him."

Kate was terrified, but not for herself. She had lived through her share of bullying and was tough enough to get through this. She was worried for the boy. She hadn't gotten a good look at him, but she'd seen that he was scrawny. A few good knocks from these larger boys and he'd be done in.

"You mean that little boy?" Kate said, breath heaving as she formulated a plan.

The minion stilled behind her, but she kept going. "The scrawny one, right?" Her gut roiled from bad-mouthing the boy, thus placing herself in league with the bullies. But this was the only way. "I saw him picking berries out by that weird tree. You know the one?"

"Yeah. Split Tree." Charles nodded, too dumb to realize she was misleading him completely.

"Right. The split tree."

"Well, go on," Charles bellowed.

Kate tried to look over her shoulder again, but Charles's brother wouldn't slacken his hold on her arms. She swallowed and kept going, trying to sound as tough as the older girls she used to share a room with at the parish orphanage. "The little runt was eating the berries I picked so I pummeled him. I took his shoes for sport and threw one of them in the stream."

A sick smile tilted Charles's lips, and he locked eyes with his brother above her head. When he turned his attention back on Kate, she felt like she might vomit. "Where is he now?" Charles asked.

She tried to shrug. "I left him cryin' by the berries last I know. Not too long ago, either."

Charles flicked his head to indicate they should take off.

Kate rolled her shoulders once she was released. She watched their burly forms head toward Split Tree and the blackberry bushes. The minion brother glanced over his shoulder and held her gaze. She was correct—he didn't have the same evil in his blue-gray eyes. But regardless, she wouldn't back down to a bully. She stood tall, watching him until he looked away.

A long sigh escaped her throat before a shudder joined it. She froze when Charles paused and turned back to her.

"How do we know you aren't lying?"

She pointed to the shoe lying on its side amidst the stones and twigs and lifted a tiny eyebrow. "How else would I have that?"

He seemed to accept this and jogged away, his brother falling in behind him.

As soon as the savages were out of sight, Kate picked up the shoe and sprinted back to where she had last seen the boy up in the tree. She made it to the stream and searched the foliage. He was either very good at blending in, or he was gone.

"Thank you."

Kate was startled by the voice behind her and spun around, ready to strike with the shoe once again. She let out a pent-up breath when she laid eyes on the sandy-haired boy before tossing his shoe to him.

"It was nothing," she said with a shrug.

His face was serious. "Not to me, it wasn't."

She smiled at him and tried to laugh, his somber tone leaving her uneasy. "They were just bullies."

The boy looked past her to where the others had retreated and then focused on her face. "Come to the water and I'll clean you up."

"There is no need," Kate said, shaking her head. "I've got to return before my uncle finds me missing or I'll be back on chimney duty." She shuddered. She needed to somehow burn her dress and create a new one, too. She didn't have any more time to waste.

The boy nodded in understanding. "Bullies are everywhere, aren't they?"

She didn't know how to respond to this. It was true for her, but she somehow didn't think the boy needed an answer. And she still had to find a way back to Split Tree Manor without going by the split tree or the blackberry bushes. She turned to leave, but the boy's hand shot out and stopped her.

His gaze locked on her, rooting her to the spot. "Someday I will repay you for what you did for me."

Kate scanned his face, trying to read through the intent and seriousness that belied his tender years. He had to be her age, at least, but he spoke so desperately.

She nodded slowly until he released her arm. Then she ran for the edge of the woods.

activity as she neared the lawns in front of the school that were overrun with townsfolk setting up booths and preparing for their games. The social on the morrow was held annually by the school as a fundraising opportunity to assist those girls that could not afford full tuition, and it was a cause dear to Kate's heart. One of Kate's first and dearest friends from Lytle's School for Girls had been one of the scholarship students. And though Emily was off using her hard-learned manners and propriety in London's ballrooms, they had remained close friends.

The sticky syrup dripped down her fingers, and she tossed the plum pit into the slop bucket beside the back-kitchen door before doing her best to wipe her hand on her dirty apron.

"Now you set those plums down just on the table there and wash up," Mrs. James said as she rolled out some kind of pastry dough on her worktable. Her youthful cheeks were rosy from exertion that caused her freckles to stand out all the more, and wisps of red hair escaped her cap to trail along her brow and neck. She wasn't much older than Kate herself, but she sure could bake a grand pheasant pie. "Mrs. Presley was in here asking 'bout you not ten minutes ago, so you best be getting yourself upstairs now."

"Yes ma'am," Kate said with a wink and a curtsy. She skirted the worktable as best she could but still felt the faint swat from the rolling pin on her behind.

Racing up the stairs to the staff bedrooms, she quickly removed her apron and hung it on a peg beside her door before pouring cold water into the basin on her washstand and cleaning her hands and face. Aside from one drip of plum juice on her collar, she was otherwise spotless, the apron having taken the brunt of the fruit-picking dirt, and she deemed herself acceptable to meet with Mrs. Presley before dinner.

On the landing outside of her room, Kate nearly ran into Lissie, the chambermaid for the teachers' rooms, and quickly stepped back again.

"Sorry, ma'am." Lissie bobbed a quick curtsy. "Mrs. Presley is waiting on you in her office. You've got a visitor."

Kate had started toward the headmistress's office but stopped short and spun back to the maid, her mouth going slack. "A visitor?"

"Yes'm. A handsome one too, if you don't mind my saying," Lissie added with a little grin. Kate absentmindedly shook her head and turned back toward the office, but her feet were fastened in place as though by paste. In her eight years at Lytle's School for Girls, she had not once received a visitor. Not *once*. Even when Uncle had revoked his financial support upon her completion, he had delivered the news via note. The footman who had brought it from Split Tree Manor had not even felt the need to wait around until the note was in the proper hands.

"Right, then." Kate took a deep breath and flurried down the stairs.

The man standing in Mrs. Presley's office with his hands clasped behind his back and his mustache carefully groomed was not what Kate would consider particularly handsome. He was not an ugly fellow by any means. His nose was straight and not overly large, and his wide eyes were a fair brown color. But his hair was too severe and his features too stiff. He seemed the preacher or lawyer type that didn't smile often, and a face unused to smiling was not, in Kate's opinion, a handsome one. With slight disappointment, she walked into the room after knocking lightly on the door.

"Miss Kingston, please come in." Mrs. Presley gestured to the open seat across from her desk. Kate swept into the room and stood behind the chair with a healthy dose of uncertainty. With the stranger standing so tall beside her, she felt uneasy. Mrs. Presley soon took care of that situation as school headmistresses are easily capable of doing. "This is Mr. Montgomery, and he has come to see you on a matter of business." Folding her hands together, she asked primly, "Shall I give you the room?"

Kate gave her a beseeching glance. Was it childish to not want to meet with this man alone? For propriety's sake alone, Mrs. Presley ought to stay.

"Or perhaps," Mrs. Presley said as she walked around her desk and closed the door to her office slowly. "I shall remain."

Kate's shoulders relaxed. It was so like Mrs. Presley to be perceptive to the needs of others.

"The choice belongs to Miss Kingston, ma'am," the stodgy Mr. Montgomery said, his voice as unremarkable as his face. He stepped to the chair beside Kate's and waited for the ladies to take their seats before subtly flipping back the tails of his coat and perching on the edge of his chair. Kate stifled her mirth. He even acted without any embellishment.

Mr. Montgomery turned to look her square in the face. "Miss Kingston, I have come to inform you that your uncle, Mr. Bartholomew Kingston, has died."

Silence sat thick in the room as Kate absorbed the information, her surprise quickly deflating. She curled her hands around the arm rests on her straight, wooden chair and squeezed as hard as she could, willing herself to feel a measure of grief appropriate for such news. But nothing presented itself. After she felt like an acceptable amount of time had passed, she looked into Mr. Montgomery's staid eyes and nodded.

"Oh, right." Mr. Montgomery seemed taken aback by her composure. Or was it simply her nod? He pulled out a folder of papers from a leather case and began sorting through them frantically as if he was not quite prepared for this part yet. She noticed a crisp white handkerchief float to the floor and cringed. The man had been prepared to offer it to her for her tears, most likely. *Tears*, for Uncle. Should she have cried? Perhaps it was expected, but she was never one to cry on cue. She would have made a wretched actress.

"I am here today on particular business for the law firm of Montgomery and Montgomery. We would like to first offer our sincerest condolences on the loss of your belov—" Mr. Montgomery cleared his throat awkwardly and redirected "—loss of your family member at this time. We are here to assist you in any way you deem necessary."

"Thank you, Mr. Montgomery, that is most kind," Mrs. Presley said, jarring Kate out of her stupor. She had forgotten that the headmistress was seated directly across from her, so preoccupied she was in her recollection of Split Tree Manor. She'd not allowed herself to think about the place in years. She had only one fond memory of it, and it involved seeing the manor out the back window of the carriage taking her away for the last time.

"Of course," Mr. Montgomery nodded solemnly, "we had some trouble sorting the will and inheritance, which is why a few weeks passed before I could locate and inform you of the situation. I am afraid your uncle was buried a fortnight past in the local parish cemetery in Larkfield. The estate was not entailed, as I'm sure you are aware."

"The estate?" Kate asked, her brow pulling down in confusion.

"Split Tree Manor."

"Yes," she said, no less confused.

"The estate in all of its entirety, along with the sum set aside by your late father are now yours, except for..." He perused a document in front of him before tapping it once with his forefinger and grinning. "Any and all horses."

"Any and all *horses*?" Kate was stunned. Surely she hadn't followed Mr. Montgomery's explanation very well. Baffled, she cleared her throat. "You are saying, sir, that I have inherited an estate from my uncle and a sum of money from my father, but not any horses?"

He delivered a self-satisfied smile. "Precisely."

"Well, now that we've got that sorted," she muttered to herself.

Quiet settled in the room. Mr. Montgomery looked through the documents on his lap, most likely trying to see if he'd missed anything. Mrs. Presley remained seated with her hands tightly clasped on her desk and her mouth pinched. Kate would have worried about her headmistress if that wasn't her regular demeanor.

Part of Kate felt an overwhelming rush of relief. Not that she'd inherited a dilapidated manor, no...that was not something she was ready to consider. She was relieved that the ever-looming man in the back of her mind was now gone. She had never actually believed Uncle would snatch her from her present life and thrust her back into one of servitude and isolation. But irrational fears were just that: irrational.

Mrs. Presley's voice sliced through Kate's musings. "Are you able to provide Miss Kingston with any numbers today? For the purpose of planning."

"Oh, of course. Of course!" Mr. Montgomery hurriedly looked through his papers. He really was a bit unorganized, so perhaps he wasn't *entirely* boring. "Let us see here...your father left you a sum total of ten thousand pounds to be—"

"*Ten thousand pounds?*" Mrs. Presley and Kate exclaimed in unison before glancing at one another briefly, both of their expressions laced with self-consciousness.

"—obtained upon your twentieth birthday or date of your marriage." He looked up at Kate. "Of course you know about *that*. You've been benefitting from the interest for some time. Now, the matter of Split Tree Manor is a different conversation. It is my understanding that—"

"I am sorry, Mr. Montgomery, might we pause for a

moment?" Kate crossed her ankles under her chair and clasped her hands together, only to release both of them, stand up, and walk to the window. The implications were clear, and Kate was intelligent enough to follow them quickly. Only, she didn't want to believe them. Certainly her uncle wouldn't have kept her inheritance from her. "Would you explain the concept of interest? You said I've been benefiting from the interest for some time, yet I am afraid I do not follow." She tried to give Mr. Montgomery a sweet smile and was rewarded with a condescending one. He turned in his chair and let out a sigh as if he was preparing to address a child, lowering his voice a bit.

Kate bristled but clenched her teeth and let her irritation pass.

"Your father was the oldest son and heir to the estate of Split Tree Manor and all that his own father possessed. The estate was not entailed, so when your father and mother died, it was passed on to you. Of course, as you were only a small child at the time, the property was placed in the hands of your guardian until you were either married or turned the age of twenty."

Despite her request for further understanding, Kate was no simpleton. If she'd heard the man correctly, then she should have gained the rights to manage Split Tree on her last birthday. An unwelcome snake coiled in her stomach. "But I've been twenty these six months past and I've heard nothing from my uncle about any of this."

Mr. Montgomery paused, as if pondering the new information. "It is my understanding that your Uncle Bartholomew was not entirely coherent this past year. His illness was advanced. He must have been unable to contact you and begin the transfer of the money and property to you, the rightful owner. Of course, with the extent of Mr. Kingston's illness, it may come as no shock that the manor has fallen into slight disrepair." At this point he looked up into her eyes and tried to give her a hopeful grin. "But it is nothing that cannot be put to rights with proper time and money, both of which you have."

"Neither of which I have," Kate said unthinkingly. "Well, I suppose…" Her mind drifted into a mass of jumbled thoughts. She turned toward the window and watched from the second story as the townspeople and Lytle's servants continued setting up for the school social. A smile tilted Kate's lips at the community she was so thoroughly involved in. She did not have a family who cared about her, but she had a family of neighbors whom she loved, who loved her in return. She wasn't prepared to leave the only pleasant home she'd ever had.

She supposed Split Tree had been that for her once, but Kate had been an orphan for so long now, she hardly spared a thought for the parents who'd once loved her. The only things she held in her heart associated with Split Tree Manor were unpleasant memories of a tyrannical, controlling uncle.

She heard the din of voices behind her as Mr. Montgomery and Mrs. Presley spoke to one another, but she couldn't focus enough to listen to what they were saying. Letting out a shuddering breath, Kate wrapped her arms around herself, squeezing tightly.

"What if I don't want it?"

"Pardon me?" Mr. Montgomery said. Kate had spoken so quietly she did not realize she had been heard.

"Shall we adjourn for the day, Mr. Montgomery?" Mrs. Presley asked, leaning forward on her elbows as they rested atop her desk. "This is quite a lot to take in for Miss Kingston, and perhaps it is better digested in small doses."

"Absolutely." He stood. "Forgive me for bearing such news." He gave Kate a sorrowful look that she accepted with a small nod and an automatic curtsy. She was vaguely aware of Mrs. Presley escorting Mr. Montgomery away before the woman returned some minutes later and closed her door with a soft snap. Gently, she guided Kate to the small sofa on the other side of the room and helped her to sit before taking a seat beside her.

"This is a lot to take in, my dear." Mrs. Presley spoke in a soft voice. "Perhaps you would like to take some time to consider your options before coming to any decisions."

Kate nodded automatically. She was obedient to a fault. While her personality had always been a bit more difficult to suppress into a small, graceful package, she was used to taking and obeying commands. It is what had made her such an agreeable student and then employee these past eight years.

"I cannot say I am surprised that he would keep my inheritance from me," Kate said, her voice sounding small. "Uncle was a tyrant and a brute."

Mrs. Presley seemed to weigh her words carefully. "I realize we've discussed this scarcely in the past, but you once assured me that your uncle did not injure you. Please, be frank with me now. Is that true? Did the man ever—"

"No, he never hurt me. Not beyond taking a switch to my backside. Which I daresay is not the height of abuse." She continued to stare ahead as memories of her time at Split Tree Manor arrived in her foremind as snatches and images. "I was four when my parents died and was sent to live with a family outside of the parish. I am unsure why, but I always assumed my uncle did not want the burden of such a small girl, so he passed me on to someone of his acquaintance."

Mrs. Presley nodded, listening intently.

"I was nine years old when I was pulled from that house and brought to live with my uncle, but never given a reason why he suddenly wished to have me at Split Tree—nor do I understand it now. When I first arrived, he merely locked me in my room with a nurse. He didn't know what to do with a child, I suppose, but he never treated me with any more regard than he did his servants. He was highly irregular, and I am certain I shall never understand him."

Mrs. Presley offered a sad smile.

"Then I came here, shortly after I turned twelve." Kate looked at her mentor and schoolmistress, warmth blooming in her heart. "I found a home here within the strict rules and rigid schedule. I thrived on it."

"What shall you do?"

Kate felt the ripple of shock flow through her once more. Mrs. Presley was asking what she was going to do? That was a first. She had a *choice* for the first time in her life. Even when she had been offered the position of art teacher, she had not had a choice—not really. She'd had nowhere else to go.

"I do not know."

3

PETER

*T*here was nothing worse than wishing to chop a full brace of firewood and being forced to cease after two puny logs.

Peter Evans tossed the chopped wood into the pile and stuck the ax into the trunk, rubbing his injured shoulder as he surveyed the land. He had been home for a year now and still the place did not feel as though it belonged to him. Although, Martin probably had something to do with that.

The land never would truly feel like it belonged to Peter while his younger brother maintained control over the management. Peter would have been happy to pass the property, house, and all it encompassed to Martin had the estate not been entailed and passed directly to him. It was out of his hands.

Closing his eyes, he pressed his fingers against his eyelids. There was no sense in lamenting that which he had no control over. He'd done his part to join up with the soldiers, to find meaning and purpose. But much like everything else in his life, his military career was ripped from him on the Peninsula, and he'd had little choice but to return to Evanslea and make of it what he could.

"Sir Peter?"

Dropping his hand, Peter lifted his face to the groom waiting patiently beside the woodshed, thumbs hanging languidly from his pockets.

"What is it?" Peter asked.

"Destiny is getting close, sir. I think it might be time."

A shaft of light broke through his cloudy mind, lighting the prospect of the rest of his day. A smile came unbidden to his lips. "Then let's go at once."

Falling in line with his groom, Peter took off across the lawn toward the stables.

Martin

Martin Evans ran his hand along the polished banister as he slowly descended the grand staircase. Ever since his brother, Peter, had inherited Evanslea and returned from the war, this home had felt less *his*. Which, given Peter's attitude, was to be expected. However, it was vastly unfair.

Most things were unfair.

Martin directed a footman to bring tea to the study and began sifting through the latest entries in the accounts book. Peter's steward was making a hash out of everything Martin had worked toward. He was spending all of the carefully acquired money on tenants and repairs and the like, things that certainly could wait. If they blew through this money the way Charles had blown through his before he'd died, they'd be penniless in no time.

Peter wasn't meant to run Evanslea, and he certainly wasn't

good at it. He should have just gone back to fight Napoleon with the rest of them.

A knock at the door preceded the maid, and she brought a tray laden with tea and biscuits into the room, setting it down softly before pouring a cup. Martin watched her go through the movements and nodded his head when she looked to him, his sign that she was free to go.

He waited until she left before drinking his tea. He couldn't stand to be bothered by the maids. They were nervous and awkward around him, and he hated them for it.

Neighing caught his attention, and he watched the stables through the window. The superior stock within those walls was simply another sign of Peter's unbefitting character. Martin shook his head, grateful his father was not alive to watch Evanslea's decline. For in Peter's hands, there was no other foreseeable outcome—not when he wasted so much of their blunt on horses.

But it would all come to rights when Martin had completed his plans. He had goals and knew himself capable of accomplishing them. He merely needed to get around the one small hurdle that was forever throwing itself in his path.

A knock at the door brought his attention back to the present room. "Yes?"

The door creaked open, allowing a man to step inside.

Martin froze mentally, but he did his best not to show it. Anger quickly engulfed the fear which had initially befallen him. "You should not be here," he snapped. "What if you're seen?"

"As a neighboring servant, I don't think it's so odd I'd be seen coming here," the man said, his low-born tone grating on Martin's nerves.

"What is it?"

"The girl has been notified and will soon be returning."

Joy erupted in Martin's chest, a cat-like smile stretching his lips to greater lengths than they were typically wont to go.

"Thought you'd like to know," the man said, satisfaction lacing his tone. He rocked back on his heels, his mouth pinched in gratification.

Martin's composure drew into place. "Is everything set?"

"It will be by the time she gets here."

"Good," Martin said, holding the man's gaze. His voice dropped to frigid degrees. "But next time you have something to say to me, send a note. The Blue Boar will do just fine. I don't want you coming here again."

The man nodded once, steel eyes unrelenting, before sweeping from the room.

Martin rubbed his chin, staring at the closed study door. Had he been foolish to enlist the help of such a creature? Especially when the man had been willing to...well, suffice it to say Martin knew his lack of conscience.

He sat back, swinging his pocket watch from its chain. Perhaps only time would tell.

4

KATE

*C*hildren ran by Kate so quickly, their movement lifted her skirts and swung them around, eliciting a small chuckle from her lips. She righted one small boy that bumped into her leg and sent him on his way.

"There are plenty of pastries for everyone!" she called after them. It was a delight to see the farmers' children in their pieced-together Sunday best, playing amidst the well-dressed schoolgirls. Various parents who lived nearby or had the luxury of travel were in attendance as well, and it did the school well as a whole to enjoy such a pleasant night of camaraderie and fellowship.

Kate paid for a slice of plum cake and took her dessert to a nearby bench before tasting the exquisite treat, nibbling small bites to make the cake last as long as possible. Her heart squeezed as she gazed over the festivities, noting people she had come to cherish over the past eight years. She chuckled when she saw Lucas Alldridge, the local blacksmith, hoist his daughter onto his knee and wipe her crumbly face with his handkerchief.

Kate had fancied herself in love with Lucas when he had

saved her from a mad pig at age sixteen. Of course, he was engaged and married within the year to Beth, the vicar's daughter, and Kate had nursed a broken heart for some time, but there was no animosity between the three. To be honest, Kate was rather sure Beth had no inkling of her past infatuation. Though Lucas would be hard pressed to forget the sappy poetry and artful sketches she had left on his doorstep.

Kate had an unfortunate habit of creating hero worship for any man large in stature that defended the lesser man. She knew within her soul that part of her attraction to the tall, thickly built men, was due to them being the very opposite of her short, shriveling uncle in every regard. It was no secret she valued a person who would stand up to a bully.

"Hiding from your throng of suitors?"

Kate gasped with recognition at the voice behind her and jumped up, grabbing at her cake before it could fall from her lap. "Emily!" she exclaimed. "But I thought you couldn't make it this year!"

"I had thought so, too," her friend replied with a wry smile before sweeping her into a tight embrace. It had been a whole year since their last reunion and conversing via post was not the same as doing so face to face. Kate had dearly missed her friend. Looking around her, she noticed an absence. "But where is Paul?"

"Back to the Continent. Napoleon is causing trouble."

Kate's heart sank. She had heard the news but had failed to consider what it meant for Emily's husband, a captain in the Eleventh Regiment of Light Dragoons. Emily gave her a weak smile. "I felt the company in London to be a little lacking and suddenly found myself in need of a good diversion. You know how I fret when Paul goes away."

Kate nodded. Emily had left school a year early to marry Paul. He was the younger son of a wealthy landowner headed for a life in the military, and she, a poor scholarship student who had been smitten at first sight.

Paul forbade Emily to be one of the women of lesser morals that followed his regiment and camped behind them on tour. Kate was positive he only wanted to protect his beloved from the sights and horrors of war, and she appreciated him all the more for it. Emily did not lack for friends and had been immediately taken in by Paul's circle with whom she spent her time frivolously enjoying the better things in life that she had not been able to afford before. Of course, if anyone deserved such a rise in station, it was the kind-hearted Emily.

"I do hope I'll have you to myself for a time," Kate said selfishly.

Emily tucked a strand of her blonde hair behind one ear and sighed, her gaze darting from the people to the festivities around them. "I have missed you." Slipping her hand into Kate's, she tugged it until they both sat on the bench. "Now, do tell me everything I have missed since you last wrote."

"Well," Kate began, settling in beside her friend. "It's funny you should ask. I received a most interesting visit from a lawyer yesterday."

<hr />

It took the better part of a half-hour to relay the details of Mr. Montgomery's visit, including the implications against Uncle Bartholomew, and Kate's options moving forward. When she completed her story, Kate sat back and watched as Emily's slender eyebrows rose high, her small mouth open. Emily was on the petite side, and she looked like a child wearing such an expression of confusion and surprise. Kate wondered momentarily if she herself had appeared the same way upon hearing the news, but she knew her sturdier frame and plain brown locks did not lend themselves to the illusion of daintiness and helplessness. She was not overly tall by any means but being perfectly average meant she was just that: unremarkable.

"And now I do not know if I'd rather sell the place outright or let it deteriorate first and then parcel off the land," Kate finished.

"Have you lost your senses?" Emily asked, sitting bolt upright. "Ten thousand pounds! *Kate,* you have ten thousand pounds! To say nothing for the estate." She slowly melted back into the bench, the awe returning to her face. "You are richer than I am."

"Oh, nonsense. What does that matter? I could never reside there."

"Whyever not?"

"Because." Kate shifted uneasily. She was grown now, it was true. But that made it all the more difficult to explain how horribly unsettled she felt each time she considered her time spent in that dreadful place.

Emily seemed to understand, however. "You could redecorate. Completely gut the place and start fresh."

"I do not know," Kate said hesitantly. "According to Mr. Montgomery, the staff had mostly been let go or left voluntarily toward the end of my uncle's life. I'm not sure if he was letting the place fall into ruin out of spite or ignorance, but I'm not positive the estate is worth living in, anyway." Reaching forward, Kate clutched her friend's hand, lowering her voice to a whisper. "What if I leave my position here and all of these people I know and love only to find a pile of stones and a curious tree? I cannot simply return to Lytle's. Mrs. Presley will have already found my replacement."

"Then your great adventure would begin," Emily said gently. She moved to take Kate's other hand and squeezed her fingers softly, her voice resolute. "And I will go with you."

Kate startled. "Whatever do you mean?"

"Well, you cannot live alone, can you?"

"I suppose it wouldn't be proper."

Emily sat back with smug satisfaction on her face. "I shall come and be your companion until you are settled enough to hire someone else. I have experience running a house, I am married—and therefore a respectable chaperone—and I've nothing else to occupy my time." Her mouth moved into a playful smirk. "It is a faultless plan, really."

It *was* a good plan, in theory. With Emily's husband off fighting Napoleon, this was a wonderful opportunity to keep her too busy to worry about Paul and the danger surrounding him.

Kate shook her head. "But that house. I am not sure I have the courage to live there." To herself she sounded small and pitiful. If she had been speaking to anyone else, she would have been utterly mortified.

Emily moved an arm around Kate's shoulders and pulled her close. "Then we will post the property for sale and return to London forthwith. You need not stay if you cannot stomach it, Kate. But do you not think, for your father's sake, that you must at least try?"

And there it was. The thought that had settled in the back of Kate's mind ever since she had first heard the news, that hovered on the perimeter of her conscious but had not previously dared to take root in her heart. The house had belonged first to her parents. It was where her father had been raised and had brought his bride to live; where Kate herself had been born and adored for the first few years of her life before her uncle had moved in and sent her away.

"Besides," Emily continued, jarring Kate out of her trance, "should you not leave poor Lucas and his wife alone once and for all and let them live the rest of their lives in peace?"

Kate looked up sharply to catch Lucas's eye. He sent her a hearty wink, which she returned with a weak wave, her cheeks warming. Of course he did not hold any regard for her; he was simply friendly. But she would take the shame of her youthful poetry to the grave.

"Very well," Kate said bravely after wiping her eyes. "I shall do it. But only for Lucas and Beth."

"Very good," Emily said, pulling Kate to her feet. "Now do tell me, is Mrs. Fernley selling her delightful wassail this year? We must go find ourselves a glass and toast to Lucas and Beth's health."

"I suppose we must."

***

Before saying farewell two days following the school social, Kate and Emily devised their plan. They settled on meeting at Split Tree Manor a fortnight following the end of term to assess damages and begin hiring as they saw fit. Kate was grateful for Emily's experience in household maintenance and hiring of servants, for when Kate had lived at the manor as a girl, she was little more than a servant herself. To fill the role of lady of the house was going to take some adjustment and time.

Mrs. Presley was disappointed but understanding, and immensely grateful Kate planned to stay and finish the term, for it gave her ample time to find a replacement teacher.

Mr. Montgomery had since returned for a final meeting to explain Kate's travel arrangements and deliver the quarter's interest on her ten thousand pounds, along with a book of bank drafts to control the household account. She was further enlightened to find that she need not touch her own inheritance, for Split Tree Manor came with a fortune of its own that her uncle, while managing to lessen significantly, had not depleted altogether. There was a goodly sum remaining that should cover all of the house's basic expenses, as well as refurbishing and redecorating it in its entirety.

Kate had left the meeting with Mr. Montgomery and walked

directly into town to buy each girl in her school a special treat from the shop, as well as splurging on fresh art supplies and a new novel for her travels—anything which might lighten the nerves she felt over returning to Split Tree.

Her spoils wrapped in thick brown paper and tucked neatly into a basket, she managed to contain her delight at the prospect of delivering the peppermints and lemon sweets to the girls. Passing the millinery, her steps slowed as she gazed longingly at the beautiful bonnets set on display in the window. Temptation nipped at her in the form of a lovely chip straw bonnet with an emerald ribbon and spray of tiny white flowers. But it would not do. She may have chosen to forgo full mourning dress in light of her uncle's brutality and lack of feeling, but she was still going to remain solemn in her clothing—her dove gray teaching uniform was perfect for it—and she decided to wait one month more before adding colors to her wardrobe.

And besides, she needed to harness her spending lest she become a spendthrift and be poor within the year. Of course, she likely could have bought the entire shop out four times and still not have dented her purse too grandly, but that was beside the point.

"Good afternoon, Miss Kingston," Mrs. James called from up the lane.

Kate brightened, lifting her hand in a wave and quickening her pace to catch up to the cook. "Good afternoon, Mrs. James."

Releasing a sigh, Mrs. James said, "How many times do I have to ask? You must call me Alice."

"Only when we are out of the school, I suppose," Kate conceded.

"I know it's the way of things, but it doesn't feel right being called a missus when I'm not married," Alice confided.

"Most people do not obtain status of head cook at such a young age, so I assume they are grateful for the title," Kate guessed. "You must appreciate being set apart from the maids and kitchen help?"

"Yes. I got lucky, is what."

"No," Kate said sternly. "You are talented. It is perfectly acceptable to appreciate God's gifts, Alice. I know I do when I taste your divine plum cake."

Alice chuckled. "You and that plum cake. I sure hope you've got yourself a plum tree when you get to that new house of yours. It'll be a right pity if you don't got a cook that can do 'em up proper for you, either." She shot Kate a side glance that held a hint of mischievousness.

"What is cooking in that brain of yours, Alice?" Kate asked dubiously, certain she already knew the answer.

Alice paused on the side of the lane, her eyes as pleading as her voice. "I want an adventure, Miss Kingston, same as you. I've lived in this town my whole life. The farthest I've traveled was up the road to Brunston's market day because our own was out of lamb. I grew up here and I've worked in Lytle's kitchen for nearly all my life" —her shoulders lifted in a shrug— "and I just want to see more of the world."

"You do realize Split Tree Manor is just on the other side of the county? It is naught but a half day's ride in the carriage."

"Indeed!" Alice agreed, her head bobbing furiously. "I'm not so far that I will miss my family. But I can go off and do something grand, something that is my own."

Kate considered Alice's three younger sisters, all of them maids in some form or another at the school. She knew Alice's parents ran a farm with the aid of her brothers and couldn't see why the girl would want to leave all of those loved ones. If Kate had any siblings, she would cling to them with everything that she had.

But she didn't. So really, she could not relate.

Kate sighed in resignation. "I am afraid Mrs. Presley would

have my hide if I stole you from her." She began walking again, and Alice fell in line beside her.

"That's just the thing, Miss Kingston," Alice said, a little guiltily. "I already asked her."

"You did what?" Kate exclaimed, pivoting to face the cook. "Without speaking to me first? Oh, Alice! Was she terribly vexed?"

"She wasn't!" Alice said hurriedly, placating Kate with a hand on her arm. "She was kindly and understanding, honest."

"But Alice, what if I take you with me and the manor already has a cook? I can't fairly boot her out of a job. That wouldn't be right."

"Then I won't be the cook. I will do something else." Alice was determined. "I've always wanted to learn to garden," she added thoughtfully.

This pulled a giggle from Kate. Alice's calling was in the kitchen, and she was masterful at what she did. To force her to dig in the dirt would be barbaric.

Kate linked her free arm through Alice's and let out a sigh. "Very well. I shall take you with me." She cut off Alice's squeal of delight with a raised finger. "But I will not fire a cook already in place, and I must clear this with Mrs. Presley first."

Alice nodded in agreement, but her buzzing excitement was telling. And now Kate needed to figure out how to approach the headmistress and request to steal away her cook.

5

KATE

*M*rs. Presley handed Kate a basket full of sandwiches and fruit, with a canister of lemon-ade. "Mrs. James packed a basket for your journey."

Kate took the offering guiltily and handed it to the coachman to set within the hired carriage before turning back to her mentor. She'd already said her farewells to students and teachers alike. The day before, she'd walked through the town and school grounds for the last time, committing everything to memory. While Mrs. Presley had not been thrilled to part with such a lovely cook, she'd replaced Alice within days and remained content.

Kate was able to meet her own replacement the day before her departure, an older woman with gray hair and hollow cheeks. She hoped this woman would be able to inspire love and appreciation of art into her pupils but knew that it was all in God's hands now.

"Where is Alice now?" Kate asked.

"I believe she is saying goodbye to her sisters, but she should be out shortly."

Kate nodded. She took one last look at the sturdy, gray

school and wondered, not for the first time, what sort of ruin she would discover at Split Tree Manor. She'd warned Alice that their jobs may largely be repairing and cleaning for a time, but then Alice had reminded her that they must eat regardless. It warmed Kate's heart to have another ally. With both Emily and Alice by her side, she was fairly certain she could accomplish anything. Even returning to such a wretched place as Split Tree.

"I'm not sure I will be able to say goodbye," Kate said in a decidedly watery tone, bringing a handkerchief up to dab at her nose.

"Nor must you," Mrs. Presley answered firmly, lifting Kate's hand and squeezing it between her own. Lowering her voice, the matron spoke with heavy, weighted care. "For you shall write and tell us all of your grand new life in your ancestral home."

Kate nodded, giving Mrs. Presley's hand a squeeze and climbing into the carriage before she lost her wits and began to cry in earnest. She had found her first home at Lytle's with Mrs. Presley and though she was now grown, it was very frightening going off on one's own.

Alice climbed into the carriage behind her, the door was closed, and Kate held the headmistress's gaze for a moment longer before the carriage rolled forward, carrying her away.

A few girls escaped to the front lawn and Kate waved to them through the glass window situated behind her head until they were out of view.

"I have the strangest feeling," Kate said in a hollow tone, turning back to face Alice, "that I am going to find happiness in this situation, one way or another."

Alice grinned and moved to Kate's side of the carriage before pulling her into an embrace. "You will, Miss Kingston. Mark my words, but you will."

When she caught sight of the symbolic split tree on the country lane just outside of Larkfield, it was not the tree itself which arrested Kate's attention, but that of the blackberry bushes on the opposite side of the lane. Her mind brought forth a rush of memories from picking a tummy full of blackberries to running for her life from two nasty, savage boys.

The scrape she had gotten from falling on her face had left a faint scar that ran through her left eyebrow and past the outer corner of her eye before disappearing into her hairline. It was hardly noticeable now, but she had never forgotten the boy she had helped get away, and often wondered what had happened to him in the time since. She swallowed a lump and sent a prayer up to heaven for his well-being before shoving those thoughts away and focusing on the matter at hand. In precious few moments, she would be pulling up to the house.

A gasp from Alice signified their arrival, and Kate took a deep breath before looking to the window and absorbing the sight of Split Tree Manor in all its glory. She was faintly surprised to see the building still standing as a whole—though largely covered in vines. A small smile crept onto her lips. Perhaps Alice would get that chance at gardening, after all.

"Let us hope the inside is in the same condition as the exterior," Kate mumbled.

Alice shot her a funny glance, but she couldn't quit staring at the house as they rounded the drive, rolling to a stop at the front door. Kate waited for the massive oak door to swing open and was faintly surprised when the coachman helped her step onto the gravel road and the door to the manor yet remained closed. She stepped up and took a knocker to it, while Alice gathered her things and the coachman began unloading their trunks. After a minute of silence, Kate unlocked the door with the key Mr. Montgomery had given her. She swung it wide and stepped into the marbled entryway, the click of her heels reverberating off the walls. Beams of light strewn through the windows in the domed ceiling, highlighting the thick coating of dust that lay on every surface.

Kate drew in a deep breath and subsequently coughed. If there *was* anyone in the house, they were certainly made aware of Kate's presence now. Clearing her throat, she stepped further into the house and called, "Is anyone there?"

Nothing but a faint echo answered her, for which she was both relieved and worried. Footsteps tapped behind her, and she turned to find Alice entering with the basket of food and her carpet bag. The coachman followed close behind with one trunk and let it down on the marble floor with a loud thunk before turning back to retrieve the others. She hoped he would be gentler with the trunk containing her art supplies.

"I suppose I don't need to worry about booting a cook from her place then, do I?" Alice said with a bit of a forced grin.

Kate glanced at her quickly and the humor dancing in her eyes was a balm over Kate's concerned, anxious heart. A giggle spilled from her lips at the absurdity of it all, and Alice soon joined in, her shoulders shaking in mirth. Laughter rang out high and clear in the marble entryway, and by the time the coachman finished delivering the trunks, he looked at them warily and tipped his hat before making a quick escape.

"I must say, I am quite glad you insisted on coming with me," Kate said, smoothing her hands over her gray gown. "I cannot imagine what I would have done had I been dropped here alone."

"You would have survived, Miss Kingston. You are capable of more than you know."

The sentiment was her mental undoing. But rather than burst into tears like she would really like to do, Kate strolled to the front door and watched the hired carriage slip around the bend before closing the large door with an ominous thud. She clapped her hands together to remove the dust and gave Alice her brightest smile.

"Shall we see what we can make of your workspace?"

Kate was unsurprised by the lack of food in the pantry. What was pleasing was the modern stove and cupboards of dishes and cooking implements. Whoever'd pilfered the food supplies must have feared criminal action, for they had left everything of value behind.

Kate watched Alice glance through the cupboards, muttering to herself before taking a peek in the still room. She disappeared into the cellar for a moment and came back up with a grin.

"Did you find some food?"

"No, miss, none," Alice said. "But I did find a cat down there, and I'd imagine it was her that kept your home rodent free."

"*House*," Kate muttered to herself. "I'd like to take a peek in the bedrooms and then come up with a plan."

They took the servants' stairs to the first floor and found four bedrooms in working order—dirty, but intact. Nothing was moth-eaten or destroyed, and most of the furniture had been covered. It appeared the house had been properly closed up before the final servant left.

Walking through the rooms, memories assailed Kate from her last stay at Split Tree. The vision of her uncle and her own role fetching things and starting fires in the early hours of the morning had completely overwritten the few cherished memories of the time she'd spent with her parents in these same rooms. Never mind his army of servants—there was no understanding the mind of a brute. A *bully*.

Closing the door to the room that had once belonged to Uncle Bartholomew, Kate shuddered. She determined not to set foot on the nursery level of the house quite yet, if she could help it. She did not wish to muster through those memories.

"Alice, would you care to take one of these rooms while we get the house in order?"

The cook balked, shaking her head, her copper curls bouncing. "No, miss."

"But all of these rooms must be put to rights—to say nothing of the main rooms on the ground floor. Until we obtain help, it might be too large of a task to see to the servants' quarters, as well."

"I can check my own room, miss. It isn't bothersome to me."

Kate nodded, turning away. Alice didn't know the details of Kate's background with the house and most likely assumed she was fatigued, but let the woman think what she would. "I'll meet you down in the parlor, then. I should like to examine the music room as well."

They parted, and the eerie quiet settled on Kate, causing prickles to run down her skin. She felt a shadow of her uncle following her as she walked from room to room, and she glanced over her shoulder more than once to ascertain that she was, indeed, alone.

To her relief, the house was whole. It would take a thorough cleaning, for it appeared as if a good majority of the rooms had been ignored far longer than just the last few months of Uncle's illness—as she'd been led to believe.

Alice came upon Kate some time later as she sat on the bottom step of the grand staircase in the foyer. She had completed her investigation of the ground floor and had pulled a small sketchbook and a pencil from her trunk to form a list of what needed to be done.

"Perhaps our time will be better suited preparing one room this evening," Kate said, bringing her gaze up to meet Alice's. "We can rest tonight and begin cleaning in the morning."

The cook nodded. "I'll fetch what candles I can from the housekeeper's stores."

"Bring them to the parlor. We ought to remain together until we are certain we are alone."

Alice located buckets for water and rags, and they set to cleaning the parlor with vigor. They mopped the floors, piled the rugs in the corridor to be beaten later, removed holland covers and dusted the furniture, and cleaned the mantel and windows. The parlor hadn't suffered as much as other rooms, and the basic cleaning served them well.

A supper of sandwiches and plums quenched their hunger as the windows darkened and they prepared makeshift beds on the long sofas, lying down with the anticipation of a long day ahead.

Kate lay awake well into the night, her gaze trimming the edges of the molding on the ceiling faintly highlighted by the light of the moon. Alice's deep, even breathing made the quiet easier to bear, and Kate thanked God for sending Alice with her. She was certain she would have cut her losses and removed to the inn in Larkfield had she arrived alone.

Questions assailed her. What had caused her uncle to allow the house to become so filthy? Why had the servants fled when surely they must have known Kate would return? And if she had inherited ten thousand pounds and an estate from her father, how could Uncle Bartholomew have been so brazen as to keep it from her for the entirety of her life?

She fell into a fitful sleep full of visions of pampering in a house that, oddly enough, did not resemble the one she was sleeping in at that moment whatsoever.

6

PETER

*P*eter lay awake, his bedclothes shoved to the side and the cool night nipping at his sweat-slickened skin. His chest heaved from the adrenaline of waking from a dream in which his men needed him, and he could not reach them.

The dream was always the same. Always. Marsh, Aniston, and Cohen in varying states of distress, calling for assistance as French bayonets bounded toward them. The vivid flashes of gunpowder igniting and the acrid scent of smoke and mud assaulted his senses, clouding his mind.

Rubbing at his eyes, Peter scrubbed the image from his vision. The dream never mimicked reality. No, in truth, each of Peter's men had sustained their injuries at different times, in different battles, leaving him one at a time until only he remained behind in Spain. Soon, it was his turn to be speared beyond repair and sent back to Britain for a proper surgeon.

Did his men feel the acute failure of leaving before the war had ended as well? Yes, there had been a reprieve when Napoleon was exiled to Elba, but the lunatic's escape had drawn able-bodied men back to fight. Everyone had gone, it seemed, except for Peter and his closest comrades.

He should write to them. It had been a month, at least, since he'd heard from Aniston, and longer still from Marsh. Cohen's correspondence was consistent, his missives arriving in steady intervals, but the man himself was responsible for that. Peter had been an utter failure of late. But given the difficulties his men faced—lost hands and nasty scars, both mental and physical—he often felt inadequate to help them.

He told himself he would be able to help them once he'd gotten a handle on his own life—the injury he sustained to his shoulder and his mental state, to say nothing for the circumstances at home—but Martin seemed intent on making that impossible. Martin was a bitter shell of the person Peter had known as a boy, and sometimes when he caught the determined glint in Martin's eyes, he wondered how well he truly knew his own brother.

Now that they were older, Peter had wondered if he and Martin could come to an accord. It seemed his hopes had been in vain—his younger brother would never forget their youthful warfare, regardless of how thoroughly Peter had apologized for the part he'd played.

Peter's butler had informed him that Martin had taken on the running of the estate in Peter's absence, after their older brother and father had both died. Reclaiming the reins had been difficult, for Martin was not only reluctant to relinquish his role, but he showed no signs of claiming an occupation that would take him away from Evanslea. While Peter would never force his brother to leave Evanslea, he was certain they would both be happier once Martin chose a path for himself that did not keep him at the family estate.

It was with relief that Peter noticed the smooth, steady intervals of his own breathing, and a sigh escaped his lips. His logical mind recognized the inaccuracy of his dreams, the nonsensical fear which gripped him. But there was little logic to be found in the hazy in-between of sleep and wakefulness.

Rising from the feather mattress, Peter crossed to the window and drew back the drapes. His view was wide and spanned a large part of his land, encompassing the woods that trailed his property and the unused pastureland belonging to the neighbor.

It was such a shame Split Tree was empty. Bartholomew Kingston was a fool for quitting the sheep trade, but Peter could not complain about the old man's desire to dip his toe in horse breeding. It had done Peter right in the end, at least.

Dropping the drapes over the window, he turned back for his bed, scrubbing a hand over his face. If only Martin would be willing to sit down and have a real conversation with him, they could discuss the future and how best to manage it. But he'd learned to walk on light toes around Martin, or else end up on the wrong side of a temper tantrum. And not the explosive kind Peter was used to battling among soldiers, but the quiet, averting, punishing type that annoyed Peter far more than a bout of fisticuffs any day.

Sliding back into bed, he pulled a blanket over his legs and sighed. They'd gone on this way for months with no alteration, and it was beginning to wear. Something needed to change soon, or Peter was liable to put his fist through a wall.

7

KATE

*K*ate woke sharply to the distant sound of pounding.

"Alice!" she whispered loudly. "Alice, wake up!"

The cook stirred behind her as Kate rushed to pull on her wrapper and locate her slippers. One had weaseled its way under the sofa, but the other was nowhere to be seen. She got down on her hands and knees and searched beneath the nearby furniture, but it was gone.

Knocking came from the foyer again, and she sat bolt upright, banging her forehead on the edge of a bulky, triangular decorative table. "Ouch!"

"Miss?" Alice asked sleepily. Kate was glad to see that Alice was at least sitting up now, pulling on her wrapper and mumbling something about her own lost slippers.

The knocking sound came again, this time louder, and Kate ran to the foyer, tying her sash as she went. It was not until she reached the door and began to open it, revealing a man, not many years her senior with stark black hair, that she recognized her own level of disarray, and her cheeks went hot.

Closing the door to ensure she was adequately covered, Kate

put her hands to her cheeks and breathed in deeply before peeking the door open a smidge and poking her nose through it.

"Can I help you?"

"I need to speak to the lady of the house."

Kate blinked, considering her response. He clearly assumed her to be the maid, and it chagrined her. But what else could she expect after answering the door in her nightclothes?

Oh, goodness. She was in her *nightclothes*. She cleared her throat and spoke with as much authority as she could muster. "This is my home. What may I do for you?"

He eyed her dubiously, his arms crossing over a worn, linen shirt. The man wasn't well-dressed himself, and she was certain by his attire that he was of the working class. Hitching a thumb behind him to indicate the lane, he said, "I saw that carriage bringing ladies to the house yesterday, and I wanted to know if it was time to report back to my duties."

"Which are?"

He cleared his throat and said, proudly, "The stables, ma'am. But since the horses are all gone, I should think I could step in and help with the gardening now. Until you've got horses back proper, o'course. Or a gardener."

Kate watched the man awkwardly rock on his feet. The sun could not have been in the sky for a full hour even. She was tempted to tell the man he could have whatever job he wished so long as he let her be. But how she acted now would determine how her servants viewed her in the future.

"You have experience as a stable hand?" Kate asked.

"I ran the stables, Miss Kingston. And I'd like to do it again."

"Are you the only servant left?"

He looked uncomfortable and fidgeted again, crumpling his cap in his hands. "Most of them left. I can get my hands on a few stable hands and the under gardener. Probably a housemaid or two."

That would help immensely. *Any* additional servants would

be an improvement on their currently deserted state. "All previously employed here?"

"Some of them."

Kate nodded. "You have yourself a deal, sir. What is your name?"

"Henry Gibson."

Sliding her hand through the gap, she poised it to shake. Mr. Gibson looked at her strangely before he grasped her hand and they sealed the agreement. Perhaps that wasn't the sort of thing a mistress of the manor did. Kate pulled her hand inside, firmly determined to learn and act her part.

Glancing at the wide expanse of lawn behind the man, she wiped her hand surreptitiously on her wrapper. "How did you arrive here today, Mr. Gibson? Larkfield is a four-mile walk."

His neck turned red, and Kate had to bite back a smile.

"I've been staying in the quarters above the stables." He threw up his hands in defense. "No one said I couldn't!"

"That is correct, sir. No one was here to say that you couldn't." He seemed to relax at her demeanor. "Can you explain what happened to the horses?"

Mr. Gibson let out a hearty laugh that let Kate know exactly what he had eaten for breakfast—something slathered with onions. Or maybe an onion itself. He slapped his cap on his knee and grinned at her. "For them horses, you'll be wanting to see your neighbors."

"Which neighbors are those?"

"Evanslea."

As if that was any more help. The name was certainly familiar, but it had been nearly a decade since Kate had last lived at Split Tree and she'd only left the prison of a house *one* time. Any knowledge she had of the people in the area came from eavesdropping on servants.

Calling on the reserves of patience she had built up through years of teaching small children, Kate calmly inquired further.

Obtaining the direction to Evanslea, she thanked Mr. Gibson and sent him to secure whatever workers he could, requesting they call at the house to finalize terms of employment with her housekeeper.

It hardly mattered that she did not yet have a housekeeper. She would find one.

Alice was missing from the parlor when she returned, though the blankets had been folded—and still the slippers remained absent.

"There has been a change of plans, Alice," Kate said, finding the cook in the kitchen. Alice had been pulling items from the cupboard, rearranging the kitchen to suit her needs. She looked up at Kate with a raised brow on her freckled face.

"We are going to get ourselves some horses."

They walked down the road and past the split tree before turning left at the lane beyond the woods. It seemed to stretch eternally before them, the road running the length of the woods with thick, dense forest on their left and a large expanse of open countryside to their right. According to Mr. Gibson, this lane led directly to the neighboring estate—though he seemed to think approaching them about purchasing a horse would be a fruitless effort. Kate disagreed. If this Evans family had just acquired the stock of her uncle's stables, then surely they had at least one or two beasts they would be willing to part with.

She had with her the blank bank drafts Mr. Montgomery had given her and hoped these people would be good and fair about quality and price, since she had no earthly idea what the going rate for a horse even was.

"What if they don't want to sell us a horse?" Alice asked, a look of worry marring her pretty features. Her freckles stood out against the pale skin that was finally receiving a bit of sun and her red hair shone in the sunlight.

"Then maybe they will agree to rent us one or two. At least until we obtain our own."

Alice nodded, but the worry did not leave her face. Kate was doing her level best to remain optimistic through each curve, but she felt as though she was trying to learn to speak Gaelic, so foreign were the troubles she faced.

"Alice, I had wondered something," Kate began hesitantly.

"Of course," Alice said.

"How would you feel about taking on the mantle of housekeeper until I have found a proper replacement? I assume a good housekeeper will need to be acquired through an agency, and I just think that with all of the servants we will need to interview, it might be wise to have someone to manage them in the interim."

Alice laughed, loosening the knot in Kate's stomach. "It was uncomfortable speaking to the stable man this morning?"

"Dreadfully so."

Alice let out another peal of laughter that unlocked the chuckles pent up in Kate's chest. She freed them and her shoulders lightened immediately. The sun shone down on her upturned face and she grinned at Alice.

"I can do that, if you wish it. You know, you really ought to laugh more, Miss Kingston," Alice said. She nodded to the pencil stuck into Kate's coiffure. "Perhaps you ought to add it to your list of things you need to do. It might alleviate some of those tensions."

Kate shot her a wry smile and then stopped dead in her tracks, pulling back on Alice's arm when she noticed a man standing just five feet before them. "Oh!" she said quickly, her body flushing cold at the startle. Kate brought a hand up to rest on her breastbone to calm her beating heart. "You startled me."

He was taller than she, but not significantly, and dressed in riding attire, leading a horse. There was something vaguely familiar about his classically handsome features and sand-colored hair, but she could not place how she recognized him.

His eyebrows hitched up on his forehead, and his gaze flicked from Kate to Alice before he delivered a bow fit for a London drawing room and quite out of place on this deserted country lane. "Forgive me," he said, his voice smooth. "May I be of assistance to you, ladies?"

"We are hoping to reach Evanslea. Might you be able to tell me if we are headed the right way?"

A slow smile spread on his handsome face, nearly knocking the breath from Kate's chest. He bowed. "I can do you one better, for I should be privileged to escort you the remainder of the way."

"That is very kind, sir," Kate said, trying to keep her answering smile demure. She figured she was more than likely beaming at the man. Such kindness and chivalry was likely to make her blush, so unused to it as she was.

He stepped closer. "I am Martin Evans, and my home is just up the road here."

"Pleasure," Kate murmured. She fell into step beside him as Alice pulled back a few paces and then to the side of the lane to avoid the horse trailing behind Mr. Evans. "I hope you will forgive our unusual behavior, but we have come on a matter of business."

"Oh?" Mr. Evans lifted his sandy brows. "With whom, might I ask, am I to do business?"

Kate blushed, glancing to the road before smiling back into Mr. Evans's stormy eyes. She felt an inkling of familiarity looking into his gaze. "I am Miss Kingston and this is my house-keeper and cook, Mrs. James."

Stepping beyond the woods, they came upon a large stone house built after the Palladian style. Long gray columns lined the front portico with evenly spaced windows in three rows. The house put Split Tree Manor to shame, and Kate found herself struck by its elegance and beauty. The long, smooth lawn that ran the distance to the house was wide and level, and she could see the edges of a flower garden toward the rear of the house that she had to assume was just as lovely.

"It is beautiful," Kate said on a breath.

"Thank you, Miss Kingston," Mr. Evans said with no little pride in his voice.

Taking his offered arm to walk across the lawn, Kate began to think that maybe moving to Split Tree Manor had not been such a bad idea after all.

8

KATE

*S*eated in Mr. Evans's study with Alice to her left and Mr. Evans across the giant oak desk, Kate felt small. Mr. Evans's kind features were fixed into a pleasant smile. He appeared as though he had all day to devote to her, and she felt silly for taking any of this man's time—let alone on such a desperate errand.

"I have recently moved into Split Tree Manor," she began, slightly gratified at the surprise in his expression. "And I was informed that all of the horses in my uncle's stables have been bequeathed to you."

"You are Bartholomew Kingston's niece? I suppose I should have gathered as much. It is not very often I find a lovely young lady and her companion walking my lane." His lips formed a generous smile. "Welcome to the neighborhood."

"Thank you." Kate dipped her head in acknowledgement. "I am prepared to do my best to bring Split Tree Manor back to proper working order once again, but I find myself in need of some transportation."

"I see," Mr. Evans said, sitting back in his chair. "Allow me to offer you the use of our horses, Miss Kingston. Our stables are at your disposal, and you may come and go as you wish." He gestured with an arm, and Kate felt all the sillier. But she had walked this far, and she was not going to back down from her original goal now.

"I had rather hoped to *purchase* some horses from you."

Lines formed on his forehead. "Oh?"

"And a carriage."

He gave her an indulgent smile. "Shall I throw in a coachman as well?"

Kate stilled. She had not come to be mocked, and it was difficult to know if Mr. Evans was in earnest. His smile spoke of kindness, but there was an enigmatic glint in his eye that left her uncertain. "I realize how extraordinary I sound. I was directed here by my stablemaster, but if you do not have what I need, I will take my business elsewhere." She rose from her seat.

"Wait, Miss Kingston," Mr. Evans said, his hands raised.

Kate paused before turning away—though she could not so easily stem the blush rising up her neck.

"I was not mocking you."

Giving her full attention to the man, it was her turn to raise an eyebrow.

"Truly," he said, coming around the desk to stand beside her. He lifted one of her hands in his own, his familiarity stealing her breath. "Our stables have recently grown substantially, and while I cannot promise you a horse that previously came from Split Tree, I am certain we have one or two we can afford to part with. As far as a carriage is concerned, I have it on good authority that Mr. Kingston had a few of good quality in his stable house that I am certain have remained in working condition."

Kate swallowed and nodded. The man looked so sincere, his stormy eyes clearing to a gray-blue that had the potential to easily sweep her from her feet.

"And what I meant by my ill-chosen words was that I would be happy to lend you a coachman until you have secured one of your own."

Chuckling softly, Kate reclaimed her hand. "I must say, Mr. Evans, I feel rather silly. Though only my uncle's stablemaster, Mr. Gilbert, remains, and I am sure he can drive my carriage until I find someone more suitable."

"Think nothing of it. I am happy to assist you in whatever way I can," he answered, dipping his head to look into her eyes like he could read her thoughts. The feeling was almost unnerving and heightened the notion that she had met this man before. He cracked a smile. "Ah yes, Mr. Gilbert. Well, as he is not here at present, allow me to lend you one of my men today."

Kate nodded, acquiescing.

"Come, I shall get you some refreshment while we await the carriage. You may borrow one of mine until you have sorted your own, and I will send someone to retrieve it tomorrow."

"That is most kind, Mr. Evans, but I feel as if we should discuss payment first."

He stopped and glanced at Alice before lowering his voice. "I cannot accept any payment, Miss Kingston."

She straightened her shoulders. "I did not come here for any favors, Mr. Evans. I am prepared to pay. My uncle left these horses to you, and I cannot feel comfortable with the arrangement unless money has crossed hands."

"Do you not know, Miss Kingston? It is I who owe you the favor."

Her eyebrows pulled together as she clasped her hands in front of her, searching his face. Mr. Evans regarded her patiently.

"Have we met before, Mr. Evans?"

"Yes, Miss Kingston. It was quite some time ago, and I told you that someday I would repay you for the kindness you did for me."

Recognition fell on her like the rays of a long-missed sun and

Kate gasped. This was the scrawny boy that had hidden in the tree all those years ago? He was not so scrawny now. He had grown into a fine gentleman, and Kate found herself thinking that if she could somehow show him to the maid, Lissie, then she would *really* know what handsome looked like—certainly nothing like Mr. Montgomery.

"I cannot believe it," Kate said softly.

"Nor I, for I did not believe I would ever lay eyes on you again," Mr. Evans said, taking her elbow and leading her from the room. He spoke to a passing footman about refreshments in the morning room and readying a carriage. Kate faintly recognized Alice's footsteps trailing behind them.

"But I do not understand," she said, once he had returned his attention to her. "How could you have known I was that same girl?"

Mr. Evans looked down at her as one would a child and grinned. "Do you think I could forget the face of my guardian angel? I have dreamed of it for many years since."

Kate felt the blush that tinged her cheeks and looked away. Maybe she was playing the demure lady correctly for once. Could it be fate that had brought her to Mr. Evans again?

"We share something, Miss Kingston, do we not?" he pressed. "Both of us having suffered in the role of victim has given us a bond of sorts, I believe. I give you my word as your new neighbor that I shall look out for you. That is, after all, what a good neighbor would do."

His sincerity and the hard gray of his eyes was too serious to trifle with. Kate busied herself with straightening her reticule on her wrist, unsure of what to make of his pronouncement.

She took tea in the morning room with Mr. Evans and Alice before loading into a well sprung carriage and wishing the man a good day. Leaning back on the squabs, she closed her eyes and replayed the previous hour in her mind through the entire trip into Larkfield—her cook remaining silent, allowing her the time to ponder.

The borrowed coachman let Kate out at Larkins, a store which doubled as the post office in town. The bell jingled above her head when Kate and Alice stepped inside. They were greeted by a round man with a florid complexion.

"Mr. Larkin, ma'am," he said, dipping his head at Kate. "How might I help you?"

"I was hoping to place this notice in your window," she said, pulling a rolled paper from her reticule. "I've recently acquired Split Tree Manor and I have need of some help."

Unrolling the sheet of paper, she smoothed it on the wooden countertop, vaguely aware of a woman approaching Alice behind her and asking how she might be of service.

"You are welcome to put that in the window," Mr. Larkin said, "but if you want help quickly, you'd best see Sims across the street."

"Sims?"

"Innkeeper," Mr. Larkin explained, taking the paper and holding it up to read Kate's handiwork. He slapped it down on the counter and sent her a wink. "I'll be sure to put this in a prime location, Miss Kingston. Welcome to Larkfield."

"Thank you," Kate said. She turned to find Alice and the woman with their heads bent together as they discussed something. Meandering the aisles, she perused the shop's basic offerings, noting a distinct lack of drawing supplies. It seemed that Kate would be required to send for what she needed when she ran out of charcoals or paints.

Alice approached. "I've placed an order with Mrs. Larkin and secured the direction for the butcher. Shall we?"

After visiting the butcher and having a lengthy conversation about cuts and quality of meat, Alice and Kate walked to the inn for lunch.

They were seated by a rosy-faced giant of a man and ordered

two meals. When the man returned with two large bowls of stew and chunks of bread, Kate gathered his attention.

"Might I ask a favor, Mr. Sims?" Kate asked the gruff-looking man. When he didn't respond, she continued. "I am looking to hire some help for Split Tree Manor. I've put a notice up at the Larkins' shop, but I wonder if you might know of anyone who would make a decent housemaid or kitchen staff."

Mr. Sims looked contemplative before nodding slowly, rubbing the stubble on his chin. "I think I could find a gal or two."

"That would be most appreciated, Mr. Sims. My housekeeper will be holding interviews tomorrow at noon, if you would spread the word."

He left them in peace to eat their meal, and Kate shot Alice a wry glance. "Have you considered that we might have been better off remaining at Lytle's?"

"Not for one moment," Alice replied, her voice firm.

Sighing, Kate finished eating before rising, and linking her arm through Alice's. "If only Emily were here already, she would probably know a better way to go about doing all of this."

They made it outside, and Alice leaned in, lowering her voice. "I thought you did just fine in there, Miss Kingston."

"Thank you. I was rather nervous. Mr. Sims is quite large."

"That he was, but you sent that smile his way, and he didn't know what to do with himself, now did he?" Alice laughed as they crossed the street. Kate couldn't help but chuckle, even though she knew her friend was embellishing for the sake of her nerves.

Regardless, she felt strong and capable for all she had so far accomplished. Food would be arriving at Split Tree in a matter of hours, she now had horses to convey her where she needed to go, and help would soon be on its way. Not to mention Emily, of course. Things were certainly looking up.

They loaded into the carriage, and Kate let out a soft sigh of contentment as it began to move forward. "Is this the adventure you had in mind when you chose to leave Lytle's?" she asked Alice.

"Can't say what I had in mind, exactly. But this is turning out to be quite an adventure, isn't it?"

"I'd say."

They fell into silence when they reached the outskirts of town. Green, rolling hills passed by the window, broken by the occasional cottage or veering lane.

A loud shout broke through the quiet tedium of wheels on a packed dirt road. A muffled, angry tone came from behind the carriage. If only this vehicle were equipped with a window in the back like the one Kate had rented to travel from Lytle's, she would be able to understand what the yelling was for.

But as the shouting ensued, volleying between the stranger and the coachman, Kate was no closer to deciphering what was being said and grew increasingly uneasy.

"Highwaymen!" Alice exclaimed. Her face lost all of its color and she clutched Kate's arm with a force that betrayed her hours spent kneading dough.

"We aren't on a highway," Kate said crossly, and she pulled Alice's hands from her arm, sure that finger marks would present themselves under her sleeve. The carriage rolled to a stop and an angry man yelled to the coachman, who said something else before the door swung open with angry force, causing Alice to scream as it hit the side of the carriage.

A man appeared in the opening, thunder written on his face. Alice's screams rent the air as the stranger's face shifted to shock, took stock of the interior, and then looked back to the coachman in utter confusion. His cravat was untidy and waistcoat askew, but the cut of his coat was exquisitely sculpted to his tall, broad torso.

"Alice, calm down," Kate tried to yell over Alice's frantic screams. "*Calm down!*" She was tempted to slap some sense into the cook but grabbed her by the shoulders and shook her instead. "He is a gentleman!"

This seemed to halt both the man outside and the maid inside, and everyone looked at Kate. She straightened herself as best she could and directed her stony gaze to the beast of a man holding the carriage door open. "What can I do for you, sir?"

"I apologize, ma'am," he said, his voice low and sincere. "I believed I was stopping someone else's carriage."

Kate held his gaze while she catalogued his features. He possessed a square jaw and height that required him to stoop to speak into the carriage. His hair was golden brown and hung longer than fashionable, falling over his ears in disarray, and his shoulders were broad enough to block light from the doorway, making it impossible to tell if his eyes were blue or gray. He was, in short, a monster of a man, and it was apparent that he was attempting to rein in some sort of temper as well, if his flaring nostrils and heaving chest were any clue.

Kate held his gaze. "Do you often flag down coaches like an errant highwayman?"

One corner of his mouth ticked up as if he was trying—and failing—not to smile. His gaze flicked away before looking back at Kate, and she was arrested by the sudden weary nature of his demeanor. "Please, forgive the intrusion."

Kate nodded once. She watched the stranger glance at Alice before nodding to her as well and closing the door with a soft click. Hoofbeats soon pounded past the carriage at a fast clip, and then they were on their way once more.

"Perhaps we shan't talk of adventure anymore," Kate said wryly, still recovering from the shock. He'd clearly mistaken them for someone else, but why?

Alice gave a watery giggle. "Or we should talk of it more often if that's the sort of adventure we're going to be getting."

9

MARTIN

"Martin!"

Martin heard the roar of his name as his brother entered the house, followed by a slam of the front door that could wake the dead. He sighed before pushing himself to his feet and walking around to lean on the front of the desk. There was nothing Peter despised more than seeing Martin completely at ease when he was furious himself.

Perhaps it was an old habit he had yet to rid himself of but getting under Peter's skin was one of his greatest pleasures.

He listened as the boot heels made their way across the entryway and down the corridor. Homer must have directed Peter to the study for him to come here straight away. Martin crossed his arms over his chest and propped one foot back against the desk, doing his best to look serene.

The door flew open and Peter crashed in much like an angry bull, headed straight for Martin. If it wasn't for years of practice in schooling his features, he would be cowering like a puppy, but he had learned long ago that that only gave the bull what he wanted.

"Martin!" Peter roared again. "What have you done with my carriage?"

"Your carriage?" Martin asked innocently. He watched a muscle tick angrily in Peter's jaw and glee circled in the pit of his stomach. "I lent it to a neighbor."

This seemed to take the wind out of Peter's sails a tad. His breathing remained heavy, but he lowered his voice to a reasonable volume. "Why?"

"She needed one. We have many. It made sense." He didn't need to tell Peter that he'd also given two of his horses away. Not yet, at least. The bewilderment on his brother's face was too good to ruin now.

"What neighbor?"

"Your precious carriage will be restored tomorrow, Peter. Why are you so angry about it?" Martin asked. The man didn't typically blow up over such minor things.

Peter grunted and dropped himself into a tall wingback chair, rubbing his temples. The exertion must have taken whatever strength he had left. Martin tried a different tactic. "Should you be resting?"

This elicited a cold glare from Peter that had Martin wanting to shrink back. But he held his ground.

Peter stood suddenly and turned for the door, causing Martin to flinch. He was only too grateful his brother was unable to see it. They were at an impasse. Peter was angry about the missing carriage, but Martin had stumped him—the man wouldn't begrudge helping out their neighbors. So now all that was left was for them to part ways so that his beast of a brother could cool off to a reasonable man again. If that was even possible.

"I should let you know," Martin said, as if an afterthought, to Peter's retreating back, "the Smithsons will be joining us for dinner."

Peter grunted.

Martin waited for the door to close again before he went

back around the desk and sat in the oversized king's chair. He pulled a ledger out of the top drawer of the monstrous desk and began flipping through the pages. He always felt so dwarfed at this desk, as if it was designed to give a man power but merely sapped him of it instead.

He found the tenant he was looking for and made the appropriate marks before putting the book away and leaving the room.

Seeing Miss Kingston today had been something of a shock at first, but then again, he wasn't lying when he'd told her that he had been dreaming of her these last ten years. Nonetheless, the prospect of seeing his childhood savior once he'd learned of her impending arrival hadn't prepared him for the lovely vision she had grown into. Her elegant, lithe figure was no less exquisite for the dowdy gown which had encased it, and everything about her was neat and tidy, from the careful way she'd tucked a fichu into the neckline of her gown, to the neat arrangement of her coiffure.

It was with anticipation that he thought of seeing her again tomorrow. Of course, she was taller than he'd thought she would be, and that gray gown was undoubtedly her idea of mourning, but he couldn't wait to see her in color and dressed up to the nines.

Now that her uncle had been disposed of and she had been informed of the inheritance which was rightly hers, everything had been set into proper motion. Martin smiled, satisfied with himself. He was planning his delightful courtship with her already.

KATE

*D*aydreams of Mr. Evans kept Kate snuggled in the comfortable feather bed long past an acceptable hour on the first morning in her room. Her maid had come in with hot water at least an hour ago and she could hear her scurrying around the room now, most likely setting out another of Kate's plain gowns and tidying the dressing table. It had been a week since she'd last seen Mr. Evans when he'd come personally to retrieve his carriage. She had felt quite disappointed to find him conspicuously absent from the church on Sunday.

Emily had arrived two days prior with a housekeeper in tow, and Kate and Alice both were beyond grateful to have handed over the reins to the seemingly capable Mrs. McKinley. A few maids had already come from Larkfield prior to Mrs. McKinley's arrival and had been working on cleaning the house, but it was a large building and progress had been slow. After only two days in the position, Mrs. McKinley had somehow acquired an army of servants and the entire first floor was very nearly set to rights.

Kate flipped over on her bed and stretched her arms high

above her head. She had not had the luxury of sleeping late in her life and she was glad to take advantage of the opportunity, but it could not be a regular occurrence. The time read eight o'clock and she smiled when she considered that it was probably still early to a great many people. Emily included, no doubt.

With her auburn brown hair coiled on her head in a neat bun and her gray gown in place, she made her way to the breakfast room, surprised to see that Emily had beaten her there and was munching on a triangle of toasted bread.

"Good morning, sleepy head," Emily said after taking a sip of tea.

"Have you recently become an early riser?" Kate asked from the sideboard where she filled her plate with scrumptious food.

"No, but there was a noise that woke me this morning, and I couldn't go back to sleep. I am surprised it did not wake you too —it was immensely loud."

Kate sat beside her friend and began preparing her own tea. "What was it?"

Emily shrugged her delicate shoulder. "I don't know. At first, I thought someone was hammering on the other side of my wall but when I got up to look, there was no one there."

"Odd. I'll have to ask Mrs. McKinley about it."

"Please do," Emily said haughtily. "I'd prefer not to be woken in that manner again."

Kate chuckled as she sipped her tea. She knew not to take Emily seriously. Instead she enjoyed her eggs and spread some marmalade on toasted bread.

"Shall we go into town today and see what their shops have to offer?" Emily asked. "What do you think?"

"I had thought to begin tackling the garden today," Kate said. "Perhaps we can shop tomorrow? Larkfield boasts one millinery and I believe one modiste, and I doubt either of them are quite up to your standards now that you have London's shops at your disposal."

"Nonsense." Emily stuck her nose in the air before shooting Kate a sly grin. "I was thinking we'd shop for you, anyhow. You cannot go on wearing those wretched gray gowns forever. You are not even mourning your uncle."

"No, I am not. But do you not think that local society will find me less than acceptable if I do not show at least some form of mourning? I would never wear black for him, but I do think coming into this house and turning everything upside down and then wearing bright colors on top of that might seem a bit... graceless."

"Then don't wear bright colors. You may choose the darkest colors you can find. Or even stick to gray if you *must*. But at least get something new. Something flattering."

"I don't know," Kate said, focusing on her toast. "I must think on it."

Emily rose from the table with a triumphant smile and danced from the room after informing Kate that she was going to change into her habit and go for a ride. She did not, as a rule, travel without her fine mare, Josephine, and she could not see the day started without a ride. As Emily walked away, Kate heard mutterings about her not being English enough because she refused to learn to ride, and she had to smile to herself. It was not that she never wanted to learn, it was merely the lack of opportunity. When others were taking riding lessons at school, Kate had been busy with her drawing and watercolors. It had seemed like a waste of time for someone that was to spend the rest of their life in a teaching position to learn to ride. Now, however, she had rather wished she had learned. *Now* it would be a practical skill.

Mrs. McKinley walked by the breakfast room just then and Kate got up to chase her down. At a ladylike pace, of course.

"I wanted to ask you if you know anything about a loud hammering sound that woke Mrs. Nielsen early this morning? She believed it to be in the room beside her own."

"Oh, I do apologize," Mrs. McKinley said in her stately way. "There was a table in the library that was stuck against the wall and Alfred was attempting to pry it away to retrieve a book that had wedged in the corner. I promise such a disturbance will not happen again."

"Was he able to retrieve the book?"

"Yes, one of the maids had dropped it when she was dusting. It was a slim little thing but too stubborn to be removed easily."

Mrs. McKinley looked tense standing in the corridor, as though she fought to hold herself there instead of attending to the many other things which she ought to be doing.

"I was also wondering how the search for a butler was going," Kate said.

"I have received a few responses to my post and narrowed it down to two candidates. They will both be coming in for an interview and we shall have a butler in place by the end of next week."

"That is wonderful. Thank you, Mrs. McKinley."

The housekeeper nodded once before briskly stepping away.

Kate watched her leave, swallowing the desire to follow Mrs. McKinley wherever she was going and ask to help. She was accustomed to being useful. Since Mrs. McKinley had come to Split Tree Manor and taken control of the household, Kate had felt oddly bereft.

She was not ready to settle down as the lady of the manor, servants silently swirled around her doing all of the work while she hosted teas and stitched flowers on pillows.

Flowers. A splendid notion.

Kate made short shrift of pulling on her half boots and locating the garden shed behind the house. She found a pair of gloves that were entirely too large but would get the job done and set off for the kitchen garden. There was staff responsible for undertaking the process of caring for both the vegetable garden and the remnants of a pleasure garden, but the head gardener had deemed the ivy climbing up the outside of the house as nearing dangerous and he and his under gardener were both making the vines their primary focus until the situation was under control. Kate located the kitchen garden easily and nearly balked at the mass of overgrown weeds waiting for her.

What had people eaten here the last few months? The garden had to be covered in at least six months of extra growth. She pulled on the gloves with determination before entering the small gated area and getting to work.

Sweat beaded on her brow and quickly cooled in the light summer breeze as Kate worked section by section through the garden plot. As the sun rose steadily behind wispy white clouds, her limbs felt weary, but she continued on, working muscles that had never before been used to such excess. It took hours, or so it seemed, for her to make it through an entire row before she looked behind her only to see an endless expanse still yet untouched. Not one to quit, however, she turned around and kept going. It was easy to fall into a rhythm, and something about pulling the encroaching, polluting weeds from the ground and tossing them into her ever-growing pile was as cleansing as it was restorative.

Hoofbeats sounded faintly in the distance and Kate assumed Emily was back from her ride. She made a mental note to consider purchasing a mare of her own and asking Emily to teach her to ride. With such an abundance of property now belonging to her, it only made sense to have easily accessible transportation. Sitting back on her heels, she looked up at the south wall of the manor. The door to the kitchen could be seen just to her right, and while the house was large and imposing, now that the ivy vines were being managed, it also looked rather serene.

Serene? She recognized the feeling with a jolt, shaking her head in wonder that she could ever pair such a word with a place that housed so many of her miserable memories.

The laugh that sounded in the distance was undoubtedly Emily's, and Kate took the excuse to leave the remainder of the garden to another day. She shed her gloves but took most of the dirt with her embedded in her skirts. With a rueful glance at the work she had yet to accomplish, Kate took off toward the stables, hoping to meet Emily. When she rounded the corner and came face to face with not only her friend, but the object of her most recent daydreams, she felt her face flush before the shock in Emily's eyes could fully reach her consciousness.

"Good day to you, Miss Kingston," Mr. Evans said in a jolly tone indicating the mirth he had recently felt.

"Good day," she mumbled, taking refuge in a curtsy.

"Mercy, Kate! You are filthy!" Emily said in an unguarded tongue. "I did not realize when you spoke of the garden that you intended on doing the work *yourself*. Whatever did you hire those gardeners for?" She seemed to remember their company and added a stilted laugh.

"They are busy tackling the vines, and I was worried about waiting too long to get the crops started. I am not very knowledgeable about these things, but I assume we must get to planting soon if we are going to yield any harvest this autumn."

"We?" Mr. Evans inquired with a bit of a grin.

Kate flushed deeper. "Well, my gardeners, naturally..." She trailed off, unsure of any excuse that would explain her odd behavior to these two. How did she explain to the posh Mr. Evans that she needed to do something with her hands? His opinion of her was not likely getting off to a good start. She looked to Emily for help.

Emily laughed, the sound strained to Kate's ear. "You shall never guess what I did on my ride this morning, and I daresay you will be woefully embarrassed to call me your guest when I tell you."

"I believe you must tell me now," Kate said, playing along.

"I took a fall from my horse in the vicinity of this kind stranger." She gestured grandly to Mr. Evans.

"Oh, dear!" Kate rushed to her side. "Are you well? Have you injured yourself?"

"Kate, I am fine." Emily laughed, tucking a blonde lock under her hat. "I was fortunate. The fall was light and the landing soft. But I'm afraid my blunder was witnessed, and this gentleman would not hear of me coming home unaccompanied."

Mr. Evans gave Emily a kind smile that caused a foolish churn of jealousy in Kate's midsection. Her breath caught at the surprise of such a feeling—and toward her dearest friend. "Do I take that to mean you require an introduction?" she asked, hoping to ward off her irrational, horrible feelings completely.

"Yes," Emily answered. "We have followed the strictures of propriety to the utmost, and I am afraid I must learn my champion's name if I am to thank him adequately."

Kate wanted to laugh. She understood her friend's jest, for it was apparent both Emily and Mr. Evans had a faint idea of who the other person was, or they would not have ended up at Split Tree Manor. Of course, propriety forbade the gentleman to introduce himself and Kate felt a small victory on the recollection that he had forgone such protocol when meeting her nearly a fortnight before. She would like to think that perhaps it meant that he'd had a special desire to learn who she was, but on second thought he had already known, in a sense, for they had met on that day in the forest ten years prior.

"Emily, may I introduce Mr. Evans, our neighbor on the south side, just closer than we are to Larkfield." Emily curtsied prettily as Kate continued. "Mr. Evans, meet Mrs. Nielsen, my dear friend and companion."

"The pleasure is mine. Will I have the opportunity to meet Mr. Nielsen by chance?"

"That would depend on Napoleon," Emily said ruefully.

Mr. Evans nodded in understanding. His head tipped as his eyes portrayed sorrow. "Was he recently sent back then?"

Emily nodded. "I shall be happy when this French nuisance is behind us." She squared her shoulders as if she was heading into battle herself. "Until then, I shall enjoy the days in this beautiful country with my favorite friend."

Mr. Evans turned his stormy eyes upon Kate, and she was lost in the magnetic pull they had over her. "How fortunate our Miss Kingston is to have such devoted friends."

"Yes, fortunate indeed," Kate agreed. The penetration of his gaze did not make her forget her current state of affairs. "Perhaps you would like to come inside, Mr. Evans? I imagine the ordeal you both endured would be greatly improved with a nice, strong cup of tea."

"That would be delightful."

The ladies left Mr. Evans in the drawing room while they retired upstairs; Emily to change out of her riding habit while Kate slipped into her own room and hurriedly wiped the grime from her face and hands and donned a new, yet identical, gray gown. Upon seeing her mud smeared forehead and cheeks in the looking glass, Kate nearly lost any desire to face Mr. Evans again, but quickly decided that reminding him of her clean face and tidy hair would be more beneficial than hiding away.

"I can see why you were so eager to see Mr. Evans again after that first meeting," Emily whispered as they walked down the stairs together. "He is charming and exceedingly handsome. I vow, when I fell from the horse, it appeared as if he was prepared to carry me all the way home, and I, a stranger."

Kate swallowed that familiar feeling of jealousy—Emily was married, for heaven's sake—and grinned at her friend. "I am not surprised. From the first moment I met him I was undone by his charismatic attitude. Not to mention those eyes."

"Well, let us see what we can do to ferret out a little more of

Mr. Evans's history, should we not? I, for one, would like to know why such an eligible man is unmarried."

They arrived at the parlor door and Kate shot her friend a look that told her to behave. She found Mr. Evans seated by the window, the glow of the windows lighting him from behind, and it took all the strength she possessed to refrain from sighing in happiness.

KATE

*N*ever before had Kate worried about the dazzling effect of her smile—or the lack thereof. Nor would she have been able to guess before coming to Split Tree Manor that she would become holed up in her bedroom, seated at her dressing table, and practicing a proper smile in the looking glass. Striking a balance proved difficult. Too large and her uneven teeth were on clear display, yet too small and she appeared as if she was trying to be coy and flirtatious. She could not stomach the idea of being forward or blatant in her attentions to Mr. Evans, but she would also like to show him that she was interested. She practiced with her mouth closed, hiding her teeth completely, but that had the effect of stretching her lips flat.

It was probably in vain anyway. Mr. Evans had not appeared at church last week, so she was unlikely to see him at the service today. But it couldn't hurt to be prepared.

During the tea they had shared a few days prior, Mr. Evans had come up with a wonderful plan to hold a large dinner party and introduce Kate and Emily to the local society. He had told them to expect an invitation shortly and had left Kate in utter suspense, fretting about things that she had previously not cared one wit for, like the degree of her smile.

Her gaze lowered in the looking glass and rested on the starched collar of her plain gray gown. She fingered a simple black button and cocked her head sideways. Perhaps Emily was right. Her self-imposed mourning period was nearly up. And anyway, acting in mourning did not mean she had to be dowdy and plain. She could acquire new gowns in somber tones and retain a proper semblance of mourning to appease any town members who had known her uncle. She wouldn't want the society of Larkfield and the surrounding estates to think her selfish or callous.

With one last attempt at a smile in the looking glass, Kate groaned and made her way downstairs. She passed the closed door beside the foot of the staircase and gave it a wide berth, as usual. Reason demanded she acknowledge that though her uncle had used the room as his study while he was alive, he no longer ruled supreme and could not hurt her anymore. She would not be called into that room ever again, for a scolding or worse. This rational line of thinking did not make Uncle Bartholomew's domain any easier to bear, however, and she had successfully steered clear of it thus far.

The ride to church was spent in quiet reflection. Emily was undoubtedly missing her beloved Paul, and Kate found herself wondering what purpose her uncle had last used the carriage for. Upon further investigation, Kate had discovered a small carriage house located off of the main stables holding a traveling coach as well as an open barouche. Both vehicles were a bit outdated, but in working order by the time Mr. Gibson had gotten through with them. Why he had failed to tell her they were there to begin with was beyond her.

The vicar gave a sermon that would have been uplifting, Kate was sure, had she been paying attention. As it was, her focus was arrested by the man that walked in five minutes after her and sat three rows before her in his graceful way—Mr. Evans. She watched him sing and imagined she could hear his voice among the worshippers, strong and clear. At the end of the service she turned to Emily to give herself a moment to prepare. It was time. She would lock eyes with Mr. Evans, deliver a smile that told him she was interested without being too forward, and then leave. The responsibility would then be his to pursue.

Emily led the way out of the pew, and Kate looked up in time to see Mr. Evans vanish into the churchyard. It was easy to escape since she knew no one from the congregation to hold her captive with conversation, and within moments she was at the door thanking the elderly vicar for his lovely sermon. His eyes twinkled as he let her on her way, and Emily turned back quickly once they were out of earshot.

"What is the hurry for?"

"I just needed to stretch my legs," Kate said defensively, glancing around the groups of people until she spotted that sandy hair and lean coat filled out to perfection. She must have looked satisfied for Emily cocked an eyebrow after noticing the object of Kate's attention.

"You are smitten."

"Maybe I am," Kate responded, surprising herself. "But is that such a bad thing?" After all, the man had shown every sign of being just as interested in her as she was in him. He'd vowed to look out for her, for heaven's sake. Was that not a declaration of *some sort*?

This could be the beginning of something great. Something considerably more appropriate than her childish infatuation with Lucas Alldridge. She was determined to not let poetry anywhere near her intended beau this time.

"Perhaps," Emily said hesitantly. "If he is not smitten back."

Kate looked up sharply to see Mr. Evans leading a raven-haired beauty to his phaeton and handing her up. The woman was short and slender, with a perfectly coiffed head of black hair under a stark white bonnet and an eye for Mr. Evans alone. The unfortunate thing was that Mr. Evans seemed to reciprocate the affection. Kate searched his face as he jumped up beside the beauty for any sense of coercion or obligation, but he was either a very good actor or thoroughly enjoying the company. A rock fell into the pit of her stomach and made a home there. She recognized Emily's hand on her arm in consolation but said nothing, only watched the phaeton disappear down the road.

Perhaps she would go home and write a verse of poetry after all. He needn't read it, of course.

Emily leaned in. "Shall we head home? Alice will want to set out luncheon right away."

"Yes, of course," Kate agreed absently, her hope deflating like a badly baked soufflé.

"I believe Alice plans to take the afternoon to catch up on correspondence with her sisters."

This nudged Kate along, and she gave Emily a rueful smile before tearing her eyes away from the place in the road where the phaeton had disappeared. She glanced up to see the man who had stopped her carriage weeks ago step from the arched doorway of the church.

They locked eyes, and she noticed in the daylight that his were a striking slate blue.

Kate swallowed, her throat suddenly dry as sandpaper. For all of the highwayman's handsome features, he possessed a large and imposing figure. His expression could be described only as fierce, though to say he looked angry would be inaccurate. He nodded once and Kate blushed to find herself staring, but she nodded back slightly.

His approach was measured and slow, his eyes locked on her as he moved.

"Who is that man?" Emily asked, leaning close, her voice low.

The highwayman paused, bending at the waist. "Good day, ladies," he said. "Did you enjoy the sermon?"

Something about the remarkable difference between his crazed, highwayman behavior, and this pleasant gentleman struck Kate as humorous, and a wide grin—no doubt larger than the mirror had proved attractive during her practicing—spread over her lips.

"It was pleasant," she said, aware of the frank cheerfulness dancing in his eyes.

"Excellent. I hope future sermons prove just as agreeable." The highwayman bent in another bow before turning from them and crossing the gravel churchyard to the line of waiting carriages.

"That was very odd," Emily said, eyebrows raised. "Do you know his name?"

"No," Kate admitted. "Though we had an encounter in Larkfield, and I find him to be an interesting man."

"Yes," Emily said, chuckling. "That was evident."

Kate let Emily pull her to their waiting carriage and climbed inside. The highwayman's vivid, smiling gaze flashed in her mind, before it was overpowered by visions of Mr. Evans and the raven-haired beauty.

Had she misread him so thoroughly?

"Tomorrow," she said to Emily as the carriage pulled onto Split Tree Manor's lane, "we will go to Larkfield straight away. I am certain the modiste can do something up for me in muted colors. If you are willing to come and give your input, of course."

"Yes!" Emily clapped her hands together. "I thought you'd *never* ask."

"For the *love* of all things," Emily whispered under her breath. "Do not go with that green for the trim—it will wash you out terribly."

Kate picked up the bolt of green that Emily so despised and pushed it to the other side of the counter.

"Did you not plan to choose dark colors to keep some semblance of mourning?" Emily asked, her pale eyebrows drawn together.

Kate looked longingly at the light blue satin and pushed it away with the green. She sighed and turned back to the modiste. "I would like to look at your selection of violet if I may."

"Certainly."

They were led to a section of the store that held every fabric possible in a variety of purple, from lavender to deep violet. It was true that by the time the ordered gowns were made and delivered, the month of mourning Kate had decided upon would be completed. She was not blind to the expectations of society, however, and choosing deep, muted colors would hopefully satisfy even the most critical neighbors.

They spent the following hour looking through fashion plates and choosing between fabrics and trims for the gowns. The modiste appeared very capable, bustling about with her pad of paper and measuring strip, promising the first of the gowns within the week. Kate only had to hope now that Mr. Evans's dinner invitation would not come before that, for she would be hard pressed to go among company as the dowdy neighbor now that she had seen the competition for his affections.

Rounding off their excursion at the bakery, Kate treated her friend to a fresh blueberry muffin and tea.

"I do miss Alice's plum cake. Have you considered planting an orchard?" Emily asked after wiping her mouth with a napkin.

Kate laughed. "Does that not seem excessive for a simple dessert?"

"That cake is anything but simple! You should be ashamed for calling it so."

Chuckling, they left the bakery and headed toward their carriage. "I would rather show you the blackberry bushes," Kate said. "Though I am afraid they are not in season quite yet. But give them another month or two and we'll have the juiciest berries you have ever tasted, and Alice will come up with confections that will put that plum cake to shame."

"Then I must come back and visit if I miss the ripe season."

Kate pulled up short, yanking on Emily's arm in the process. "Do you plan to leave?"

"Well, yes," Emily said as if it was obvious. "When Paul returns, I cannot very well stay here."

"I understand that," Kate said softly. "I suppose I did not think it would be so soon. The sooner the better, naturally; I had just not thought about it."

"I know." Emily nudged her gently. "When the time comes, I will not leave you without a proper chaperone; do not fear on that account. But do not fault me for wishing Paul was here already."

"I could never!" Kate said with a dramatic hand to her heart. "It would be my dearest wish to have him back in England and safe. I simply want two things at the same time when I must only have one."

"Then let us enjoy what time we have while praying that it will be short."

———

Kate did her best the following day to copy Emily's ladylike habits. She stayed in bed as long as she was able. Which, admittedly, was not very long. Then she met with Alice and Mrs. McKinley to handle household affairs while Emily went for her ride. Following that, the ladies sat in the parlor and embroidered or read until lunch, which was followed by short naps, more embroidery, and then changing for dinner.

After two days of this behavior, she was restless, antsy. Ladylike pursuits were devilishly boring.

She was pleasantly surprised when she finished breakfast on Thursday to find that a gown of green muslin with lace trim and an ivory embellished bodice had already arrived. Kate set it aside to don an old teaching gown instead, and promptly went out to the garden. The gardeners had already done quite a bit of the weeding but there was still a section to be done before the earth could be tilled and replanted. She retrieved her gloves and set to work, enjoying the feeling of the earth in her fingers and the satisfying pull of a weed from the ground, roots and all.

The woods on the far side of the property called her attention, and she paused, tracing the outline of the trees with her eyes. Kate's chest tightened, a heavy feeling settling on her heart. Something did not feel quite right, though she was unable to pinpoint precisely what it could be. Temptation to drop her gardening gloves and walk to the woods nipped at her, but what purpose would it serve? Shaking off the unease, she turned her attention to the weeds. It was merely leftover anxieties from her time here as a child, and she needed to grow up and put aside those irrational woes.

It was well past an hour later when the garden was completely free of obnoxious weeds. Kate sat back on her heels and grinned at the barren plot, picturing the overgrown mess it had been when she had begun. She wiped the perspiration from her forehead with the back of her hand and breathed in the smell of damp earth and salty sweat that came together in a feeling of accomplishment.

"If you're gonna do the work of those maids there, you may as well come in the kitchen for a cup of tea," a snarky voice called from the kitchen doorway.

Kate chuckled, crossing to where Alice stood, bowl in hand

and a wooden spoon stirring while she talked. She'd rather be painting, but until she acquired supplies, she had to occupy herself however she could.

Alice cocked her head. "I've got a pot right here and a fresh batch of biscuits cooling on the table."

Kate's stomach gurgled in response, and she walked past Alice to where the tea and biscuits sat waiting for her. She had worked up an appetite, and the bitter liquid soothed her stomach and warmed her body at the same time. It was getting cold outside and if the clouds in the distance had anything to say for it, a storm was well on its way.

"I did not realize how long I had been out there," Kate said, swallowing a hot biscuit and burning the side of her tongue.

"You were going after those weeds like they'd done you wrong." Alice laughed. "If you're wanting exercise, I can set you up with a lump of dough that needs kneading."

"I will leave that to the expert." Kate picked up another biscuit and ate it in two bites, ignoring convention and propriety since it was only Alice and her in the kitchen. "Where are your scullery maids?"

"The still room," Alice said while stirring the bowl, nodding her head in the direction of the narrow workroom. "I sent Tilly to find the extra jars and then Mary to find Tilly."

"Are you working well together?"

Alice nodded. "I'm right glad I came with you, Miss Kingston. Can't say I have much time to leave the kitchen, but when I do, I know just where I like to be."

Kate raised an eyebrow and watched Alice look out the window toward the stables. "Is there a stable hand that has caught your fancy?"

"Perhaps," Alice said coyly.

Kate laughed with gusto. The woman was incorrigible.

"Miss Kingston?" a voice said from the stairwell. Kate turned to see one of the new footmen—David? John?—standing there with a look of worry.

"Yes...?"

"Daniel."

Kate nodded acknowledgement. She'd been close.

"We've had a message from Mr. Gibson. Mrs. Nielsen's groom returned a half hour past. He doesn't want us to be alarmed..."

"Yes?" Kate pressed, apprehension swirling in her gut.

Daniel swallowed, and she wanted to shake the information out of him. She clutched her hands in her lap and willed herself to sit still.

"Mrs. Nielsen's horse took off and he lost her." Daniel looked to the window as he said this. He didn't need to finish his thought, for it was the same one that Kate was having.

A massive storm was rolling in, and her dearest friend was out there somewhere, lost in the midst of it.

KATE

*I*mages flashed in Kate's mind of a prone Emily lying helpless on the ground, thrown from her horse, the rain drenching her thoroughly. But Kate shook her head, doing her best to shove these fears aside. Until she confirmed the fate of her friend, she needn't jump to the worst possible conclusion.

All of the able-bodied men in the household were dispatched in every direction possible. Kate ran to the woods herself, the last known place the groom had seen Emily, and a very easy place to become lost.

Mr. Gibson had sent two of his stable hands to the neighboring estates to check if Emily had sought refuge from the oncoming storm, but since they were using the only two horses on Split Tree property, aside from the one Emily had brought with her, everyone else was forced to cover what ground they could on foot. She knew the woods were technically not on her property, but they skirted the line, and Emily had mentioned more than once how she loved the serene little brook that ran through the trees. Kate knew precisely where that was.

She had seen it herself as a young girl the day she had met Mr. Evans.

She made it to the edge of the woods before the rain began to fall and was grateful for the canopy overhead that kept her mostly dry. The daylight was fading behind thick clouds overhead, but there was still enough light to see her immediate surroundings. She made it to the brook and began walking alongside it, searching the area on both sides for a figure. Grateful she had thought to run and grab her cloak before venturing outside to search, she pulled the hood over her head as raindrops began to make their way between the leaves.

Kate sent up a pleading prayer and pulled her cloak tighter around her neck. She had to find Emily. If only she'd had the sense to listen to the inkling of a feeling warning her when she had been gardening earlier. Maybe she would have found Emily sooner, or before the woman had fallen at all. She couldn't help but regret her foolishness.

She took a step around a larger tree and stopped. There before her was a chestnut colored horse with an empty saddle.

Peter

Pulling his hat lower over his eyes, Peter scanned the ground before urging Domino on. The groom that had come from Split Tree was nervous enough about the missing woman to beg caution. They had said the lost lady was an excellent horsewoman, merely unfamiliar with the area.

If Peter was a betting man, he'd guess that she'd intentionally lost the groom for some time alone with a suitor. But with the storm sitting on the horizon like a bad omen, it was better to be safe than sorry.

And he'd been sorry too often to risk it again.

A bird let out a cry that stole his attention before his eyes went back to scanning the ground. His senses were tuned in, and he could feel that he was getting close. His arm began to ache, and he shook it out, more vigorously than he should have, but he needed to chase those demons away. It wasn't the time or the place.

Turning Domino away from the stream, Peter pushed the horse up a small incline and paused. He should have been surprised, but he wasn't. He had sensed her before he had even gotten close. He'd always felt his intuition was strong, sharpened further by his military experience. That niggling feeling had once caused him to lift a fallen soldier and find Cohen underneath, his hand too far gone but the rest of him salvageable. Or there was the time the hair had stood up on the back of his neck and he'd found his brothers facing off in the woods; he was certain Charles would have thrashed Martin for landing them in trouble with Father once again, had Peter not intervened and separated the brothers.

But now was not the time for soiled memories. Frustrated with himself for allowing his mind to venture where it ought not, he swung off his horse and tried to focus on the matter at hand. Checking the lady's pulse, he was relieved to find it. It was faint, but she was alive. Though for how much longer was uncertain, for the bump on her head was atrocious. Blood ran down her face in two lines and he swallowed before bending to lift her. He needed to get her to a doctor—and fast.

Peter registered a chestnut nearby and whistled once. Domino came to his side obediently, and he examined his horse, trying to decide how to best get the unconscious lady home. His house was nearer, and the chances of getting a doctor to her there were quicker as well.

He turned to lay her on his horse when he caught sight of the figure standing five feet away, her face pale as a ghost and eyes wide with fright. He found himself impressed that she hadn't screamed, for he recognized her from the churchyard and knew her to be in some way related to the comatose woman in his arms.

Speaking of arms, his left one was rather weak, and the unconscious load wasn't helping.

"Is she..." the lady began, but apparently could not finish her thought. Peter followed it well enough. He may not have inherited any of the brains in the family, but he did understand basic human emotions. Most of the time.

"She's not dead," he said, sounding gruff even to his own ears. But truly, his arm was beginning to ache immensely. "I need to get her to a doctor."

The lady swallowed visibly and nodded, unable to tear her gaze from her friend.

"Come here," he barked, suddenly seeing a usefulness in having someone else nearby. "Are you alone?'

"Yes."

He sighed. It would have to do. He laid the unconscious woman across the saddle. "Hold her still while I get on."

The lady looked from her friend to him like he was insane. She stepped forward, and he could see right away that she knew nothing about horses from her awkward, uncomfortable steps. "Just hold her," he said, showing her where to put her hands. They trembled under his own and he had to force himself to remain focused. He could not comfort the woman now.

Peter made quick work of climbing into the saddle, afraid that one or both of the ladies would drop off if he didn't, before securing his load and turning away.

"Will you ride her horse?"

You'd think he'd asked the lady to raise the dead from the look she gave him. He wanted to curse. The rain was growing steadier. He needed to get this unconscious woman home now, but he couldn't leave the other one alone or he'd end up coming back for her lifeless body next.

"You'll have to do it," he said. "I can't leave you here."

"Yes, you can," she answered forcefully, taking him by surprise. "I will follow. Just take her to Split Tree."

"My house is closer, and she needs a doctor now."

Apparently, she could not find fault with his logic.

"Take her. I will be fine." The conviction in her tone was no match for the determination he saw in her eyes. There was no sense in arguing, particularly when a life hung in the balance. He turned Domino toward home and yelled over his shoulder, "Do not go anywhere!" before speeding away. He could only hope she would be there and well when he got back.

13

KATE

*K*ate was neither stupid nor lazy, and the increasing rain decided for her that she could not stay put. She secured the reins on Josephine and began to pull her in the direction that she knew would lead to the road. She was heading the opposite direction that Emily had just been taken, but she'd rather walk the long way that she knew than risk getting lost trekking through the ever-darkening forest.

When she had come upon the highwayman carrying Emily, she'd wanted to scream, but the sound had lodged in her throat. She had never been so scared in her life. All that blood…

Swallowing, Kate pulled her hood further over her head and yanked Josephine along as fast as she could. She glanced over her shoulder at the horse, and the beast seemed to sense her animosity, for she stopped short, causing Kate to slip in the wet leaves and slide onto her back. Groaning, she stood again and clutched Josephine's reins. She pulled against them with shaky hands, but the animal stood stationary.

"Come on, girl. I need to get to Emily," Kate muttered as she yanked again. "Ugh! If only I understood you ridiculous animals!"

Josephine threw her head back and neighed, as if she was laughing at Kate's ignorance.

"Please?" Kate tried again. She took a deep breath and softened her tone, hoping to gentle her demeanor as well. "We must be off. Let us go see to Emily."

Josephine stepped forward hesitantly and Kate continued to talk to her sweetly until they were moving along at a decent pace again. She wasn't quite running—for if she got the horse started, there would be no keeping up—but she walked as fast as her legs would carry her. They made it to the edge of the forest and onto the road before it occurred to Kate that she had no idea where she was going. Standing there in the pouring rain she realized she was stupid after all, for she had not asked the man which estate he called home. Part of her was tempted to return to Split Tree, for then at least she would be able to change into dry clothes and gather what she needed of Emily's, but would the man know to come for her there?

Kate looked toward the iconic split tree and shivered in the now pouring rain. The canopy of forest was behind her and it only took moments for the rain to drench her clothing. How could she not have asked where he was taking Emily?

Common sense said that he was taking her to Mr. Evans's home, for it was the only estate that was closer than Split Tree to the forest. But he said that he was going to take her to *his* home. Perhaps he was Mr. Evans's steward, or held another role in the house. His clothing was too nice to belong to a servant, but poor gentility often had to take on roles like that, and the man, though seemingly a brute, was obviously a gentleman.

"I suppose we'll take our chances," Kate muttered to the horse before turning down the lane toward Mr. Evans's house. She knew it was about a mile from this turnoff to the main house, and she could handle that.

She was not the one hanging unconscious from a strange

man's horse with a welt on her forehead and blood dripping down her face.

Tears welled up in Kate's eyes and then mixed with the rain. She dashed them away, letting out a shuddering breath. She would not cry. She would be strong.

Her resolve hardened, Kate picked up her skirts and continued mucking through the mud toward Evanslea.

Thunder rumbled overhead, and she was chilled to the bone. Not for the first time, she wished she could just jump on Josephine's back and ride away. Not only would she most likely be dry by now if she was able to ride a horse, but she would have also been able to ride home and tell the staff to call off the search party.

She gulped. Hopefully they'd had the sense to call it off themselves. But why would they? If they didn't know Emily had been found already then it would be even more important to keep the search going with this onslaught of rain.

A black horse with white socks jumped from the forest and splashed mud onto the front of Kate's cloak, drenching the side of her face. She pulled Josephine's lead to stop the horse and then tried to wipe mud from her eye with her wet sleeve, but the mud only smeared. Trying not to get frustrated, she opened the cloak and wiped her face with the inside material, but since it was just as wet as the outside, the action didn't accomplish much.

The man on the horse swung down and stepped toward her with fury on his brow. "I told you to stay put," he hollered.

Kate's instinct was to shrink away from the shouting, but she was grown now, and this man was not her uncle. She straightened her spine. "You hold no authority over me, sir, and I would ask you to refrain from ever speaking to me that way again."

He gave her a look full of incomprehension before turning away, the muscles working in his jaw the only tell against his outer stoicism. "Forgive me. I am used to shouting orders. If I give you a leg up, can you ride the rest of the way?"

"I wouldn't know. I've never tried."

This gave him pause, and he looked at her once more like she was a talking beast rather than a woman. "We need to get out of this rain or you risk catching cold." He flashed her a brief smile. "Should I carry you back the way I carried your friend?"

"I'll try to ride," Kate said, throwing the reins over Josephine's head before the giant of a man could pick her up and sling her over his shoulder. She *assumed* he was jesting with her, but he was a stranger, so one never did know. She stepped to the side saddle and put her hand on the pommel, much like she had seen others do countless times. She turned toward the giant and gave him an expectant look. At least, she tried to. The rain was making it increasingly difficult to see.

"I am Peter," he shouted as he stepped up to her. She watched him approach, his light brown hair matted to his forehead and rain dripping down his cheeks in little streams. She could not tell if his surname had gotten lost in the wind or if he'd intended only to share his Christian name. Strange, to say the least. But there were more pressing matters to attend to now than the intentions of a stranger.

His large hands snaked inside her cloak and closed around her waist. His face so close now, she admitted to herself that the man *looked* exactly like a Peter, before she yelped from the force of being thrown up into the saddle. She scurried to hold onto the saddle, suddenly feeling very, *very* high from the ground. Sound would not transfer through the rain, but she thought she could sense Peter chuckle as he picked up Josephine's reins from where they lay, inches from her own fingers, and then pulled them back over the horse's head. He led Josephine much like a groom teaching a child to ride a pony, but Kate was beyond caring. Her priority was staying on top of the horse.

Peter reseated his horse and set them both to a slight trot.

Kate would have yelled for him to slow down, but she was too busy keeping herself from sliding off the slick leather. Besides, he probably wouldn't have been able to hear her anyway.

Within minutes they were pulling up to the front door of Mr. Evans's house. She was momentarily mortified when Mr. Evans himself swung the front door open and looked right to her, but his gaze slid from her to Peter before she could so much as quirk her lips. Had he not recognized her then? That was not necessarily a good thing.

Peter lifted her down from the saddle and set her on the steps, but she teetered and clasped his forearm to right herself. A steady hand came around her waist ready to guide her, warming her with his solid support.

But the rain was unrelenting. Kate hurried up the steps and through the door faster than her guide and stood dripping in the foyer in all of her muddy wetness a few moments before she realized that she'd entered the house alone. She turned back to see Peter holding both of the horses' reins and leading them toward the stables.

Mr. Evans approached her. "Miss Kingston, the doctor has been sent for. Please come in and get warm."

So he *had* recognized her, then.

"Emily?"

"Your friend is being cared for by my very capable house-keeper. Allow me to direct you to a chamber to make yourself suitable, and I can bring you to her."

Kate faltered. She wanted to argue. What did mud or water matter when Emily's life could very well hang in the balance?

She stood on the ledge between wanting to please Mr. Evans and needing to see Emily when a hand grasped her under the arm and began leading her away. She trembled as the cold registered over her clammy skin and the idea of warm clothes won out. She could not very well be much help to Emily if she was on death's door herself.

99

Martin

Leave it to Peter to try and play the hero.

Martin scoffed, disgusted. He waited on the other side of the door a moment longer, listening to his maids administer to Miss Kingston's needs. It wouldn't be much longer before they were her maids as well. At least, not if he had anything to say for it.

His plan to spark her jealousy in the churchyard had seemed to work well enough. All he did was ask Miss Smithson if he could escort her home from church, and the next thing he knew, Miss Kingston was seen in Larkfield ordering herself a new wardrobe. Quirking his lips in a half smile, he mentally patted himself on the back.

Miss Kingston could have no idea that she was twice the woman Miss Smithson could ever hope to be. Miss Smithson did not understand—*she* had never been bullied.

Martin placed a hand in his pocket and glided down the stairs just in time for the door to open to Dr. Styles.

"Please come in quickly, doctor," Martin said as Homer took the doctor's coat and hat.

"The girl?" Dr. Styles asked.

"I shall direct you to her chamber straight away."

"They say she hit her head."

"Yes," Martin said sorrowfully. "It appears she lost a great deal of blood. Her friend, Miss Kingston, happened upon her in such a state. I believe you may be treating her for shock as well."

The doctor nodded as if he expected this. Women had such fragile constitutions, and it was important to protect them when able. Of course, his woman understood how to protect herself. He had seen it firsthand.

A smile tilted his lips as he led the way to Mrs. Nielsen's chamber and knocked on the door. "Shall I fetch you anything?" he asked as he stepped away.

A maid opened the door and Dr. Styles glanced in the room. "I shall send someone if I have need of you."

With a curt nod Martin walked away, hearing the click of the door behind him. Now to make sure that Miss Kingston had everything she needed.

Kate

Kate was impressed by the grandiosity of the room. A maid was already waiting for her with a heated tub of water, and she undressed and stepped into it, thawing at once.

"How did you know?" she asked the maid, who looked up, startled.

"The master sent Benny to Split Tree right away, ma'am, with a note that the lady was found and instructions to return with dry clothes for the both of you."

Kate smiled to herself as she dipped under the water and let the maid wash her hair. Mr. Evans was so thoughtful. Of course he would foresee her need for dry clothing. As a bachelor, it was unlikely that he had anything to lend her, so she was grateful to see her own gown lying on the edge of the bed. It was one of her older teaching gowns, but at this point, she could not afford to be picky. It was dry, and that was all that mattered.

They worked quickly to rid Kate of the grime and dirt and make her presentable enough to go to Emily's sickroom. She flew down the corridor behind the maid and entered the room as a man in a crisp black coat was leaving it. "Are you the doctor?" she inquired.

"I am," he answered with a little uncertainty.

Kate curtsied. "Miss Kingston. Tell me, how is my friend?"

"Head injuries are unpredictable, Miss Kingston. I wish I had better news to deliver, but that is all I can do for now. I left express instructions to send for me the moment she wakes, or if she worsens."

Kate nodded, swallowing a lump. "Is there anything I can do for her?" Her voice sounded small to her own ears.

The doctor placed a hand on Kate's shoulder and squeezed softly. "Pray, dear."

Kate's shoulders seemed to slump with the gravity of the word. She watched the doctor retreat down the corridor before leaning against the wall and dropping her face into her hands. *Paul.* What would she say to Paul?

A hand rested lightly on her shoulder and she glanced up, startled to find herself looking into slate blue eyes framed by damp golden-brown hair. She found herself lost in the look of compassion that overwhelmed his face.

"Peter." His name was hardly more than a breath on her lips.

"Has she awoken?" he asked quietly.

Kate shook her head. "The doctor's advice was to pray."

"Then we shall," Peter responded without hesitation. "Do not grieve before there is a need." The gentle rebuke went straight to her heart. He was correct—she was mourning the loss of a friend who was still very much alive.

Nodding, she turned toward the doorway, feeling the loss of companionship when Peter's hand slipped away. What was he doing up here anyway? She looked to him and found him gazing at the closed door as well.

"Thank you for bringing her here," Kate said. She realized it would be impossible to show Peter exactly how grateful she felt for his role in the ordeal. The minor *thank you* hardly seemed sufficient.

He cleared his throat softly, obviously uncomfortable with gratitude. "You know her well?"

"Yes. She is my dearest friend. She is acting as my companion as I sort out my inheritance." She gazed at the door and said apologetically, "I must go to her."

"Peter," a sharp voice called down the corridor. Kate turned to see Mr. Evans striding toward them, his mouth pinched. "Dr. Styles would like to see you before he leaves." He gave Peter a pointed look, and Kate was impressed that he would care so much after the welfare of his servant.

Peter nodded and backed away, but not before giving Kate one last searching gaze. She thanked Mr. Evans for being so generous and thoughtful, indicating her warm clothes, before going into the sick room. Emily lay on the right side of a massive four poster bed, her head wrapped in white linen and her skin decidedly pale. A woman sat in the chair beside the bed, and another was busy cleaning up what looked like the remnants of a sponge bath.

"I am Miss Kingston," Kate announced when neither woman seemed to notice her. The one sitting by the head of the bed jumped up and curtsied.

"Marianne, ma'am. But you can just call me Mary. I'll be watching Mrs. Nielsen until she wakes."

"Thank you," Kate said. "May I join you?"

Mary moved to drag over another chair, and Kate went to help her. She took the seat closer to Emily and picked up her friend's limp hand, holding it between her own. She felt so helpless sitting there with nothing to do to wake Emily or ease her discomfort. A fresh wave of regret engulfed her, rising up her body like a slow-moving flame. She *knew* now that the feeling she'd had to go to the woods had been directly related to Emily

—what else could it have been? If only she'd been wise enough to heed the impression.

But she could not go back and change her actions. She could only look to the future and make certain she never made the same mistake again. Taking the doctor's words to heart, Kate closed her eyes. If praying was the only thing that she could do to help her friend, then that is exactly what she would do.

Peter

"Can you rotate it fully for me?" Dr. Styles wanted to know.

Peter lifted his arm slowly and sucked in a breath when he hit the angle that made him wish he'd just had the arm amputated. Of course, that was an absurd notion, but it hurt like the devil. Dr. Styles caught the wince.

"Have you been doing those exercises I showed you?" he asked as if he was scolding a small child.

Peter managed not to look ashamed, but barely. "I will now."

"You really ought to if you want to recover full use of that arm. Today could have ended much differently if you were more diligent in those exercises."

"I would have saved that unconscious woman faster?" he asked with a bite.

"No, but you wouldn't be hurting so much now."

Successfully chastised, Peter promised to work harder at the exercises Dr. Styles had shown him when he'd first began to recover from the injury to his arm. The older man took his spectacles off and placed them within his doctoring bag before snapping it closed and pushing himself to a creaky stand. He let out a slow breath.

"I hope the best for that filly," he said. "I must say, I am rather surprised. I expected Miss Kingston to show more signs of shock."

So that was her name. It made sense now. He had heard that Split Tree was inhabited again, and she had mentioned the need to sort out her inheritance. She must be related to old Mr. Kingston somehow. Hopefully distantly. Very, very distantly.

"She is a strong one in the face of a trial, I gather."

"Hmmm." Dr. Styles nodded agreement. "A good one to have in your corner, I'd say. Or as a nurse in my surgery—I am always wishing for assistance from a female who doesn't lose her wits when faced with blood."

"If gentlewomen took employment like that," Peter said.

"Ah, so it is. So it is." Dr. Styles dipped his head to Peter and took his leave. Peter moved to the sideboard and poured himself a drink, taking a small sip before wincing and leaving the glass beside the bottle.

He dropped into a chair before the fire and watched the dancing flames, picturing the steadfast Miss Kingston as he had seen her that afternoon. Not only was she drenched, but she had been covered in mud. A large smear ran down the entire side of her body. He had watched his own horse splatter a significant amount on her cloak and face when he had found her, but he'd been so frightened when he'd returned to find her missing that it had taken a second longer than acceptable for him to be appropriately sorry about splashing her with mud—accidental as it had been. When he'd returned to the brook to find her gone, he'd gone through stages of fear, anger, and frustration before letting his emotions go and doing his part to locate her. It had not taken long once he'd seen the direction the horse's hoofprints had taken; he had assumed she would be on the lane. Sure enough, she was.

She had been predictable. But it was easy to predict because her logic had made sense, even to him. For some reason that point was important to him, but he did not know why. Perhaps he was only grateful to have a neighbor he could get along with. If she had installed her friend as chaperone in a house she'd inherited, it was safe to assume that there was no man in the picture. Well, no husband at least.

Though, only a simpleton would have missed the flare of jealousy on Martin's face. His brother clearly wished himself that man. Peter only wondered why Martin had not already staked his claim. Was he trying to play the courting game?

14

KATE

For two days, Emily remained unconscious, and Kate refused to leave her side. Mr. Evans was the soul of compassion, arranging for a chaise longue to be brought into the room for Kate to catch a bit of sleep here and there, and had all of her meals brought up on trays. He stayed for dinner the second night, telling her that he'd much rather dine informally with her than in the cavernous dining room downstairs any night. This had caused a blush to steal over her features, and though she could not be entirely certain, she felt like she had delivered the perfect demure smile in that moment.

Morning crept behind the thick burgundy drapes and filtered light into the room. Stretching her arms over her head, Kate yawned widely. She pulled on her dressing gown, tying the sash around her waist before a flutter of movement claimed her peripheral vision. Turning sharply, she saw it again, swallowing the gasp that rose to her throat.

"Emily?" she said softly, picking up her friend's hand and squeezing it gently. A soft flicker of eyelashes was Emily's response. Kate held her breath, waiting for Emily's eyes to open fully. "Mary. Mary!" Kate called frantically over her shoulder.

The maid had been awake with Emily for the last few hours but had slipped from the room when Kate had awoken.

Footsteps sounded in the corridor, and the door flew open. Kate was startled to see Peter but swallowed her surprise and shouted her orders. "She has awoken. We must fetch the doctor immediately."

He glanced to the bed and nodded before rushing back into the corridor with no hesitation.

Kate sat beside Emily on the edge of the mattress and lowered her voice, the smile on her face full and unrelenting. Gathering Emily's hand in both of her own, she leaned forward. "Good morning, dear friend. I have never been so glad to see those lovely eyes of yours."

Emily attempted to sit up but fell back to the pillows, her hand coming up to the dressing on her forehead. She opened her mouth to speak but only delivered a croak.

"Have you a massive headache?" Kate asked. "No, do not nod. I understand. I shall send Mary for some tea, and the doctor will be here straight away. Alice has sent over a pot of beef broth each day and a delightful restorative calf's jelly. I am certain once you have eaten you shall feel more yourself."

The answering smile pierced Kate's heart, tender and small. She swiped at her cheek as a fat tear rolled free, and she laughed self-consciously. She had been so afraid.

Mary returned, nearly dropping the ewer of hot water she carried to the washbasin, and was soon dispatched for hot tea and to alert Cook to warm the broth.

A soft knock at the door preceded Peter's entrance, and he came silently to her side as she rose and stepped away from the bed.

"I've sent the fastest horse. Dr. Styles should be here shortly."

Kate looked up into his blue-gray eyes and smiled. "Thank you."

His gaze traveled the length of her body before glancing away sharply. She was conscious of her state of dress and pulled the dressing gown tighter around her neck, toying with the ribbon at the end of her braid.

"Is there anyone else we should inform?" he asked, his voice gruff.

Kate screwed up her nose in thought. Paul. There could be no other that needed to know as he did. But would sending the news be his downfall? It would break Kate's soul to deliver such information, only to have Paul lose his head in battle.

Peter's voice lowered, his gaze roaming her face. "What is troubling you?"

"It is her husband," Kate replied automatically, stepping closer to Peter. She was sure they were far enough away that Emily wouldn't overhear, but she wanted to be careful just the same. Peter towered over her, but when he spoke in that gentle way, she felt cocooned in comfort which loosened her tongue. "I cannot know if this will be harmful or helpful information. I have yet to write to him." She glanced up to find surprise on his face, shortly followed by chagrin. Had he not known Emily to be married? The poor man. Perhaps he was suffering a hero's trial and found himself drawn to the lady he'd rescued.

"I can send another man—it does not matter how far. I should think her husband would want to know."

"All the way to Brussels?"

Stunned, Peter leaned back. "He is fighting?"

Kate nodded. "It has been my duty these last weeks to keep Emily occupied. She worries excessively."

"Naturally," Peter agreed.

They stood in comfortable silence, each wrapped in their own thoughts. Kate glanced over her shoulder to the pale face of her friend and sent up another prayer of gratitude that she had awoken.

The door opened then, and Dr. Styles came in, his cravat in

disarray and wrinkles lining his coat. He had either dressed in yesterday's clothes or had yet to change out of them.

"Your groom caught me on the road home," he said by way of explanation, passing Kate and leaning down to speak directly to Emily.

A hand came to her elbow and gently nudged her from the room. "Shall we give them some privacy?"

Kate nodded and followed Peter into the corridor. He cleared his throat and she looked up, caught by how very tall he was.

"I can see why you've hesitated, for it would be dreadfully distracting going into battle with such worries on his mind." He paused as if weighing his words. "But I cannot help but think that if my wife were lying in bed across the sea with a head injury, I should like to know. If nothing else, so that I could pray."

She realized with a start that she had not even considered this. "Of course," she said quietly. "I am embarrassed the thought hadn't occurred to me."

"It cannot be a bad thing, I'll add, that you've waited until she has awoken. After speaking with the doctor, you will have a better idea of your friend's condition, and you may be able to give her husband less anxiety."

"That is true. Thank you, Peter. You cannot know how you have eased my burdens."

He smiled down at her ruefully. "I believe it is the least I can do after our very first meeting, Miss Kingston. After stopping your carriage like a mad highwayman, it is I who stands in your debt."

"Nonsense," she said, grinning. "You gave my cook quite a fright, but she still tells the story to anyone who will care to listen. It is the highlight of her young life thus far."

His chuckle was almost a low growl, and she could feel it from where she stood, shivers chasing her spine. "Glad I could be of service," Peter said, doffing an invisible hat. "Is there any other way I can assist you this morning?"

"No, I shall wait for the doctor here. I cannot think he will be much longer, and I would hate to miss him."

"I can wait here if you would like to..." Peter cleared his throat awkwardly, his cheeks pinking. "And, um, tell the doctor you'd like to speak with him before he leaves."

Kate felt her neck grow hot. Somehow, she had forgotten again that she was not yet dressed. She stepped away, avoiding Peter's face. "Actually yes, that would be wonderful. And..."

"Yes?"

"I cannot help but think that perhaps your master would like to be informed."

Confusion shot across his face. "My..." Peter raised both eyebrows, and Kate had the dreadful feeling in the pit of her stomach that she had somehow made a blunder. Was Peter not in Mr. Evans's employ after all? Oh, dear. Could he simply be a poor relation?

"I can make sure Martin knows, of course," Peter said tightly. "And I will send a maid to fetch you as soon as the doctor is finished." His tone was a clear dismissal, and Kate delivered a brief curtsy as a reflex before turning to her own bedchamber a few doors down. She shut the door behind herself and leaned on it, closing her eyes and willing the last few minutes to be erased from Peter's mind. How foolish of her to speak of his master to him without any sort of confirmation. She wanted to sink down into the carpet immediately.

Instead, she changed into the clean, violet gown that had been brought over with other fresh clothes the day before. It had ivory ribbon on the hem and under the bosom, with lavender embroidery throughout. It was simple yet pretty and made her feel considerably less dowdy than the dove gray teaching gowns she had been so used to wearing for the last few years.

She washed her face and neck before styling her hair in a simple chignon.

She opened her door at the knock and was slightly disappointed to see Mary on the other side. Of course Peter could not come to her door, but she had hoped that he would, nonetheless. She was anxious to apologize.

She followed Mary downstairs and to the breakfast room where Dr. Styles was just sitting down with a loaded plate. Her appetite was absent, so she chose a chair across from him and waited to hear how Emily fared. Mr. Evans walked in behind her and she gave him a strained smile, but she could do no more than that at present.

"It is hard to say this early," Dr. Styles said around a mouthful of sausage. "But I have high hopes for Mrs. Nielsen. I believe lots of rest and good, solid meals should see her up and on her feet within days."

"That is grand news, doctor," Mr. Evans bellowed before taking his own seat beside Kate.

"When may I take her home?" Kate asked.

"To Split Tree?"

She nodded.

"I will come and check on her again tomorrow morning, but if she is able to get up and move about then I see no reason why she could not sustain such a short carriage ride." He placed a hand up in surrender. "She may choose to wait longer, for that bump is bound to be the cause of a nasty headache for some time, but the sleep and the broth should help to ease it. And I have left her maid with plenty of headache powders and laudanum. Only time will tell."

Kate nodded. She faintly recognized Mr. Evans beside her offering to fill a plate, but she shook her head. She could not stomach the idea of breakfast while her conscience was so disheveled.

Standing, she gave a thankful look to the doctor. "Please send me your bill; I am very grateful for all you've done."

He shook his head. "It has already been covered, Miss Kingston. Don't worry your little head over such things."

"Has Mrs. McKinley…" Kate shook her head. No, the house-keeper was unlikely to have known she needed to handle the doctor's fees already.

"Let us say your host here has been very generous," the doctor said mischievously, offering a wink.

Kate looked to Mr. Evans right away and saw his eyes shift uncomfortably before turning them to her and delivering a handsome smile. She smiled in return and thought belatedly that she had not opened her lips, so they must have been dread-fully stretched across her uneven teeth. Somehow, she did not care.

"I must write to Captain Nielsen right away."

The men stood and bowed her from the room. She raced upstairs and checked on Emily, only to find her sleeping with Mary beside the bed once more, before going to her own room and beginning a letter to Emily's husband. She explained the entire situation as best she could— apologizing for the delay but hoping he would be forgiving since she was able to send him news of Emily's awakening as well—and signed it with a post-script that she would write again if there were any changes. She added a reminder that Emily was expected to make a full and speedy recovery, for good measure.

Blowing on the letter, Kate paced her room. She was uncom-fortable. Emily could not be moved yet, but Kate could not stay. Not until she had cleared her conscience. Was that selfish of her? Perhaps Peter wanted nothing to do with her ever again after such a dreadful *faux pas*. Disappointment snaked its way through her. She had begun to think she was making a friend.

Locating Mary at Emily's bedside, she sat in the chair beside the maid's and looked her in the eye. "Have you worked here long, Mary?"

"Going on two years, I am," Mary nodded proudly.

"And who do you answer to?"

She looked confused at first. "Mrs. Bradley? She's the house-keeper. Or do you mean the master?"

"Does Peter work here in any capacity?"

Mary reeled back before taking on a thoughtful look. "I suppose he does, Miss. He helps the tenants when they need something fixed. And he spends more time with those horses of his than he does in this house."

She had been right, then. "Is he not Mr. Evans's steward, then?"

"Mercy, no!" Mary laughed. "Sir Peter is Mr. Evans's older brother, Miss."

Kate could feel the blood drain from her face. "Did you say *Sir* Peter, Mary?"

"Yes." Mary's eyebrows screwed together. "Are you feeling well?"

"No, I don't believe I am. I think I need to lie down for a minute if you think you have things under control here."

Mary nodded, and Kate made her escape. She did not know what was more embarrassing: that she had refrained from calling Peter by his proper title, or that she had referred to his younger brother as his master. And what would Martin think of how she had disrespected his brother? He would be appalled, surely.

All of her experiences with Peter thus far flew in and out of her mind as she analyzed each way she had erred. Just this morning she had *commanded* him to fetch the doctor. She fell onto her bed and closed her eyes. Perhaps if she took a nap then she would wake from this wretched dream.

PETER

*P*eter reined Domino in, entering the stable yard at a canter. He had ridden long and hard to remove the anger that had come over him when he'd realized that Miss Kingston thought he worked for Martin. Of all the crazy things to think... He shook his head again, loosening the irritation that welled up in his mind. He could not be mad at her, for she could not have known better. It was his idiot brother he blamed.

Was Martin really so desperate to be distanced from Peter that he would give the impression that Evanslea was his? Actually, that didn't surprise him one bit. Martin had acted like he ruled the estate long before Peter had returned from fighting on the Peninsula.

Jumping from his horse, he tossed the reins to a nearby stable hand and began walking briskly back to the house, jerking his riding gloves from his fingers as he went.

"I'd like a bath," he mentioned to Homer as he entered the house. He took the stairs two at a time and turned sharply toward his bedroom before running straight into a maid.

No. Not a maid. "I apologize, Miss Kingston," he said, placing a hand above her elbow to steady her. She was dressed in dark violet now, the look of worry over her features so apparent, he was suddenly stricken. "Is Mrs. Nielsen—"

"Oh, no! I mean yes. Emily is fine," Miss Kingston said, offering him a pitiful smile. "I had hoped to run into you."

"Perhaps not literally, though?" Peter said. He could not help it, and the small smile he received was worth the bad jest.

"I feel I need to apologize, Sir Peter."

He cringed. So she had discovered his status, then. He'd left off the title intentionally when he'd met her, irrationally hoping she'd never discover the truth.

"You do not like the title?" she asked, her brow raising slightly.

Was he so easy to read? "I find I quite prefer 'Captain Evans' to 'Sir Peter,' if I am completely honest."

Her mouth dropped. "You are a captain?"

"Was," he corrected.

"So you understand," she said quietly.

Yes, he understood. Miss Kingston was referring to their conversation earlier about Mrs. Nielsen's husband.

He nodded.

Miss Kingston brought her fingers to her temples and rubbed them gently. "I feel my list of blunders is steadily increasing."

"You cannot be faulted for what you did not know."

She peered up at him, unconvinced. "You are not dreadfully angry with me?"

"Not with you," he said easily.

Her face lit up briefly before it fell. "You cannot be angry at Mr. Evans—he never said he was master here. I am afraid I made assumptions."

Peter nodded. There was no sense in discussing Martin.

A hand on his arm stilled him, the touch putting his nerves on high alert. "Can we be friends again, Sir Peter?"

"I wasn't aware that we were not," he said truthfully. He wasn't aware that they were ever friends to begin with, to be completely honest, but that was not something she needed to know. He had been happy previously to gain an agreeable new neighbor. He would take her friendship as a win.

She pulled back her hand self-consciously, and he tried to smile away the awkwardness.

Kate

"Are you in need of anything else?"

Kate looked up into his smile, one she was sure he did not use frequently enough, and thought of all of the kindnesses he had bestowed on her in the last few days. She was suddenly aware that all of the many things she had assumed Mr. Evans had done for her could very well have been Peter.

"Is something troubling you?" he asked.

"I was told the doctor's bill has been taken care of."

"That is the last thing that you should worry about at present. You need only to care for your friend and her health."

"I have taken advantage of your hospitality quite enough," Kate said kindly but resolutely. "I would find it a great disservice if you do not give me the opportunity to pay my own bills."

Peter nodded. She felt that he understood, only she could see that he also found it pointless to argue. "I will have my steward send a bill to yours."

"Actually, have him send it to me. I have yet to acquire a man of business, and I have been handling all of the business items myself thus far."

She thought Peter looked impressed, but she might only have imagined it. "Are you planning to acquire any help?"

Kate nodded. "Our new butler only just arrived, and I hoped

he would go about the business of finding me a steward. I've just discovered quite an expanse of land on the north side of my property that I'm told would be perfect for an orchard. But I cannot set any plans in motion until I have fully staffed the house."

Peter nodded. "The stretch of meadow that lines my western field. I had never thought of orchards before, but I believe you are right. Apple?"

"Plum," Kate said with a smile. "My cook makes a fantastic plum cake."

"Quite worth the orchard, I assume?"

"Oh, indeed. Though I miss living beside an apple orchard immensely, I must say."

"And you cannot do both?"

Kate raised a shoulder in an unladylike shrug. "I had hoped to find a land steward who would help me discover exactly what I can and cannot do."

Peter nodded, clasping his hands behind his back. He began to step down the corridor toward the stairs, and Kate fell in beside him. "Have you any other developmental plans? I know the previous owner had sheep, but Bartholomew Kingston did not."

She pulled up short. "The owner before Uncle Bartholomew? That would have been my father."

Peter shot her a sympathetic glance. "I was quite young when he was master there, but it was my understanding that he had a successful sheep venture going for a few years."

"I know nothing about my father's time at Split Tree," Kate said quietly. "Did you know him?"

"Only vaguely. He met with my father here on occasion, and I knew him in passing, but I was young then—a child."

Kate was disappointed. Knowing that Uncle Bartholomew owned and ran Split Tree had tainted the estate in her mind. When she had discovered that he'd never really owned it all along but had only acted so in the capacity of her guardian, she'd never fully considered the legacy of her father's role in the estate, or that he had given it to her. The house, the lands...they were all Kate's, all along. The concept completely fueled her curiosity. She had always mildly wondered about her parents, but now she found herself yearning to know everything about them and how they had lived in and run Split Tree.

"Would you be able to tell me what you remember?"

"I do not recollect much, but I can share with you what I recall."

Kate grinned. "That would be marvelous. Only" —she glanced back up the stairs— "I should probably sit with Emily for a good while after I take care of this letter. Mary is likely in need of a break."

"Perhaps later. I am in no hurry," Peter supplied.

"Wonderful. Thank you, Peter," she said. "Oh! I do apologize, *Sir* Peter. I believe I have already formed a habit."

"I would consider it an honor if you would address me without that blasted 'Sir,'" he said, before hurriedly adding, "Excuse my language."

Kate chuckled. "Only if you call me Kate. And only, perhaps, when we are not in mixed company." She would hate to give the impression that she and Peter had some sort of agreement.

Peter nodded, and she was grateful he understood. "Now I must post this," she said, waving the letter that she'd written to Paul.

She walked away from Peter with the express feeling that she was going to learn a great deal from him.

KATE

*L*ate the following morning, Kate closed the door to Emily's room softly, leaving her snoozing friend behind with Mary as she went in search of Peter. Dr. Styles had come and gone and determined that Emily would need to remain abed until she could comfortably walk about the room. Since she had not been able to kick her headache long enough to try such a thing, she had agreed to do her best to sleep as much as possible. Not a difficult task, Kate assumed.

Locating a liveried footman standing sentinel near the bottom of the stairs, Kate asked him where she might find Peter and was directed to the study where she had first met Mr. Evans when she had come inquiring after the purchasing of horses. Peter fit behind the large, oak desk far better than Martin had.

She swallowed that unfair thought. Mr. Evans could not help that he was smaller in stature than his brother.

Peter had not heard her come in, and she watched him, head bent, face earnest as he poured over the open account book on his desk.

"Is this a good time to visit?" Kate asked, stepping further into the room and leaving the door open behind her. She hated to disrupt his concentration, but had he looked up and found her watching him, he'd have thought her odd.

He slid a finger down the page in front of him, holding it in place before glancing up and meeting her gaze. "Of course. Please, come in." Retrieving a quill from the drawer, Peter dipped it in the inkwell and made a note on his paper before putting it away and turning his attention on Kate.

She slipped into the chair opposite him, lowering herself onto the soft leather seat and arranging her hands in her lap. "Yesterday was quite distressing. I hope you don't mind that I've sought you out so we might continue our conversation. I would very much like to hear what you recall of my father."

His expression turned soft. "You might find yourself disappointed in my report. I was very young, and I only remember images of him coming to the house to speak with my father here, actually" —his hands and face lifted, indicating the room — "in this very study."

Kate glanced around, looking at the room as though fresh light was shining through the window. Her father, such a distant, absent creature in her life, had spent time in this very chair—this very seat, perhaps—in matters as mundane as business or local political chatter. She'd never know what the men had spoken of, only that they had been neighbors. Kate had spent so much time hating Split Tree and the negative connections it held for her regarding her uncle, she had not given proper consideration to the realization that before it was in her uncle's hands, Split Tree had been her parents' home. There might even be positive memories of the old house in the very recesses of her mind.

"Are you distressed?" Peter asked, his voice soft.

"No." Kate shook her head, firmly leveling the man with her gaze. "I did not have a pleasant experience living at Split Tree with my uncle, and I dreaded returning to his house. I suppose I haven't given credit to the idea that Split Tree was my father's estate first."

"And his father's before that? Split Tree is part of your history far deeper and longer than Bartholomew Kingston's ownership." Peter rose, towering over her and the desk as he came around to the front of it and took the seat beside her, where Alice had sat when last they were in this room. "There is very little a child understands when listening to the conversation of adults, except for the way those adults make him feel. I recall your father smiling at me in a way that eased my discomfort, and while that is all I really remember, I think it is enough to note that he was a man of good character."

Peter's steel-blue eyes bore into her, flicking back and forth as if he was trying to read her expression. A hot tear welled, dripping down her cheek and she dashed it away, chuckling. "I am usually far too practical to cry," she said.

His smile was warm, comforting. "There is nothing wrong with crying, Kate."

Sucking in a cleansing breath, she gave him a weak smile. "Perhaps not. But the last few days have seen more tears than they ought."

Peter's large hand came around the arm of his chair, and Kate was arrested by the sight of it. She hadn't been around men very often in her life. Did men always have such strong, capable hands? Kate didn't know, but she certainly didn't think so. The lawyer who had come to see her in Mrs. Presley's office did not inspire this sort of comfort and ease. He'd fumbled the papers far too much to inspire any confidence in his hands.

"I think you must allow yourself some grace in this instance," Peter said. "You did not know for a time whether your friend would awaken. That would distress a great many people."

"Anyone with a heart, surely," Kate quipped.

Peter

Anyone with a heart. Well, Kate had one of those, clearly.

Peter leaned back in his seat, creating more space between them. Kate's strength of character had been made obvious with her clear head multiple times over. When he'd idiotically stopped her carriage like a mad highwayman, when she'd discovered him in the woods holding her friend's limp body, when she'd had to wait for two days for the woman to wake. Kate had kept a level head through each circumstance.

Dr. Styles had said so first, but it was true: this was the sort of woman one wished to have on one's side.

"Perhaps this whole thing would have been avoided if I rode." She turned her gaze sharply, catching his eye. "This is the second time Emily has fallen since coming to Split Tree, you see, and she is typically an excellent horsewoman. I'm not sure what has her so distracted, but perhaps she would not have grown so careless had I ridden out with her."

"You cannot blame yourself," Peter said. "You can only look to the future." He held her gaze, taking advantage of the opportunity to roam her face. What was it about Kate that was so familiar? He was certain he'd never met her before in his life, but she had a quality about her that nipped at him, that led him to believe they *had* met before.

"And in the future, I ought to ride?" she asked with a quirk of a smile.

"If you are comfortable with it, yes. It would be useful for a woman in your position to have such a skill."

She bent her head.

Had he gone too far?

"I really need to get myself a land agent," she said. "Otherwise I will be forced to learn to ride."

124

Leaning back in his seat, Peter rested his ankle on the other knee, crossing his hands over his stomach. "Why not both?"

Kate chuckled. His body tightened and he decided in that moment the sound of Kate's laughter was one of his most favorite things.

She lifted her eyebrows. "Shall I apply that same line of thinking to the dilemma with what I ought to do with my land?"

"Sheep or an orchard?" Peter asked. Now they were veering onto steadier ground. This was safe. "If you chose both, you would only be able to give half an effort to each. It would be wiser to focus all of your resources into making one of them successful. Then later, once the first was established, you could venture into the second."

Kate nodded, her mind clearly elsewhere. But Peter was not in a hurry. He would sit and discuss these business ventures for as long as he could.

Kate

Kate spent one more day taking advantage of Peter's hospitality, and Mr. Evans's companionship, before Emily's head felt recovered enough to endure the carriage ride home. Emily retained her dignity by walking herself down the stairs and to the carriage, however heavily she leaned upon Mr. Evans's arm. Kate thanked both of the brothers all they had done and proceeded to help Emily into the carriage, before stepping up to sit beside her, trying to remain unalarmed by how exhausted her friend looked. She was still recovering, and it would be some time before Emily fully regained her strength. The doctor had told them this was to be expected.

Dr. Styles planned to call on them that afternoon to check in with his patient anyhow, after giving her ample time to rest, and Kate was glad to have such a diligent man watching over Emily's health.

The carriage moved at a crawl, but that did not bother Kate. She was grateful to be returning home.

The word stuck in her mind as she came to realize what she had unconsciously thought. She had referred to Split Tree Manor as her home. It was a surprise, though she found it was not an unpleasant one. Once Peter had helped her to look past Uncle Bartholomew's ownership and recall that her ancestors held much more history in the house than her uncle did alone, she was able to see the estate in a new light. Perhaps she could erase his black mark on the place forevermore. She had already done that to a small degree by cleaning the house and opening up previously closed rooms. Perhaps it was time she redecorated the parlor and dining rooms. A wisp of revulsion snaked through her as she thought of doing the same in the study or library. *No, not yet.* She would take this one step at a time.

Kate spent teatime in the parlor after helping Emily up the stairs and into bed. She had brought down her sketchbook and a charcoal pencil and began reimagining the parlor in a variety of colors and styles. Of course, the colors were all neatly labeled, but she would have to go over them later with watercolors if she was planning on showing anyone else her vision. After an hour or so, the redesigns became something of a game, and she went from decent, classic ideas to the most far-fetched themes she could conjure.

One particularly amusing rendition of the room entirely done over in the Greek sense, complete with statues, gauzy drapes, and gold-leafed furniture, was interrupted by the arrival of Dr. Styles. Kate accompanied him upstairs and remained nearby while he examined the recently awoken Emily, then spoke with him in the foyer on his way to another patient's house.

"She is coming along nicely," he said. "If you will continue to ensure that she rests adequately, I believe her body and mind will heal quickly and efficiently."

"Absolutely. Thank you, Dr. Styles," Kate said.

He gave her a fatherly smile before glancing around the foyer and back to her. "It is nice to see Split Tree looking so warm again. It feels like so long ago now, but your mother did throw the best parties."

Kate stilled, her brain taking a moment to catch up to her ears. "Did you know my parents well?"

"Oh, yes," Dr. Styles said, tilting his head in compassion. "Quite well. I grew up with both of them. And the sweetest couple they were."

Kate's eyes began to tear of their own accord, and she cleared her throat quietly. "I am afraid I know nearly nothing about either of my parents."

"Is that so? Well, what a shame." Dr. Styles tsk-tsked. "Mrs. Styles and I must have you over for dinner one of these nights, and we can fill your ears with larks from their younger years."

Kate nodded, trying not to appear as eager as she felt. The doctor gave her a sympathetic smile before leaving Kate to cry in the foyer uninhibited.

She went to pull a handkerchief from her sleeve and realized that she had forgotten to get a clean one that morning. Wiping her face as best she could, she returned to the parlor and her sketchbook, but she could not focus, her mind running wild with the things she had just heard. Having been placed in a stranger's home by her uninterested uncle until the age of nine, Kate had very few memories of her parents. And when she was brought back to Split Tree Manor for the years of nine until twelve, there was no illusion of love or familial affection in the household. She had not even connected Split Tree Manor to her own parents until quite recently. Of course, she had tiny snitches of memory of her beautiful young mother singing to her in bed, or her curly-haired father throwing her into the air and catching her once again, but they had died when she was four, and the memories were neither full nor very reliable.

Spreading out her various designs on the low table in front of the sofa, Kate had to snicker at the Egyptian room with hieroglyphics on the walls, and the jungle room with furniture carved to resemble animals and a multitude of potted ferns and trees lining the walls.

"Miss Kingston?" a maid said, curtsying at the doorway. "Mrs. James would like a word on Mrs. Nielsen's diet requirements when you have a minute."

"Thank you, Jane. I will come now," Kate said, leaving her drawings to finish later and following the maid downstairs. She really was so fortunate to have been able to bring Alice with her. Not only was the woman a mastermind in the kitchen but having worked in a school for girls that had seen every illness imaginable, she had a thorough understanding of what Emily would need to heal fuller and faster.

KATE

*T*he following day brought an invitation from Mr. Evans to dine at his home on Wednesday. Dr. Styles had sparked a yearning within Kate to meet the families that had been around for years, and she hoped to make the acquaintance of those who might remember her parents. But Emily was still in something of a delicate situation, and Mr. Evans, of all people, ought to have considered that when the very purpose of the dinner party was to introduce Kate *and* Emily to the local gentry.

She brushed aside the concerns to worry over later. Emily would know best how to handle this situation.

A second missive arrived with the invitation, and she opened the note to discover Peter's sure, tidy scrawl. Trailing her eyes down the page, she read a full accounting of the bills she had accrued while staying at Evanslea. A laugh escaped her throat when she read the line where Peter had charged her a pittance for *rescuing the damsel in the rain* and then a slightly larger sum for *going back for the lady who would not stay put,* as well as a small fee tacked onto the latter for *undue stress in searching for said woman.*

His sense of humor was in sync with her own, which she had

discovered while they talked sheep and orchards, debating the merits of the two until the orchard had ultimately won out. She liked the idea of raising sheep as her father did, and maybe she still would one day, but if she ever wanted an orchard on this land then she needed to begin straight away.

She set the note from Peter beside the invitation to dinner, noticing a small scrap of paper falling onto the floor. It was a postscript from Peter—the name and direction of a trustworthy land agent, should she still be in need of one. She laughed aloud when she read the tiny print on the back that told her this man was particularly gifted at purchasing fine horses, should she be in need. Was this what it felt like to have a brother? A man she could speak easily with, who made her feel comfortable while discussing unladylike pursuits? She had confided in Peter that she thought it was time for her to learn to ride, though the concept terrified her even greater after her bout with Josephine in the rain.

Horses in general were so very tall.

She carried the two cards up to her room and set them on the fireplace mantel. One to make her laugh and the other to give her hope. Mr. Evans had been quite attentive during her stay at Evanslea, and regardless of who owned the estate, she was not one to turn away an interested, eligible man. Besides, she *had* her own estate. What would she do with it if she married someone that came with a house of his own?

She made her way to Emily's room and knocked on the door softly.

"Come in."

Kate found Emily seated in a plush chair near the fire, her face drawn, a slight bloom to her cheeks. She was beginning to look more herself, but she seemed to tire very easily. "I had thought to go into Larkfield and pick up a novel from the lending library. Is there anything I can do for you while I am there?"

130

"Why would you go all the way into Larkfield when you have a perfectly nice, fully stocked library right here?" Emily asked with a raised brow. Kate knew she was being baited, albeit good-naturedly.

"Perhaps I would like a more modern selection, thank you," Kate countered with as snobby a tone as she could muster. "I will bring you one of those gothic novels you love so much if you promise to keep that tongue in check, missy."

Emily smiled. "I promise. Now tell me, has anything arrived from Paul?" The eagerness in her voice was heartbreaking.

"Not yet, I'm afraid. But remember that he cannot have even received my letter yet, so it is unlikely you shall hear from him until at least another week has come and gone."

"I know. I just miss him." Emily sighed. Her gaze flitted to Kate and away, her jaw working as if trying to determine what to say. "I do not know what came over me that day in the storm. Or, well, maybe I do."

Kate waited a moment. The silence stretched, and she tried to find a balance between giving Emily the space she needed and prying for information too quickly. It was clear that Emily wanted to talk about what happened, but it was delicate. She had never before fallen from a horse, and yet she'd been unseated twice already at Split Tree.

"I always worry when Paul goes away. It is natural, I believe." Emily turned her gaze to the fireplace, and her eyes glazed over. "We have been planning on settling more permanently. He was going to sell out and find an occupation that could keep him home. But of course, we were not quick enough. Once he was called back to fight, he couldn't back out; it isn't in his nature."

Kate nodded. "Paul is noble. He would have felt it his duty to go."

"Precisely," Emily agreed. "And though I know it is irrational, I find myself worrying about him constantly. So many of his friends have been coming home injured. Or worse," she added, her voice falling to a whisper, "not coming home at all."

"Becoming so distracted with worry that you make careless mistakes and injure yourself will not bring Paul home faster," she admonished quietly. "So you may as well take care of yourself."

"Yes, the logical part of me understands that; the irrational half wants to panic relentlessly. That half usually wins."

Kate put an arm around her friend and gave her shoulders a squeeze. "Perhaps you ought to refrain from riding until you can do so without losing your head. Or falling from Josephine."

Emily's lips bent into a wry smile. "That would probably be best. I'm just not myself."

"Do you feel like coming with me into town?"

"No, thank you. I have been walking circles about the room for exercise, and I think I am due for a nap. My head pounds relentlessly."

"Then you rest. I can take Jane."

She left the room with a heavy heart. It was not like Emily to be melancholy, and if she was saving her sorrow for her rides, then she was most likely trying to hide it. Kate determined to check in with Emily at regular intervals to make sure she understood Kate was there to share in both hardships and happiness.

Her maid, Jane, was agreeable to a trip to the library, and it was not much longer before they were in the carriage and on their way to Larkfield. They passed the split tree and Kate had an image pop in her mind of a crude drawing she had done of it as a child the day she had met Mr. Evans for the first time and saved him from those wretched, savage boys. She should locate the drawing when she returned home and come out with her easel and paints to do a better job one of these days. The idea excited her, for she hadn't painted since leaving Lytle's School for Girls.

The lending library was located next to Mr. Larkin's shop, and Kate took her time selecting a novel called *Pride and Prejudice* for Emily that had just recently come to the shelves but came highly recommended from the woman sitting behind the desk of the library. Kate assumed anything written by *A Lady* must certainly be worth reading.

She perused a small section on gardening in search of a book on orchard care but walked away empty-handed. It would be wise to send a note to the man that Peter recommended as steward—hopefully he was knowledgeable about such things. Or at least amenable to learning.

Kate stopped in the Larkins' shop for some peppermints to take to Emily and chatted with Mrs. Larkin for a few minutes while waiting for her purchase to be wrapped. The bell above the door signaled another customer, and Mrs. Larkin excused herself to see to the raven-haired beauty Mr. Evans had driven home from church a few weeks past.

Kate attempted a smile at the lady. The woman paused, her gaze dragging from Kate's neck to her toes, before flicking away in clear dismissal.

Swallowing the bitter sting of rejection, she tried not to be offended. It was true that they had yet to be introduced. But honestly, a *small* smile would not have been a trial.

Returning to her carriage, Kate did not notice the men approaching until she nearly barreled into them, so intent she was on not being offended by the lady in the shop.

She glanced up, catching Peter's eye. "Pardon me, gentlemen, I'm afraid my mind is somewhere in the clouds," Kate said with a stiff smile.

Jane stepped away to remain appropriately close but not involved in the conversation.

Peter glanced at Kate, a small tick in his brow indicating he did not believe all was as she said it was. "Allow me to introduce my steward, Mr. Balham. Miss Kingston."

"Pleasure," Kate said, dipping her head. "I have just come from the lending library and hoped to find some literature to guide me in my orchard endeavors, but alas there was nothing in stock. Perhaps you have a title to recommend?"

Mr. Balham nodded. "I do, Miss Kingston. I have a few which might be of some use to you. I can send them to Split Tree."

"That would be wonderful, thank you," Kate said. Interesting, that. He knew where she came from. Had Peter been discussing her? Well, of course he had—she was his agricultural neighbor. What else would he discuss with his steward besides the land and what the neighbors were planning to do with theirs?

"We have just come from a horse auction ourselves," Peter supplied. "They had the sweetest little docile mare, absolutely perfect for a new rider."

"You don't say," Kate said flatly. "Perhaps you already purchased said mare and are planning to pawn it off on your neighbor?"

"Perhaps I have." A smile tugged at Peter's lips. "As I mentioned, it was an auction. The price was just too good to pass up."

Kate was briefly struck by the handsome grin he sent her way but recovered rapidly. "You are serious then?"

He held her captive in his steel-blue eyes. "Yes."

Kate did not know whether to tremble in fear or exclaim her gratitude. She had been wanting to learn, naturally, but this was coming together all too soon. Once she owned the horse, the next step would be actually getting on it. She swallowed a lump in her throat. It was not as if the beasts themselves scared her, but she was fearful of putting her trust in an animal that she did not know.

"You need not fear, as I said; this little mare is extremely docile. I was told she would be perfect for a child."

"I'm not sure whether to take that as a compliment, sir," Kate said dryly. She hoped Peter could catch the glint of teasing in her eye.

"Then simply consider it good fortune," Peter said, his voice becoming low and serious. "Surely we must appreciate the blessings which are placed in our paths."

"You stump me there. I must not tease such a righteous opinion."

"Sir Peter, how wonderful to see you!" a high-pitched voice called just down the street.

Kate turned to see the woman who had snubbed her in the store and irritation swept through her that the lady would feel it appropriate to approach her now. Even if she was directing her greetings to Peter.

"Miss Smithson, I hope this day finds you well," Peter said as he dipped his head in a bow. His tone offered none of the levity it had previously held, but rather portrayed the Lord of the Manor role that he most likely took with subordinates. Kate was briefly stunned by the authority in his voice and manner but shook it off. "Do you have the pleasure of knowing Miss Kingston here?"

Miss Smithson flicked her gaze to Kate, her mouth forming a feline smile. "No, I am afraid we've yet to be introduced." She dipped into a graceful curtsy which Kate replied in kind, before turning back to Peter.

Kate was only slightly gratified to note that Miss Smithson ignored Mr. Balham as well, but then scolded herself on her less than kind thoughts. Mr. Balham probably resented being cast aside quite as much as she did. Though judging by his contented expression, he was feeling no worse for the wear, currently.

"I received the invitation to dine at Evanslea, and I must say my sister and I are only too happy to accept." She shot Peter a smile that revealed even, white teeth, and Kate hated her all the more. Running her tongue over her own slightly crooked front teeth, noting the jagged edge where they didn't quite line up, she glanced to Peter, flushing hot when she caught him watching her.

Glancing over her shoulder to where Jane waited beside the carriage, Kate turned back to Peter and dipped in a preemptive curtsy. "My maid is waiting. I must be off. It was good to meet both of you," she looked to Miss Smithson quickly before giving Mr. Balham a warm smile. "And I await your book recommendation, sir. I am only too eager to begin."

Turning away before anyone had a chance to waylay her, Kate climbed swiftly into her carriage and tapped the roof the moment Jane was seated beside her. She blew out her frustration and wondered which was more unnerving—that Peter had caught her comparing herself to Miss Smithson, or that she cared.

KATE

*E*mily was thrilled the following Monday when Kate informed her that she would be learning to ride. Peter had cornered her in the churchyard following the service the previous day and asked when it would be a good time to bring her horse by, and she'd decided not to put off the inevitable. She had been wanting to ride over to the north pasture and look at the plot of land suggested to her for the orchard but had yet to make it. Mostly because she did not know how.

Instead, she had spent the last few days devouring the books sent over from Mr. Balham and corresponding with Mr. Cruikshank, the steward recommended by Peter. He was set to arrive within a week and begin the job on a trial period. Her butler had agreed that it would be safe to test the man's methods in this way and see if he was a good fit for her personality and household. Not having a man in the house to answer to was very likely difficult for a lot of men, and Kate was concerned that Mr. Cruikshank would find this a trial as well.

After picking at her breakfast, she tried on the riding habit Emily had surprised her with. It was a deep forest green that set off the auburn highlights of her brown hair and warmed her skin tone considerably. She had been shocked when it had arrived with the remaining gowns that she had ordered in Larkfield, but Emily had been convinced Kate could be persuaded to learn now that she lived on so large an estate and had spoken with the modiste about it privately.

Now she was grateful Emily had had such foresight, for she would never have been able to fit in Emily's habit and was glad to have her own.

When the door knocker sounded, Kate found herself rooted to the sofa. Her stomach did not hold much more than half a cup of tea and a few bites of toasted bread, since the more she thought about being on a horse, the more terrified she became. Emily loved her horse so much that she considered Josephine the daughter she did not have, and the horse had still dropped her twice since she had come to stay at Split Tree. Although, that was due to Emily's lack of concentration, not Josephine's. But still.

"Are you ready?" Peter said from the doorway. He looked taller in his riding attire than anything else, Kate decided, when she took in his full form. His golden-brown hair was still slightly damp at the neck, and his eyes were looking more blue today than gray—but piercing as ever.

"I do not know if I ever will be," Kate responded. "Forgive me for my rudeness. I am finding myself very stuck to this cushion."

Peter laughed, the sound loud and clear, which she responded to with a wry smile. "Must we do this today?"

"Yes." Peter crossed the room and sat beside her. He took one of her hands in his own, warm and safe. "We will start small and walk circles in the paddock. The fence will remain closed, and your horse won't be able to run off, I promise."

Kate smiled, feeling warmed by his consideration. "What is her name?"

"That is for you to decide." He patted her hand once before standing and pulling her up with him. "Now let's be off."

Kate followed, swinging her skirts over her left arm. Every step she took felt like she was trudging in deep mud, so reluctant she was to begin her lessons. She placed her hand on Peter's elbow and let him guide her outside and to the paddock directly next to the stables. It was on the tip of her tongue to inquire about Martin—she would've liked for him to have joined them. Peter's eyes positively shone as he gestured with pride to a beautiful, light brown mare with white spots under her belly and on her neck, a lady's saddle fitted around her middle.

"She is beautiful!" Kate sized her up. "And not so very big, I think," she finished.

Peter looked down at her and smiled. "You'll see that she is just right for you, I think."

Kate's gaze was riveted to the beast, watching muscles bunch in the powerful thighs as the horse examined the paddock. "Thank you for letting me borrow a saddle."

"It was found in your tack room," he explained. "It is old, and you may need to order a new one if it does not fit right, but in the interim it should do the job well enough."

Kate nodded, determination settling on her shoulders. "Let's begin."

Peter guided her into the paddock and toward the mare. Settling the beast with soothing words and a calming hand on the horse's nose, he looked to Kate. "She is ready. Are you?"

"No, but I do not see how that makes the slightest difference."

Peter's low chuckle swept through her, and she closed the distance between herself and the side of the horse, resting her hand on the top of the saddle. She amended her earlier notion that the horse wasn't overly large. She felt quite the opposite when standing right beside her. Begging the heavens for a measure of courage, Kate glanced at Peter over her shoulder. She held his gaze as he came around to help her up, and his eyes seemed to speak to her, to reassure her that he would not let her fall. And she believed him.

Bending forward, Peter laced his fingers to give Kate a foot up, and she placed her boot in the safety of his large hands.

"And, up," he said, and with little warning, Kate was rising into the air until she made contact with the saddle. Hooking her leg around the pommel, she arranged her skirts over her legs and squeezed her knees together, feeling far more secure than she had anticipated. This was far more enjoyable than the last time she'd been on a horse.

His smile broad, Peter nodded approvingly. "Do you feel comfortable?"

"Yes," Kate answered, surprise evident in her tone. "I feel as though this saddle was made for me."

The lessons were slow moving. Kate made certain Peter was aware of her fears and he gently moved her forward a little at a time. He did not release the reins at all, and after a good deal of time gently walking around the paddock, he gave Kate the reins and instructed her on how to direct the horse. She was beginning to feel somewhat confident when Peter called the lessons to a halt, saying that Kate was progressing splendidly, and they should not push their luck for today.

They returned to the house for tea, and Kate insisted on paying Peter for the horse straight away.

"Have you chosen a name?" he asked.

"I must think on it still. This is my first time naming an animal, and I am determined to do right by her."

Peter nodded. "The name will come to you."

Kate was positive that he gave her a low number, but Peter insisted the horse was a steal and he had gotten her for a very good price. She let it slide eventually, determining that it was fruitless to argue, and paid the man what he asked. "I should add a good sum for your lessons too, I suppose," she said after handing him the bank draft.

"My lessons are free, Kate. That is what we call being a good neighbor."

"So you teach all of your neighbors to ride?" she asked teasingly.

"Only you and Mr. Brummel. But don't tell the others."

Kate had to laugh at the image of Peter teaching the eighty-year-old man that she had seen at church how to ride a horse. His back was stooped, and he relied heavily on his cane, which he used on Sundays to hit the floor when he felt that the children were being too rowdy during the service.

"Shall we resume tomorrow? Say, the same time?"

Kate was taken aback but recovered quickly. "I do not want to put you out, Peter. I had thought we would do this once a week until I grow comfortable with the horse."

"Certainly not," he replied, his eyes dancing with amusement. "I plan to have you riding around your estate by Friday."

"You have too much faith in me," Kate said dryly. "I shall believe that when I see it."

"You'll be doing it by Friday, mark my words. Now do not argue with me. We have gotten you started, let us keep up the momentum."

Kate nodded once, determination setting in. He was right; she just needed to conquer this, and the quicker the better.

Martin

Spinning the glass of brandy on the table, Martin watched the amber liquid slosh up the side of the cup. When he'd ridden over to Split Tree earlier that day and seen Peter teaching Miss Kingston to ride, he'd wanted to throttle his brother. The man was incredibly dense if he imagined Miss Kingston would look upon him favorably after she learned of the role he had played on that fateful day in the woods a decade ago.

Peter didn't qualify as a suitor. He was a bully.

And the Miss Kingston he knew would *never* fall in love with a bully.

It was a good thing Martin had chosen to turn directly around and go back home, or he likely would have said something to Peter and Miss Kingston that he would later come to regret. It was a pitiful truth that Peter brought out the worst in him. But what could he do about it? Their relationship would never heal, and that was Peter's fault alone. It was Peter's choice to stand by Charles through every childhood altercation, forever creating an impenetrable barrier—one Martin could *never* overcome.

Peter stepped into the library, caught Martin's gaze, and paused. He hovered in the doorway, so clearly uncomfortable. It was delightful watching Peter squirm, but Martin needed to put an end to it. He had something more important to accomplish this evening.

"How did the lesson go today?" he asked, holding his brother's gaze.

Peter stilled. Stepping into the room, he crossed the rug and lowered himself in the chair opposite Martin. "Really well. Miss Kingston is a natural."

Martin sipped at his brandy. "Of course she is."

"You are welcome to join us tomorrow," Peter said, his hands clutching the edges of the armrests.

"I've too much to do," Martin said, waving the offer away. He would not encroach on Miss Kingston's lessons, not when he wouldn't be the man in charge. He never wanted her to see him in a position of less authority than Peter. "I have sent the invitations for the dinner party to introduce Miss Kingston and Mrs. Nielson to Larkfield society."

Peter nodded, no doubt relieved.

"It is my understanding that you've engaged a man to act as Miss Kingston's steward as well," Martin said, his voice even. He chuckled, the sound void of mirth. "One would almost believe you've set your sights on her."

Silence settled between them, Martin holding his brother's gaze. "Brandy?" he asked, lifting the decanter. Peter nodded and Martin filled a cup before adding more to his own. The splash of liquid against glass was loud in the quiet room.

"It is no secret that I've paid Miss Kingston special attention since her arrival," Martin continued, handing his brother the glass. "I am prepared to request permission to formally court her, and I'd like to have your blessing."

Peter's eyes were hard, unyielding. Had he begun to fall for Miss Kingston too? Well, Martin spoke first. And they couldn't both have her.

Peter brought his cup to his lips, taking a sip. "Has Miss Kingston given you any indication that she would welcome your suit?"

"Of course," Martin said, leaning back in his chair. "I wouldn't have planned anything otherwise. I need to make a formal request to court her, of course, but I wanted to speak to you about it first, to ensure that you would bless the union."

"You plan to offer for her already?"

"No, not yet. But that will be the inevitable result."

Peter nodded. "Of course."

"I am glad you are treating her so kindly, brother. She will become your sister after all."

Peter drained the rest of his brandy and set the glass on the table beside his chair. "Is that all?"

Martin nodded, refilling his own glass. He could only dampen his smile so much—he didn't want Peter to see the immense joy this conversation had given him. It was strained, uncomfortable, effective. Peter could assist Miss Kingston all he wanted now, their lessons tainted by the steadfast truth that she would become Martin's wife.

KATE

*T*uesday's ride had Kate comfortably trotting around the paddock by herself, and Wednesday she was testing the horse in the field behind the stables. Peter refused to let her off of the stable, flat grounds yet, and for that she was grateful. Peter had ridden Domino as well for that lesson and they'd stayed out in the field for a good deal longer than she had before, causing Kate to feel no small degree of soreness by the time she was lifted down from the saddle.

"Perhaps we will take a break tomorrow and resume Friday?" Peter suggested. "I happen to know that there are a great many things planned for entertainment this evening at the dinner party, and if my brother has his wish, then you shall not be leaving Evanslea until the wee hours of the morning."

"Mercy, it sounds like a ball."

"Do not be surprised if it turns into one," Peter said resignedly. "Martin's dinner parties often do."

Arranging the skirt of her habit over her arm, Kate swallowed. Of course she hadn't completely forgotten about the dinner party, but it had not been entirely at the forefront of her mind of late, and now the realities of the evening were making themselves very clear. "Perhaps I should have brushed up on my dancing a little more and worried about reading those agriculture books a little less this week. My head is spinning with soil content and sun angles and percentages. I am afraid I won't know the difference between a minuet and a reel."

"I think you will manage," Peter said. "Martin fancies the waltz, anyhow."

Kate peered at Peter, trying to gauge whether or not he was in earnest. He looked down at her as they walked across the lawn to the house. "Are you scandalized? I understand that in London it is becoming widely more acceptable. In our circle of society here we still have a few that refuse to dance it; but for the most part it has been tolerated."

"I am afraid I will have to sit out the dancing regardless. Not only do I not know how to waltz, but I am sure my legs won't carry me around tonight as it is."

"That sore?" Peter asked, before looking away. A blush crept into his cheeks and Kate smiled at such an innocent display on such a large man.

"I am still growing accustomed to the saddle, yes."

Peter cleared his throat awkwardly, holding the door open for Kate and then following her into the parlor. "Have you thought of a name yet for your horse?"

"No, not yet," Kate said, grateful for the change in subject. She realized she had left her drawings all over the low table again that morning and rushed to gather them up before Peter caught sight. She was too late.

"These are marvelous," he said over her shoulder. "May I?"

Kate handed over the stack of various parlor redesigns with a sheepish smile. "Most of them were just to amuse myself." She had brought out her watercolors and added color here and there, and a few of the drawings weren't too bad. Only, she could not decide which direction she wanted to go. Peter chuckled at a few of the more elaborate renditions, and she had to laugh a little too, to ease her awkwardness.

He glanced up and the smile on his lips was dazzling. The Evans men were certainly quite handsome. "I think the jungle room is my favorite."

"That is one of mine as well," she said. "Though I am not sure where I would locate an armchair carved to look like one is seated in the large, open mouth of a lion."

"Or a sofa that resembles a relaxed bear."

"I think the giraffe candelabras could be easily made though," Kate said as if she was truly considering that design. She was gratified by Peter's easy laugh as he finished looking through the sketches.

"This one," he said, pulling out a basic room redone with tasteful furniture and simple colors. It was a clear blend of classic styles and modern colors.

"I was leaning that direction as well. I only wonder if it is not too boring."

"Classic is not boring. It seems to me that sometimes by trying to outdo others we lose our sense of self; and this vision, to me," he said, holding up the sketch, "is very *you*."

Kate did not know what to think. She understood the compliment, and found his no nonsense way to be reassuring, in a sense. She had developed a great friendship with Peter over the recent weeks and appreciated his candid nature. She assumed it had gone a long way in commanding his troops during his years as Captain. Yet she was also a woman and would be lying to herself if she had pretended not to notice the lack of flowery praise.

"Now I must go help Martin prepare for this evening," Peter said, standing. "Martin has a great deal in store for you."

"For me?" she asked, unsure what to make of his pointed stare. "Whatever could you mean by that cryptic comment?"

He shifted his weight to his other leg. "He laid out his plans to me a few nights past, and I must say, I understood them perfectly. I hope you will be happy."

Kate stared, trying desperately to think of something to say. Was Mr. Evans planning to court her? To make his intentions known and public? It was precisely what she had wanted when she met the man, but the prospect made her nervous, nonetheless. At least she would have Emily with her that evening to aid her. Kate hadn't the least notion how to flirt with a gentleman.

Peter cleared his throat, calling her back to the present. "Do you look forward to meeting some of your neighbors?"

"Some of them, yes," she responded truthfully, her mind flitting to Miss Smithson.

Peter smiled as if he could read her mind before setting the sketch on the table and taking his leave. Kate lifted the paper. She remained in the parlor a moment longer, studying the sketch of the simple design and wondering precisely what Peter saw when he looked at her.

Peter

It took all of Peter's restraint not to run to his horse and gallop away. A bruising ride would clear his head, but he didn't wish for Kate to glance from her parlor window and catch him in a fit of pique.

He hadn't meant to tell her of Martin's intentions, but temptation had grown too strong and the words slipped from his tongue like an oily snake.

Peter received his punishment watching Kate's face move between expressions of surprise and excitement. The thought of courting Martin had clearly given her pleasure, which was vastly different from the feeling it had ignited within Peter. When Martin had told Peter of his intent to court Kate, an unwelcome feeling had settled in his stomach, growing heavy and thick.

That feeling had returned speaking to Kate in her parlor today. But a woman such as she deserved the best of everything. She deserved whatever it was her heart desired. And Peter would not stand in the way of that.

He couldn't. He'd given Martin his word. As a gentleman, it would be in his best interest to strive to view Kate as the sister she would one day become. After taking so much from Martin during their childhood, falling into whatever plans Charles had concocted or standing by and doing nothing to stop Charles from his angry pursuits, Peter had no other choice now but to step aside and let Martin and Kate find happiness—however difficult that might be.

Swinging up into the saddle, Peter turned toward Evanslea and clicked his tongue. He would return to his stables, check on Destiny and her foals, and rid his mind of visions of Kate.

20

KATE

he carriage ride to Evanslea was short. Kate had found herself in a melancholy mood for the remainder of the day after Peter had left, and while she was glad Emily felt well enough to go to the dinner with her, she was also grateful that her friend's fatigue would most likely lend itself in helping her to end the night early. She was not intending to dance.

In opposition to Kate's dreary mood, Emily had received a letter from Paul in the afternoon post and her spirits had soared. He seemed to be doing well, and while he worried over Emily's careless riding, he had faith that she was recovering nicely and had extended his thanks to Kate for caring for his precious wife. It seemed, to Paul, as if the war could not possibly go on for too much longer, and he had every hope of being reunited with his love in a reasonable timeframe.

Kate would only be too glad when that time came. Perhaps she could even convince Paul to take a restorative couple of months at Split Tree before returning with Emily to London.

It was as she mused over this that they pulled into the carriage drive at Evanslea and a footman helped her step onto the gravel road. Mr. Evans greeted them at the door, expressed his happiness at Emily's recovery, and gave a special smile to Kate that had butterflies batting their wings in her stomach. They were not the first to arrive, and Mr. Evans introduced them to Mr. and Mrs. Kettlewell and their son, Albert Kettlewell; Mrs. Gressle and her companion, an elderly Miss Juniper; and Mr. and Mrs. Smithson and their daughters, Miss Smithson and Miss Annie Smithson.

Kate had already met Miss Smithson outside of Mr. Larkin's shop, but she found that she rather liked the look of the younger sister, Miss Annie, considerably more. Miss Annie had the same raven hair and perfectly plump red lips, but the smile on her face and the glint in her eye lent themselves to an unpretentious attitude, and Kate thought she could see something of a kindred spirit in the girl.

They had only to wait on Mr. Faile and his Uncle, Mr. Horace, and their dinner party would be complete. Peter stepped into the room with Mr. Balham, the sight both familiar and comforting. Mr. Evans stepped away to see to the last of the arriving guests—a portly young man and his frizzy, white-haired uncle—so Kate and Emily approached Peter and his steward.

"I must thank you for the books, Mr. Balham," Kate said after introducing him to Emily. "They have been excessively useful."

"I had rather thought they would be," he answered with a smile. "I'm glad they are of some value to you, but if you find yourself with any questions, I would be more than happy to discuss them."

"So *you* are the reason my friend is holed up in that parlor day in and out with her nose stuck in those massive books," Emily said with a playful glare, her nose scrunching beneath drawn brows. "I vow, between all of the riding lessons and those wretched books, I have scarce seen her at all this past week."

"I must apologize for taking away your companion, Mrs.

Nielsen," Peter said dutifully. "Though I cannot regret my part in it."

"It has been a blessing, I think," Kate said. "If I pestered you day in and out, do you think you would have healed as quickly as you did?"

Emily relented. "I suppose you make a valid point there."

Mr. Evans returned, pulling Kate away, and apologized to the men without a hint of remorse. "I have it on good authority," he told her, "that dinner shall be announced soon. And call me selfish, but I would like to find myself at your side when it is time to take in the guests."

Kate smiled up at him prettily, or at least that was her goal. Were her teeth showing too much? Perhaps she ought to practice in the mirror again. "I should like that above all things."

Mr. Evans's answering smile was interrupted by the butler announcing dinner, and she glanced over to find Mr. Balham offering Emily an arm before allowing her own hand to rest on Mr. Evans's. She watched Peter cross to Mrs. Gressle, the older woman, and startled a little at Mr. Evans's voice in her ear. "Mrs. Gressle is the niece of an earl. She is the highest-ranking woman in the room until Sir Peter marries." Kate nodded, ignoring the hint of malice that colored his words, and followed him into the dining room. It must be tiresome to plan and execute a dinner party without a woman to assist. Surely he was merely weary from the evening's responsibilities.

"As our guest of honor, it should be you in the right-hand seat," Mr. Evans continued, nodding to where Peter led Mrs. Gressle. "But I cannot say I am upset by Peter's insistence that we show Mrs. Gressle her due. She does get persnickety if we do not remember her esteemed uncle."

Kate chuckled at this, unsurprised by Peter's gallantry in observing Mrs. Gressle's need for recognition. "I would rather give up the seat of honor than ruffle any feathers. I am not entirely sure anyone else here sees Emily or I as guests of honor, anyhow. I quite received the impression that they couldn't care less." This was delivered in an amused tone, but she found, upon looking at Mr. Evans, that his face was stricken.

"Have you been mistreated?"

"Well, no," Kate answered truthfully. "And I did not expect to be wholly accepted right away. Perhaps you misunderstood," Kate said softly, laying a hand on top of his arm after he seated her at the table. "I only meant that it will take time for the gentility of Larkfield to feel like a comfortable group of friends."

Mr. Evans looked relieved, if somewhat confused. "Such is the way of things, I suppose."

Kate nodded, waiting for the rest of the men to seat themselves. Through the dinner she found her gaze straying down to Miss Smithson at the other end of the table, irritation prickling her every time she heard the lady's stilted laugh or high-pitched teasing. Eventually she forbade herself from looking there, but that ended up being worse. She was afraid Mr. Evans would find her a dull dinner companion and it was with great relief that the meal came to an end and the women were ushered into the drawing room to wait for the men as they enjoyed cigars and port.

Mrs. Gressle took on the hostess's responsibility to ensure that all of the ladies were comfortable. Turning to whisper a jest to Emily, Kate pulled up short—her friend's face drawn and pale. Directing Emily to a sofa, she seated her against an array of pillows.

"Shall we leave now?"

"No," Emily said, as if it was a preposterous idea. "Your Mr. Evans has a whole evening of entertainment planned, does he not?"

"Yes, but I had not intended on staying for the entire evening. You need your rest if you are to continue healing."

"And rest I will get, against these marvelously comfortable pillows."

"Emily, Paul is trusting me with your health," Kate said with the severity she felt. She would not let Paul down.

"And my health requires a bit of entertainment," Emily snapped. "No, do not look so offended, Kate, but remember that I have been holed up for a fortnight now, and longer still if you count the days I was unconscious. I am not ready to leave yet so quit looking concerned for me. I promise I will let you know the moment I am ready to go."

Kate nodded. How selfish of her to forget that Emily must have been bored out of her mind of late. "As long as we do not have to play any ridiculous games like charades or hunt the slipper, I will stay as long as you like."

The men entered the room then, filtering in to fill the spaces left by the women on various chairs or sofa cushions.

"I noticed that you have your piano prepared, Sir Peter. Would you like me to sing for you?" Miss Smithson asked, her lashes batting as she coyly dipped her head. False coyness, clearly. The woman seemed too calculated for it to be otherwise.

"Perhaps later," Mr. Evans cut in, moving to stand at the head of the room. "I thought it would be exceptional to first play a round or two of charades."

Miss Smithson clapped her hands in glee, an apparent attempt to override her irritation at not being asked to sing, while Emily smothered a laugh. Kate elbowed her in the ribs.

"How do you feel about charades, Miss Kingston?" Mr. Evans asked, turning to her. He searched her face for something, but she could not guess what.

She gave him her widest smile, while staying cautious of exposing too much of her crooked teeth. "I should like it above all things, sir," she said with the sweetest voice she could muster. The party was then broken into two teams and Kate geared herself up to play a game that she, in fact, quite detested above all things.

Martin

The party was moving along splendidly. Martin saw the way Kate had lit up when she entered the drawing room on his arm and he didn't think he was being excessively conceited to think she was pleased to go into dinner with him, either. It had irked him to find her comfortably discussing something with Peter and Mr. Balham, but he had righted that situation quickly. Ladies of distinction had no business in discussing anything with a steward. She was far too high above him in station.

The game of charades was rapidly dying down and Martin had thought a lively game of hunt the slipper would give him ample time to walk the corridors with Miss Kingston alone, but the group was looking a little wan, and he was afraid that suggesting such a game would throw them deeper into the doldrums. This was the problem with country society. His options for dinner guests were limited to country bumpkins, single, older women with companions, or hopeful, young gentility trying to pawn their daughters off to anyone of title or rank.

Not that he qualified. No, *he* was not the head of this household.

"Miss Smithson, would you care to play for us now?" Martin asked, glad when her eyes lit up that she would not hold his earlier deferral against him now. She looked as though she was trying to catch Peter's eye tonight, and it was hideously obvious she was doing so in order to try and make Martin jealous—and failing, miserably. If the news she had brought to him earlier that month had not succeeded in dragging Martin to the altar, she should realize that none of her antics would force him to propose. She could flirt with his brother all she liked. Of course, Peter refused to be baited, and that was all fine by Martin. It gave him more time.

Miss Annie moved to the piano to accompany her sister, and it was apparent that the two had been practicing. Their delivery was superb, every note perfect. And while Martin was not a connoisseur of music, he could appreciate a well sung sonata.

He suffered through a few more pieces of music delivered by the Smithson sisters before asking Miss Kingston if she cared to play for them. She refused politely, stating that none of her talent lay in music. Mrs. Nielsen was apparently gifted with a lovely alto, but she was looking rather pulled and no one argued with her when she declined. This was turning out to be a sorry party indeed.

Martin threw out his plans of rolling up the carpets and getting Miss Kingston into a waltz, and instead suggested whist. It was universally accepted, and the group split up perfectly into four tables. He had played two exceptional games with Miss Kingston as his partner before she was pulled from the table mentally, if not literally.

"Is something troubling you, Miss Kingston?" he asked, trying not to be irritated. Her eyebrows pulled together to form a perfectly concerned brow and he longed to smooth out the wrinkles and force her problems away, that they might return to enjoying their evening.

Miss Kingston looked to the other two people at the table, Miss Annie and her partner, the portly Mr. Faile, before returning her gaze to Martin. He was gratified that she had hesitated to share something with him because of their company, for he knew she would not hesitate if it was only him. She trusted him.

"I really must get Emily home," Miss Kingston said regretfully. "She is still healing, you know. I only wish I did not have to cut the evening short."

Oh, was that all? Martin gave her his most compassionate face. "Of course you must do what is best for Mrs. Nielsen. I will have your carriage brought out straight away."

The look of pure gratitude she gave him was worth cutting a million nights short. He tossed the rest of his hand on the table while Mr. Faile began gathering the discarded cards.

It took a moment's work to instruct Homer to have Miss Kingston's carriage brought round to the front, but when Martin returned to the drawing room, he simmered at the sight that greeted him. Peter had swooped in and helped Mrs. Nielsen to her feet, leading her to the door while Miss Kingston said her farewells, Mr. Balham guiding her behind Peter. The *steward*. He had only been invited because they were short by one male and he usually fit in perfectly, blending into the background of the dinner table and conveniently making his escape after dinner. Only tonight, Balham hadn't made his escape. He had held on and continued to be a part of the activities. Of course, it ended up being beneficial during their impromptu games of whist, but that was beside the point. He had usurped Martin's place, sliding in and escorting Miss Kingston to the foyer.

Martin maneuvered his way beside the party putting on wraps and cloaks in the corridor and stepped in to guide Miss Kingston's hand to his own arm. After leading her outside he received a blessed few moments with her alone before they were joined by Peter and Mrs. Nielsen, Mr. Balham having *finally* disappeared.

"Perhaps I may call on you tomorrow?" Martin asked as he helped Miss Kingston up the carriage step.

"I should like that. Only, perhaps not too early," she said, chuckling.

Martin delivered a handsome bow and moved aside for Mrs. Nielsen. He stood beside his brother and watched as the carriage was closed up and began rolling away.

"Say, Martin," Peter began, his hands clasped behind his back as he rocked on his feet, watching the carriage in much the same way that Martin was. "Care to explain why two of my horses are pulling Miss Kingston's carriage?"

"I owed her a favor," Martin replied simply.

Peter turned and gave him a searching look, his eyebrow raised. "And she accepted this gift so easily? You must forgive me if I find that hard to believe."

"Believe what you want," Martin said with a shrug. He loved knowing something that Peter did not know. Of course, it wasn't nearly as sweet as the blow he was about to deliver.

"And what was this immense favor? She has only lived at Split Tree for two months now."

"It was not a favor acquired in the last few months," Martin said easily, watching as the lantern swinging on the carriage grew dimmer and dimmer before turning out of sight. He shifted, looking his brother square in the face. "It was from a long time ago when she risked her neck to save me from two savage boys intent on doing me harm in the woods."

Confusion clouded his brother's brow and Martin waited patiently for the realization to hit. Understanding dawned in Peter's eyes, and his jaw went slack. Martin had to work excessively to hold in his grin. "Of course, those were *her* words. But neither of us have ever forgotten how we bonded that day through our pure hatred of those who willingly abuse another man. Or woman."

Martin left his brother with that parting shot and strolled back into the house. He had not gotten this far in life from his lack of intelligence, and it had been clear to him that while Peter made special care not to single Miss Kingston out, the man's eyes had followed her the entire night. But *she* had preferred Martin's company. The win was a sweet wash over Martin and made him appreciate Miss Kingston all the more.

The rest of the party had moved into three separate games of whist by the time he returned, and he stationed himself near the

Smithson's table, watching and flirting while keeping an eye out for Peter. When his brother finally returned to the drawing room, he looked pleasant and social. Almost too pleasant, and certainly too social. Martin soared. He could not wait to see what this new information did to bring Peter down a notch in the world. The man was just too conceited. It was delightful to know that Martin still held the power to lower Peter's ridiculously high opinion of himself.

Now to just let this eat at Peter until the precise opportunity arrived to mention it to Miss Kingston, and she would dissolve, securing Martin's place by her side. He smiled to himself with the surety that she would be running to his arms within a matter of days, a week or two at most. And he couldn't wait.

21

KATE

he world was still waking when Kate went outside to see her horse. She had gone from being afraid to ride to caring so deeply about the animal in such a short time—it was amazing what conquering a fear could lead to. She was determined to name her horse today, and it was while making plans to ride out to the location for the orchard that it came to her; she would call her Apple.

It had been an easy thing to decide on planting an apple orchard. They were hearty trees and according to the books lent by Mr. Balham, had more likelihood of success in her particular region. But it would not stop her from finding a wonderful location for a plum tree somewhere on her property. Alice would not let the matter drop until she did, anyway. And she would be glad of the plum cake.

Kate leaned an arm over the gate on Apple's stall and smoothed her neck. She had surprised herself when she had awoken early that morning, especially after the late night they'd had at the dinner party. It worked out for the best, though, since Peter was not planning on coming to ride this morning, and Kate could go out before breakfast.

She'd had an unsettling feeling since leaving Evanslea the night before, but she could not quite place it. She was being courted, and it was such a remarkable, breathtaking feeling to be desired—something she'd never before experienced. And yet, unease had taken residence within her during the dinner party and had refused to leave her be.

The trouble was, she was not unhappy with Martin's attentions, so she failed to understand what caused her the discomfort. She had told Emily of Mr. Evans's desire to call on her today, and when she thought of his dashing smile a flurry swirled in her midsection.

She inhaled a deep breath. This fresh air would clear her head, she hoped.

A groom saddled Apple for Kate while she waited, then placed a mounting block beside her. She situated herself on the saddle with a little more ease than she had the day before, and slowly walked Apple out of the stables. A groom had been commissioned to accompany her, and she did not complain about his company. It made her feel a little less uneasy being in the unfenced wild as such a new rider. He hung back a little distance to give her the illusion of isolation, but she liked knowing he was nearby should she need him.

Kate swung Apple in an arc around the house toward the empty fields. They had once been grazed by a good many sheep, and she tried to picture her father out there with them, shepherding his flock and watching over the land. Whether or not he actually would have done this, Kate liked to imagine it.

The serene image touched her soul, the faint breeze dancing across her, tickling her jaw like her father might have done, had he been here. The sun crested over the side of the earth, and Kate could see the frost beginning to melt. Her face warmed in the new sun and she breathed in a deep gulp of the crisp morning air, enjoying it before the heat of the day melted it away.

A figure on a horse passed over a nearby hill, disturbing her daydreams. She startled before recognition set in, warming her like a comforting cup of chocolate. It was far easier to feel content atop the saddle when Peter was nearby, and even more of a treat when she had not expected to see him that morning. It was really too bad Mr. Evans didn't enjoy riding as much as his brother did. She would have liked to see him this morning, as well.

She expertly maneuvered Apple to meet her friend and gave him a wide grin.

"I did not expect to see you this morning."

"Nor I, you," Peter said, coming to a pause beside her. Domino was a good deal larger than Apple, and Peter's added height caused him to tower over her.

"Must I inquire why you are trespassing?" Kate said playfully.

He gave a nervous chuckle and said, "I am not sure, to be honest. I was discussing your plans for the apple orchard with Mr. Balham and thought to take a look at the proposed fields this morning."

"I am headed there now. Shall we go together?"

Peter nodded, turning Domino to fall in line beside her.

Kate looked over the hills as the sun began to thaw the glittering frost and create a sparkling effect. It was magical, and she was hit with an overwhelming gratitude for the home she was making her own. She turned toward her neighbor, a very kind man that willingly shared his opinions with her and listened in return. It was not something Kate had experienced before, and she wondered again if this was what it felt like to have a brother. "You are taking a great deal of interest in my land."

"Yes." He searched her face before continuing. "I find I must do things to occupy my time, or my mind suffers."

Kate understood. It was the very reason she had spent so much time weeding the kitchen garden while the gardeners were taking care of more important things. She could not sit idle. "And Evanslea does not keep you occupied?"

"It most certainly does." Peter chuckled, though his smile was tight. "But a new campaign like this is much more interesting."

"Are my fields something to be conquered, then?"

"In a sense, absolutely."

Kate studied her friend. She had the feeling that though he seemed composed, there was something troubling him. His playful words lacked levity and his smile seemed the least bit strained. "You must think in those terms easily after your years in the military."

"I am afraid it is ingrained in me."

"And yet you are not there..." Kate bit her tongue. She was prying now, and it was not only unladylike, but it was unfriendly as well. If Peter wished to confide in her, that was his choice. She should not have pressed him, and she wished she could swallow those words back up. She searched for something to say to easily guide the conversation onto safer ground, but her mind was at a complete loss.

"I am not there now," he finished anyway. She turned to him and saw the strain in his eyes, the anger that glittered, turning them from a soft blue-gray to thunder and steel. She would never wish to be on the wrong side of such passionate dislike—but with Peter that would never be a concern.

"We need not discuss this, Peter," Kate said gently. "It was wrong of me to pry."

Peter stopped Domino, and she pulled on her reins to come even with him. He gave her a serious, hard look, though not unkind; it was as though his thoughts were heavy, and he was determining whether or not to burden her with them. "I was injured and sent home right after Napoleon was exiled. I had thought the war over—I think a great many of us did. And when I came home and saw that I was needed here, I sold out, hoping to heal in peace and finally fulfill my duty to my father and the estate."

"That is very noble of you."

"It is noble to be shot in the arm?" Peter said, a self-mocking bite to his voice.

"Yes, it is noble to be injured fighting for King and Country. But I am referring to your desire to take your place as the leader of Evanslea. For your family, your future posterity, it is not wrong to take an interest in the bettering of your home and legacy."

He faced her, speaking softly. "Is that how you have justified coming back to Split Tree when the idea was so repugnant to you?"

Kate was startled by his words. Of course he knew that she was struggling with letting go of the memory of her uncle, for she had mentioned it to him. "I suppose so. I must think of how the estate was when my father owned and ran it, and how he would want me to prepare it for future generations. My uncle was a small mark on a greater story, and soon he shall be erased completely."

"You are scrubbing his mark from the estate, I assume. Have you chosen a design for the parlor then?"

"Yes," she said, giving him an arch look from the corner of her eye as their horses resumed walking. "But do not be conceited that I agree with you on the simple layout. I believe it is elegant and will be a great starting point for the redecoration."

Peter grinned, and it did her heart good, like every smile he sent her way filled her reserve a little more. *This* had to be what having a family felt like—that comfortable, encouraging joy one received from another person. Kate did not wonder if Peter enjoyed her company, if she was saying the right thing, or smiling too wide, she merely felt at ease in his presence. Emily had provided this for her over the years but receiving this sort of encouragement from a man—an equal—was different.

They arrived at the fields and spent some time going over potential boundary lines and discussing how many trees they could feasibly fit in the area. By the time they were finished Kate was sore from the saddle and in need of a break. She unhooked her leg and slid down from Apple, pulling the horse's reins over her head to lead her on.

"I am still getting used to riding so frequently. I'm afraid my legs need a stretch."

Peter slid down easily and fell into step beside her.

"You need not walk with me, Peter. I have my groom, and I am sure after a few minutes I'll be ready to ride Apple the rest of the way home."

"A fitting name," Peter said. "And not much of a surprise."

"Oh, do you like it? I only thought of it this morning."

They walked halfway back to Split Tree discussing the best and worst horse names they had heard when Peter grew quiet, wistful. Calm enveloped them a moment before Peter spoke, his voice serious. "I never thought I would inherit Evanslea." His gaze flicked to her, hesitating, before he swallowed. "When our older brother was killed in a reckless carriage accident racing a friend of his a few years ago, it came as a great shock to all of us. But I think my father most of all. It was eventually his downfall. I know it is a strange concept, but I am certain he died from disappointment."

"I am sorry," Kate said, unable to help the sheen of tears that filmed her eyes and pricked her nose. She'd had no idea that Peter and Mr. Evans had an older brother. "Your father must have been heartbroken."

"I believe it was more a case of realizing that the son he brought up to take over everything was gone, and his legacy was going to fall into the hands of the less than capable middle son."

"Surely not," Kate said, troubled on his behalf. "There could be no better man to care for the people and estate than you. Your military training aside, you are more than capable."

"You need not flatter me, Kate. I understand that I was not blessed with the cunning of my brothers, nor a head for numbers and business and such. It is why I rely so heavily on Mr. Balham."

"It does not make you a lesser man to understand your strengths and weaknesses." Kate slowed to a stop and looked Peter in the eye, her head tilted and her gaze willing him to know that she was sincere. "Surely you know that it only builds your character to recognize where you are limited and to have the humility to allow yourself to rely on others. None of us are meant to do everything alone."

Peter studied her, and she found herself closer to him than she realized, his scent lifting on the breeze and tickling her nose —shaving soap and the outdoors. She caught a trace of emotion in his eyes and wished it would not be inappropriate to pull him into a hug. Human connection was not something she'd had regularly in her life, and the sudden desire for it now shocked her.

"You appear stunned," Peter said softly, his brows knit together. "Whatever can you be thinking?"

Kate hated that she felt her cheeks grow warm. Now it could not possibly matter what she would say. Hopefully Peter would be a gentleman and let it go.

"Now I *really* must know," he said with no little amusement.

Kate turned away and began fitting her hand to the pommel of the saddle. "You know, I believe I am ready to ride the rest of the way."

Peter chuckled and she felt it through her back as he came behind her. His hands fit around her waist and he lifted her into the saddle, searing her skin where they touched. She refused to look in his eyes as she got herself situated and arranged her skirts around her legs. She waited for him to leave, to mount Domino, but he remained standing beside Apple.

"It's quite a novelty to look up at a woman," he said.

Kate laughed, unable to help herself and the tension drained away. "Yes, I imagine monsters of men are not quite used to that feeling."

Peter shot her a rueful glance before turning away, reseating his horse in one fluid motion. "Shall we race back?"

"Not on your life," Kate shouted as Peter flew away. She watched him exercise Domino with no little wonder, contemplating if she would ever feel comfortable enough to push Apple to breakneck speed. Perhaps one day she would, but for now she was content to canter.

Kate had enough time to change out of her riding habit and consume a small breakfast before Mr. Evans was announced. She met him in the parlor with Emily who sat in a chair near the window with her novel from the lending library, doing her duty as a chaperone while giving them adequate space.

It was a strained beginning, for Mr. Evans had only a few small remarks to make about the appearance of the house. It was left to Kate to lead them into a comfortable conversation about the dinner party the night before. Their topics ranged from Mr. Horace's wild, frizzy hair to the fantastic cut of lamb prepared by the Evanses' cook. The proper thirty minutes was observed, and Mr. Evans took his leave after begging permission to take her driving on Saturday.

"I should love to, but where does one go for a drive in the country? I have only once been to London on a holiday with my headmistress, but I recall the fashionable set driving around the parks."

"There is a lovely vista only thirty minutes north with a view that will steal your breath. Trust me," he added in a lower voice. "It is stunning."

"Shall we make up a party?" Kate asked hesitantly. She knew riding in an open phaeton was above reproach, but spending time alone admiring a vista seemed questionable.

"That is a grand idea," Mr. Evans responded, to her relief. "What do you think, Mrs. Nielsen?"

"I think that sounds lovely," Emily said, raising her head from her book briefly to give him a smile. "I confess I would not mind if Mr. Balham was in attendance—I had the most diverting conversation with him at dinner last night."

Mr. Evans looked stunned. He recovered quickly, his mouth flattening into a thin line. "I will see what I can pull together."

"And a picnic?" Kate added. "Perhaps we should make an outing of it."

"Splendid idea, Miss Kingston. I shall have my cook put something together."

They bid farewell, and Kate watched him leave from the front window before rejoining Emily, her mind clouding with concern.

Emily let out a long-suffering sigh, placing her bookmark in her book and laying it on the windowsill. "What is the matter?"

"I wonder if Mr. Evans appreciated being persuaded into an outing," Kate said.

"Into an enjoyable outing with friends and a picnic luncheon? You are right. That sounds terrible."

"When you say it like that, I feel conceited for thinking that he'd rather spend time with me alone." Kate pulled her feet onto the chair and tucked them under her skirts.

"Of course he would," Emily said matter-of-factly. "You are courting. But the outing he originally proposed was not exactly proper."

Kate sighed, leaning back in her chair. "Indeed. I don't know if I like courting. It almost seems like a waste of time. But I suppose there are no other ways of getting to know one another."

Emily brought a finger up as though she had an idea. "Other ways of getting to know one another? You could go riding together every morning and discuss the details of running your estates."

Kate decided not to gratify Emily with a response.

"Oh Kate, don't sulk. I am only teasing. It is true, though, is it not? That is how you and Sir Peter have become friends."

Kate blinked. "Yes, but that is just it. Peter is my friend. Someday he'll become my brother. I want to get to know Mr. Evans with a different relationship in mind."

"But dear," Emily said, scooting to the edge of her chair and tilting her face with a soft smile. "That is how the best relationships begin. You need a firm foundation, and friendship is the strongest."

Emily was happily married, so it stood to reason that she would know what she was saying. But that did not mean Kate had to agree fully. Every relationship was different, and while she appreciated and admired Peter, he was her friend, and would remain so. Wouldn't he?

It was time to speak about something different. "Have you written to Paul today?"

"Yes," Emily said, moving back into a comfortable position. "This morning."

The butler came to the door and asked if they were home for visitors. It took a quick second's work to tidy themselves and move to the sofas positioned in the center of the room before Mrs. Smithson and her daughter, Miss Annie were announced. Kate requested a tea service and was pleased when Mrs. Smithson left Miss Annie to most of the conversation—after begging pardon for Miss Smithson's absence, of course.

"She had the most dreadful headache this morning and remained in bed," Mrs. Smithson said by way of explanation.

Her own black hair was littered with strands of silver, causing her to look like an older, more dignified version of her missing daughter.

"Do convey our best wishes for a speedy recovery," Emily said diplomatically.

"I am so glad you've come to Larkfield," Miss Annie interrupted, seemingly unconcerned about her sister's headache. "Society here has been dreadfully dull, but I have a feeling it is about to become so much more interesting."

"It cannot have been that bad. The dinner party last night was exceedingly pleasant."

Miss Annie sighed dramatically. "Charades? Please. I was certain Mr. Evans was about to start up a game of hunt the slipper when he asked my sister to sing."

"Hunt the slipper is not so bad," Emily said, biting back a smile.

"If you are ten years old, perhaps not."

Kate could not help herself, and she laughed a little too loudly before using her tea to smother the unladylike sound. The twinkle in her eye was reciprocated in Miss Annie's.

"It must be something in the air. We've had to hunt our own slippers frequently since moving into Split Tree," Emily said.

"It is true," Kate said with an air of resignation. "I have replaced both of our slippers once, and my cook's, and still they continue to go missing. I am convinced we have ourselves a slipper thief."

"How strange," Mrs. Smithson said. Her gaze betrayed her doubt.

Kate and Emily were invited to return the call for tea the following week and Kate ended visiting hours with the comfort and promise of growing friendships.

KATE

*T*he vista was every bit as breathless as Mr. Evans had described it to be. Large rolling hills fanned out in every direction, dotted by homes and farmsteads, and bits of white and black here and there of sheep or cattle grazing. The only downfall to the glorious view was the overcast sky and threat of rain.

Mr. Evans's cook had outdone herself, and the picnic luncheon shared by the party left more than one of them with the desire for a quick afternoon nap. Peter and Mr. Balham were not among that set and decided to take a walk, in which they were accompanied by Emily and Miss Annie further up the hill and out of sight. Mr. Evans, Mr. Faile, Miss Smithson and Kate remained on the blankets overlooking the view.

"Has anyone seen such a lovely view before? I really ought to sketch it," Kate said, pulling out her book and a small case of charcoals.

Miss Smithson eyed her but shrugged her dainty shoulder while Mr. Faile mumbled something incoherent under his breath. He was beginning to slouch, and it was apparent that within minutes the man would be asleep.

"I should love to see what you can make of the view," Mr. Evans said graciously, leaning back on his elbows and stretching his legs out before him.

"I believe I will go on with Annie and the others," Miss Smithson said suddenly, rising to her feet. She put a hand down to stop Mr. Evans, who had begun to rise as well. "I know the direction and they left less than five minutes ago. If I cannot catch up with them within ten, I will turn back." Though she spoke in a tone that brooked no argument, Kate was a little surprised that Mr. Evans had not insisted on accompanying her. She herself took solitary walks when she was at Lytle's School for Girls on a consistent basis, but an independent school-teacher could not possibly be compared to a young gentlewoman.

"Do you think it safe for her to go alone?" Kate asked as the woman walked away.

"Oh yes, of course," Mr. Evans responded without hesitation. "We have been coming to this place for years—she knows the way."

Uncertainty tugged at Kate, but she pushed it aside and focused on the sketchbook in her lap. She drew a few strokes for the distant hills before working her way down the paper, concentrating on her task while Mr. Evans chatted about his favorite London sights.

He leaned forward and lifted a bottle of wine to refill his glass, but it came up empty. Rummaging through the basket, his mouth pressed into a firm line. He looked up, and his gaze trailed the distance around them before settling on Kate. "Servants are never around when one needs them," he said, irritated. Rising, he pasted a pleasant smile over his irritation. "Probably gathering near the remaining food. I will return shortly."

The silence—punctuated by Mr. Faile's deep, even breathing —was a blessed relief. Birds chirped from the high trees and distant laughing could faintly be heard from the group that had gone exploring. Taking to her paper, Kate focused on replicating the glorious scene before her, doing its majesty as much justice as she could manage.

"They are insufficiently prepared," Mr. Evans said, returning empty-handed, his expression tight. "Perhaps I should have checked the number of bottles myself, but I expected my servants to do an adequate job."

Kate shot him a small smile before focusing on her task. She did not wish to argue with the man, so she held her tongue, but he was being harder on his men than the situation called for. It was merely wine, and they had had plenty during their meal. But Kate had the odd circumstances of having lived as both a member of the working class and then moving up in the world. It was a truth she could acknowledge to herself that she likely wouldn't see eye to eye with members of gentility at all times. She'd had experiences the likes of Mr. Evans would never understand, a window into the kitchens and the life of the maids. At Lytle's, she had been friends with Mrs. James, her cook, and had spent an evening chatting with the housemaids on occasion.

She could never do so now, but that didn't erase her past experiences and how they colored her viewpoint. Mr. Evans's ignorance, likewise, could be understood.

Mr. Evans lowered himself beside her again, disturbing the peaceful setting with talk of the differences between London's theater and its opera. He explained the merits of each but thought the opera had a much more refined audience, so it was slightly preferable to sitting in a room with all manner of ruffians. Kate wanted to laugh but quickly realized that Mr. Evans was not joking, so she swallowed her mirth in an awkward hiccup. Did one really notice who stood in the back of the theater when one was engrossed in the play? And even then, what did it matter who else was in attendance?

"Perhaps I shall go to both of them one day, and then we may see if we share that opinion," Kate finally said.

Mr. Evans looked at her with a tilt to his head and a condescending smile. "I should love to take you."

Kate's stomach flipped over, the butterflies in full force. Her pulse sped, but the longer he watched her, his gaze flicking to her lips, the less enjoyable the butterflies felt. But why? Should she not be satisfied by his attention? She tore her eyes away, focusing back on her sketch.

"Are you planning to go to London at all?"

"Not any time soon," Kate said, unable to focus. She needed to shade the hillside, but prickles ran down her skin and she felt antsy—though at a loss to explain why. "I cannot now because of my mourning, and so many things could change before next year. I suppose it depends a little on Emily and Paul."

Mr. Evans nodded in understanding. A snort came from the next blanket and they both looked to Mr. Faile, who had succumbed to an even deeper sleep.

"I leave on Monday for a fortnight in the city. If you find yourself going that direction, then I should love to take you to the theater."

"That is most kind, Mr. Evans," Kate said. "But I feel I must wait for my mourning period to be over before I can venture that far into Society. I might have chosen to forgo proper mourning attire, but I ought to refrain from a trip to Town until the full three months has been observed."

Mr. Evans looked stormy. "I suppose that is true, but it seems unfair for you to continue to suffer at the hands of that brute."

Kate was startled by his vehemence. "I do not suffer, Mr. Evans. This mourning period is exactly what I've needed to help me adjust to my new life at Split Tree."

He did not look convinced, but he did not press her. The silence was only momentary before he dove into a discourse on the value of various hotel dining rooms and which one was best to reserve for a night after the theater.

Kate half-listened as she shaded in her sketch, her mind wandering to the sheep dotting the hillside. She absentmindedly drew in a shepherd among the sheep and with the flick of her pencil gave him the distinct nose that her own father's portrait portrayed in the corridor at Split Tree Manor. She was imagining the repositioning of that portrait to the parlor when her mind wandered to the study and what things of her father's could potentially be found in that room.

It was with these possibilities on her mind that she heard the high-pitched scream that suddenly pierced the air and caused a large black mark to dash across her page.

Peter

He knew it had come from somewhere below them, but precisely *where* was impossible to pinpoint. Peter's hair had stood on the back of his neck for a quarter of a minute before the scream sounded, and his heart had sped in anticipation. Of course, he could not have foreseen the cold wash of fear, but even as he wondered who it was that screamed, something told him Kate was safe.

Mr. Balham caught his eye and gestured toward the ladies, both white with fear. He jerked his head back down the hillside and Mr. Balham nodded slightly. "Let us return and locate the rest of our party," he said gently, pushing Mrs. Nielsen and Miss Annie back the way they had just come.

"Kate," Mrs. Nielsen whispered in question.

Mr. Balham nodded in understanding. "Let us find them before we panic."

He ushered the women away before Peter turned toward the edge of the nearby cliff and peered down. He winced at the image below him and made quick work of the steep downhill slope. If he had known he would be rescuing ladies from peril so often, he might not have left the military so readily. He reached the form lying on the bank of the cliff and recognized Miss Smithson's black hair immediately.

"Miss Smithson?" he asked, gently nudging her shoulder. His breath came out in one full puff when she stirred, relief coursing through him.

"Sir Peter?"

"Yes." Peter knelt closer, helping her turn toward him. He was glad for his familiarity with wounds when he first saw the gash on her arm and was able to look her in the eye unflinching. The last thing he needed was to deal with another unconscious woman; his injured arm could not handle more stress. "It appears that you have fallen. Does it hurt anywhere, or may I help you to stand?"

Her nose wrinkled in thought, and he waited for the panic to set in and the hysteria to come. She surprised him by nodding concisely, though her eyes remained wary. "I can stand."

With his arm around her waist, Peter helped Miss Smithson to sit. He untied his cravat and fastened it around her arm to slow the bleeding. "Can you walk back to the carriages?"

"I will try."

Peter guided her to her feet and let her lean on him heavily as they made their way toward the path that would lead them through the hill and back toward the carriages.

He keenly felt the vast difference in their heights as he helped Miss Smithson up the hill and toward the group. Servants were scurrying about, quickly cleaning up the remnants of the luncheon while Kate was throwing things into a small bag and Miss Annie was sobbing in Mrs. Nielsen's arms. When she noticed her sister, Miss Annie squealed and ran the distance toward them, but Peter held out a staying hand to halt her.

"Harriet! What happened?" Miss Annie said as her tear-stained cheeks glimmered in the light, her hands clutched tightly in front of her.

Miss Smithson glanced around the group quickly before looking back to her sister, a stunned, uncertain look in her eyes. "I scratched my arm, and I should like to go home."

The men immediately moved into action and they were soon ensconced in carriages on the road home. Miss Annie had insisted on riding with her sister and Peter, while Mr. Balham took the last seat in their vehicle. Peter directed the coachman to drive straight to Dr. Styles's home so he could take a look at Miss Smithson's arm.

Martin had not seemed too bothered by the series of events and had graciously led a worried Kate to the second carriage. Peter had watched him help her and Mrs. Nielsen inside before jumping in himself, followed by Mr. Faile, and he found that he resented his brother in that moment. Martin had done nothing useful in this crisis, much like the last time around.

Peter fumed as he recalled that series of events. When the servant from Split Tree Manor had arrived that dreadfully rainy day to ask for all available men to assist in the search for their missing guest, Peter had sprung into familiar action, organizing his men and heading for the place that he deemed her most likely to have become lost. It had come as something of a surprise to him when he directed Martin to prepare to ride out and his brother had only looked at him blankly, as if he had been surprised by the notion that he would also go out and look.

"The *servants* are searching," he'd said. Peter had been so dumbfounded, he'd stared at his brother momentarily before taking off for his own horse.

When he had returned later with the missing woman in his arms, his butler had been helpful in locating a footman to run to Split Tree Manor, call off the search, and collect the necessary items for both Mrs. Nielsen and Kate. It had been apparent to Peter at the time that Kate would not only insist on staying at his home with her sick friend, but she would not leave Mrs. Nielsen's side the entire time either.

That was when he had directed a footman to carry the chaise longue to Mrs. Nielsen's bedside, so Kate would have a place to rest. Martin had been just as useless then, and Peter had to smile at the recollection that Kate had believed Martin to be his master. *Martin.*

The weaselly boy had grown into a somewhat better man, for he no longer felt the need to battle Peter on *every* single thing— now he only argued about half of the time instead. In truth, Peter hoped to have forged a closer relationship with Martin once their older brother—and largest wedge between them— had died. But alas, it was not to be.

He faintly recognized feminine voices and realized that Miss Annie was asking him something. "I am sorry," he said guiltily. "I was woolgathering."

"Can we not go any faster?" Miss Annie repeated. "My sister is looking quite pale."

"It is but a scratch," Miss Smithson snapped. "I shall be fine. Quit your fretting."

Duly chastised, Miss Annie seemed to sink against the squabs.

"You are certain you suffered no other injuries when you fell?" Mr. Balham asked softly.

"Yes," Miss Smithson whispered. "But I did not fall."

"What was that?" Mr. Balham asked, leaning forward on the rear-facing bench.

Miss Smithson looked toward the window, her gaze on nothing in particular. "I was pushed."

23

KATE

*K*ate could not get her heart to calm down. She did not fully understand why, but she was anxious, restlessly pacing the front windows that lined the parlor, her gaze scanning the gravel drive outside. The events of the day replayed in her mind as she searched for the component that did not fit, the part that she was missing. Miss Smithson had seemed frightened almost, anxious and fretful. But why would a fall cause the woman fear? Kate was missing something; the details did not add up.

Guilt had plagued her for allowing Miss Smithson to hike the rest of the ridge alone—particularly after feeling the tightening in her gut, the same feeling which had warned her in the garden the day Emily had gotten hurt. The quiet carriage ride home had increased the feeling that something was not right and that once again she had failed to heed the warning sign.

"Would it be too early to call on the Smithsons?" she voiced.

Emily lifted her head from the book she was reading in a chair near the fire. "If they have even arrived home yet. I know Sir Peter intended on driving directly to Dr. Styles's home."

"Right," Kate muttered, resuming her pacing. It was selfish

181

of her to be so eager to assuage her curiosity. Though she would admit she worried about the state of Miss Smithson's arm, she needed to know what had happened. Fully capable, strong women did not usually just fall from smooth ledges.

"I must go," she finally said. "I cannot sit here a moment longer."

"You haven't *sat* here at all," Emily said under her breath.

Kate ignored the comment. "Are you coming with me?"

"No."

Kate swallowed her irritation. "Why not?"

"The poor girl probably wants to be left alone, Kate. You would if you suffered such a fall."

"But what if she didn't fall?"

Emily looked bewildered. "What in heaven's name are you talking about?"

"I..." Kate sighed and slumped into the chair opposite her friend. "I do not know. I just feel like something doesn't quite fit."

"Something doesn't quite fit?" Emily repeated slowly, dubiously.

"I know I sound mad," Kate whispered. "I cannot explain it, but I *feel* like something is not right."

Emily gave her a kind smile. "Perhaps we should call it an early night and things will look better in the morning?"

Kate shrugged. "There is no way I could fall asleep right now. I think I will use what light I have left to exercise Apple. Perhaps that will clear my mind."

She quickly donned her riding habit and flew out to the stables before Emily and her voice of reason could be any more sensible. Kate waited impatiently while Mr. Gibson saddled Apple, his grooms busy at dinner and he already in the stables, then used the mounting block to seat herself while Mr. Gibson saddled his own horse. She had not asked him to come with her, but she supposed it was wise.

She took off once Mr. Gibson had mounted his horse and surprised herself at Apple's speed. The horse was quick to adjust to Kate's mood, it seemed, for she flew over the pasture with ease. She could faintly feel the warmth seep from the air as the setting sun lowered slowly, and she pushed Apple toward Evanslea. Kate considered finding an excuse to see Mr. Evans when she arrived but relaxed in relief when she came upon Peter and Mr. Balham leaving the stables.

"Peter!" she called from atop her horse, pulling the reins to slow Apple as she came upon the men.

Peter turned in surprise and quickly glanced behind her.

She came to a stop and slid less than gracefully down Apple's heaving side.

"Have you come from Dr. Styles's house? Is Miss Smithson well?"

"Yes, we have," Peter said. His voice was strong, but his eyes told a different story. She wanted to beg him to explain to her whatever he was keeping to himself but restrained for Mr. Balham's sake. Given her current behavior, however, it was probably already too late for that. "Miss Smithson's arm was cared for and she has been escorted home. Dr. Styles anticipates a full recovery."

Kate stood completely still, the reins clutched tightly in her fist. She considered the situation. She could not very well tell these men that she expected something nefarious about Miss Smithson's fall—not when her only evidence was a simple feeling and the fear in Miss Smithson's eyes—but she could not exactly keep her mouth shut, either. Not when failure to act had twice caused women to suffer now.

Still, she hesitated. It made no sense. Every member of their party had either been on top of the cliffs or sitting on the blankets—there was no one left to have the nefarious intentions Kate feared. She squeezed her eyes closed, letting out the breath she had been holding and using a hand to cover her eyes. Her thoughts were a mess.

"Why don't you come inside for some tea?" Mr. Balham asked kindly.

"No," Kate said. "But I thank you. I must get home before it is too dark to see."

"I believe you have already reached that point," Peter said, his mouth quirking into a kind smile.

Kate looked up again and realized that they were moving from twilight rather steadily into night. "Oh, dear," she said under her breath.

"You can take my carriage," Peter said.

"No, thank you. Mr. Gibson knows the way home—we will be fine."

Peter glanced at the stable master behind her and then looked at her again. "Then allow me to accompany you. I could not rest if I wondered for your safety."

She couldn't help the laugh that bubbled out of her. "I believe I will be safer with Mr. Gibson than anyone else. No one could possibly know this land better than he."

"I think I might," Peter said dryly. "I did grow up here."

Kate nodded, acquiescing. She hadn't thought of that much before, but he had a point. If her uncle had allowed her to leave the house, to play outside as other children did, would she have made Peter's acquaintance when she was young? Potentially formed a friendship with him as children?

Peter turned toward the stables again and beckoned her to follow, where he pointed out their mounting block. He was able to get Domino saddled rather quickly and bade Mr. Balham a farewell before turning toward Split Tree and leading the way.

Apple fell into step beside Domino, and they rode in silence until the bend in the road beside the woods, Mr. Gibson falling behind.

"There is something you are not telling me," Peter said softly.

Kate swallowed. She pretended to focus on steering Apple and the reins in her grip. "I am just being a silly girl."

She could feel the stare he directed her way, but she did not give in and look back. They spent a few minutes like this before she relented, shrugging. "It is just a feeling, Peter. I am not sure why, but I just know that something...untoward...happened on that mountain today." She took a deep breath and spoke in a rush. "Miss Smithson could not have just fallen," she said defensively. "Not when the ground was so smooth and she so young and healthy."

By the time Kate realized she was riding alone, she was a few yards ahead of Peter. She turned back but the dark made it hard to see.

A voice floated toward her and she knew that it was his. "She was pushed."

Kate swallowed the gasp. "But who...?"

Domino moved closer. "She doesn't know. But she is convinced that two hands pushed her forward, and she tumbled down the hillside. I didn't know whether to believe her, but now..."

"No." Kate swallowed hard and shook her head. "My feeling is no confirmation."

"It is to me," he said, his gray eyes serious, glinting in the moonlight. "We are not given specific feelings and thoughts like that without purpose. Though we don't always know God's reasons."

She could not deny that the very same thought had gone through her own mind numerous times within the past few hours. But could it mean anything? What would *she* be able to do for Miss Smithson? Furthermore, who would want to hurt the woman?

"I have been trying to figure out the same thing."

Kate startled. She must have spoken aloud, though she had not realized.

Peter's eyes glittered in the dark, but his face was otherwise difficult to read. "I will figure this out."

"This is not your responsibility," Kate reminded him as they began toward her home once again.

"I have the unfortunate burden of a conscience, Kate," Peter said. "I cannot do nothing."

"Then we are of the same mind."

Peter

Peter delivered Domino back to the stables and carried himself wearily into Evanslea. This was one mystery he did not want to solve. Kate had voiced his very thoughts, for who would want to harm Miss Smithson? Aside from a slightly overbearing demeanor, she was harmless. And he assumed she had only been overbearing because she was on the hunt for a husband.

And Kate had been so concerned, her furrowed brow touching his heart. Peter needed to come clean, to tell Kate he was the savage boy from that day in the woods when they were children, but how? Time and again since Martin had revealed their youthful connection, Peter had wanted to discuss the matter, to be certain Kate was aware of his role. Remembering the way he'd held her back while Charles had ruthlessly questioned her about Martin's whereabouts brought a pang of sorrow to his heart. He'd been uncomfortable with it then, but now that he knew Kate, knew her kindness and her wholesome soul, he was even more ashamed.

So many years had passed, and their relationship now was

such that Peter held hope she would forgive him, but there had not seemed a good time to mention it yet. Though, he knew he must.

Shaking his head, Peter shelved that thought away and went in search of Martin, who he found in a tall wingback chair beside a fire, swirling amber liquid in a glass.

"That took long enough," Martin said, lifting the glass to his lips.

"I saw the ladies home safely."

Martin did not acknowledge Peter beyond a flick of his eyes and quickly returned his gaze to the fire. It was apparent he was bothered by something, but Peter could not blame him. Kate had easily come to the conclusion that Miss Smithson had been pushed, and Martin was intelligent. He'd likely come to the same conclusion.

"It had started out as such a promising day—what a pity."

"Yes," Peter agreed. "Only now—"

"I had a romantic proposal planned, and it was wrecked by that dreadful accident. Kate was beside herself, naturally. Dashed ruined everything."

Peter's eyebrow raised of its own accord, and he promptly ignored the swirling sensation in his gut. "What was the nature of your proposal?"

Martin gave him an incredulous look. So, marriage then. Peter could not help but feel relieved that his brother had been unable to fulfill his plan that day. "I doubt Miss Smithson intended on ruining your afternoon."

"No," Martin agreed. "Just rotten luck."

Peter studied his brother. So, he was irritated then, not worried for Miss Smithson. "Do you think perhaps you are acting rather quickly?"

"I have known her since we were children," Martin replied instantly.

Peter wanted to argue that one encounter with a girl ten

years prior was no basis for a lifelong relationship, but Martin was in a mood. It was better to just let him stew. He rose to his feet, the question of whether Martin was aware that Miss Smithson had been pushed on the tip of his tongue.

But he refrained from saying anything, too tired to argue. His feet carried him silently from the room and to his study. He'd begun to pull away from Charles not long after the incident in the woods, when he'd noticed how his older brother didn't seem to recognize when he was taking things too far. Despite Peter's efforts to act as a barrier between Martin and Charles, the brothers never seemed to forgive one another, and Martin clearly had never absolved Peter, either. One could only beg forgiveness so many times before it grew repetitive and pointless.

He pulled his account books from the top drawer and noted where Martin had made a few marks before perusing the recent purchases. It was fruitless to remind his brother that he had assumed all responsibility of Evanslea. Old habits were hard to change, apparently.

Replacing the account books, Peter found his butler and sent for Mr. Balham. If his steward was as exhausted as he felt, then he would not refuse a light dinner taken in the study. Little did Mr. Balham know, Peter was eager to discuss Miss Smithson and the possibilities surrounding her fall. He would get to the bottom of this, one way or another.

24

KATE

A restless night preceded the early morning. If, indeed, it could be called morning before the sun had so much as peeked over the horizon. Kate let out a frustrated breath and turned over again, squeezing her eyes closed and willing herself to fall asleep. Another eternity of lying in the warm bed within the still, quiet room and she was finished trying.

She jumped out of bed and threw her wrapper around her, tying the sash and searching for her slippers. Kate had purchased new ones when she had ordered those gowns weeks ago and had since come to the conclusion that little fairies were stealing things from her, for she had never found the missing slipper in the parlor room, or the others since. She had also since lost a jade earring and a soft, tan riding glove. She could not even wonder if there was an untrustworthy servant among them, for she never lost both items of a pair.

Locating her new slippers just under the foot of her bed, she slipped her cold feet into them and found her way to the door, one small candle lighting the way. She was distracted by the shadows cast from the flame, the familiar house seeming foreign in the cover of darkness. She reached the door to the library before she knew it and found her hand resting on the doorknob without conscious effort.

An onslaught of memories flooded her mind. Her uncle had reigned supreme from his study, except for the evenings when he'd sat in the library. His schedule had been predictable and consistent. She thought of the time she had sat at the top of the stairs and watched him go from the dining room to the library for his brandy; he'd caught sight of her and she'd run and hid so quickly she hadn't known if he'd followed. She had sat in the corner of her wardrobe for a good portion of the night before she had gained the courage to crawl into bed.

But she would never forget the sneer Uncle Bartholomew had sent her way. Nor could she erase from her mind the animosity in his eyes.

"I can do this," she said to herself as her grip tightened on the handle. She twisted and pushed the door open slowly, light spilling onto the library floor from her candle. The door swung open, a slight creak accompanying it. Kate lifted the candle and lit what she could. Bookcases lined three of the walls, floor to ceiling, leaving the fourth wall empty but for the long drapes that hung over the windows. She glanced to the fireplace and startled at the portrait that hung over the mantel. Her first order of business when the servants awoke would be to order that horrid portrait of Uncle Bartholomew removed to the attic. She would locate something else to replace it. Anything would do.

It would be the first step in removing the darkness from the room and replacing it with light.

Stepping back into the corridor, Kate noticed the faint light of morning through the foyer windows. That was quite enough demons to conquer for one morning. Footsteps sounded above her, and Kate returned to her room, deciding not to shock any of the servants by roaming the corridors in her nightdress.

Kate felt at least an inch taller on her return, and she wondered if conquering demons did that for a person.

"Miss Kingston?" The faint voice sounded far away, but when it repeated her name a fourth time, Kate found herself curled up in a chair of some sort, her feet tucked beneath her and her head resting on her folded hands against the arm of the furniture. Her eyes opened to a sideways Peter, and she immediately shot her head up, banging it against the back of the carved sofa.

Peter's smile immediately turned to concern as he crossed to her, and she found her hand rubbing the tender area of her skull as she brought her feet down and obtained a proper position.

"Does it hurt?" Peter asked as he took the seat adjacent to her, leaving the rest of the sofa free. She noticed the door open behind him and wondered where Emily was.

"Not badly. I am sorry you caught me dozing."

Peter's eyes indicated amusement, but he was too much of a gentleman to call her out for her exaggeration. "When you did not show up for our ride, I decided to check in with you."

"Is it that late already?" Embarrassment warmed her neck. She had come into the parlor after breakfast knowing she had two hours before she would need to meet with Peter. She did not remember much after the first few minutes of sitting on the sofa. And where had her embroidery gone?

"We can skip our ride today," Peter offered.

"Oh, but I was looking forward to it." She could hear how indifferent she sounded and winced. "Truly! I am just so tired." Kate yawned as if her body was helping to prove her point.

"Nonsense. We can ride again another time. Besides," Peter added, gazing at her with his amused, steel-colored eyes, "I was quite impressed with your riding last evening, and I am convinced you have outgrown the need for a teacher any longer."

Kate was surprised by the disappointment that laced her feelings. "Oh, right."

"Although," he continued, "I would not be averse to a riding partner. Particularly if said partner was a neighbor with an orchard project that needed regular advice."

She gave him a wry smile, his returning grin infectious. "It is true that I'd like your consultation. Though I cannot understand what you will get out of it."

Peter's smile turned soft. She basked in his warmth, grateful to have such a dear friend. And one that was a brute of a man, too. Though, brute hardly defined Peter. Perhaps *giant* was accurate, but he was always so courteous and considerate.

"I would like to call on Miss Smithson today," Kate said. "Do you think she will be up to receiving visitors?"

"I imagine so," Peter said on an exhale, leaning back in his chair and crossing one ankle over the other knee. "Shall I escort you? I would like to check on her myself. In fact, we could go now."

"In your riding attire?" Kate asked with the lift of a brow.

"Perhaps I had best ride Domino home and return for you and Mrs. Nielsen in a half-hour."

Kate nodded. "I'd like to question Miss Annie as well and perhaps even your brother. If there was another person on that mountain besides our party, then it stands to reason in a group as large as ours that someone would have seen them."

"Potentially," Peter said, his voice businesslike. "But not if the criminal is trained in the art of stealth. It is reasonable that they slipped in and out without being seen."

Kate leaned down and picked up the embroidery from the floor. She placed it on her lap and smoothed the edges, considering the gravity of what Peter said. "But who could ever have such heinous motives? Miss Smithson cannot possibly have any enemies. And I believe we would know if there were any terrible men in our vicinity, would we not? It would be hard to hide such a vile character."

A shrug lifted Peter's massive shoulders. "How can we

know?" He stood abruptly and glanced at his pocket watch. "I will return for you at one o'clock. We will get to the bottom of this."

The determination in his gaze sent a chill through Kate, and she found herself unable to stand. Peter left soon after, and she considered what had tipped him off. It must have some relation to his military training, and she was once again grateful to have found such a friend.

25

KATE

"*I*t is kind of you to ask after my sister, but I'm afraid she has been quite overset since her wretched fall yesterday," Miss Annie said, sipping her tea in the over-decorated drawing room of the Smithsons' home. Her black hair was swept high and her porcelain neck glowed in contrast. She was certainly going to break hearts one day.

"Of course," Kate said, taking refuge in her own teacup. Emily came to the rescue by asking after Miss Annie, and Kate took the opportunity to glance over Emily's head at the gentlemen. Seated on the sofa opposite them, Peter listened intently while Mr. Evans idly swung his pocket watch, lazily tracing its movement with his gaze.

"Perhaps we can visit again once she is feeling more herself," Peter said as he stood. Kate glanced at the mantel clock and noticed that the correct thirty minutes had been achieved just barely, but she shot Peter a look of confusion anyway. Where was the rush coming from?

"I'll go see that our carriage is brought around," Peter continued, bowing once and then leaving the room.

Mr. Evans chuckled awkwardly and lifted his shoulders in a

slight shrug. "Forgive my brother, Miss Annie. I am afraid too many years in the military has stunted his social graces."

The room offered a polite chuckle in return, but Kate felt uncomfortable. Peter did not lack any social graces—most of the time. Although, given the circumstances, the words were slightly true. Surely he had a reason for his actions. He was anything but foolish.

Ten minutes later, Peter returned to announce that the carriage was waiting and escorted Emily outside while Mr. Evans took Kate's arm. They sat in silence for the majority of the ride home, and Kate waited until she had exited the vehicle and watched the Evans men drive away to turn to Emily. "Something is going on."

"Not this again." Emily sighed, casting her gaze to the sky before turning for the house.

"Miss Smithson might be small, but she is not delicate. The abrasion on her arm would not keep her from two eligible bachelors in her own house."

"Unless she was napping, and the household decided not to inform her just who was calling. She likely needs a good deal of rest to heal."

"I had considered that, but Miss Annie looked right to Mr. Evans when she told us that Miss Smithson was *very* sad to miss us. That was a pointed statement, and you know it."

Emily scrunched up her little nose, tilting her head in thought. "That could be so, but then perhaps the mystery is why Miss Smithson would single out your Mr. Evans and not whether she was pushed."

Kate took a deep breath to abate her frustration. "It is not *whether* she was pushed, Emily, but by *whom*."

They stared into one another's eyes for a moment more before Emily gave her a tight smile. "Shall we agree to not let this come between us? I think you are overreacting, and you can think I am being too relaxed about the situation."

"Perhaps we should not speak of it any longer."

"Agreed."

Emily slipped her arm through Kate's and dragged her up the stairs and into the house, but Kate stopped in the foyer. "I think I would like to draw." It was on the tip of her tongue to invite Emily along, but she was out of charity with her friend at the moment and the time spent apart would likely be beneficial for both of them. It was a moment's work to collect her sketchbook and charcoals and she soon found herself walking down the lane toward the famed split tree.

There was a small boulder off the road, just far enough to see the entire expanse of land behind the tree, but close enough for details. Kate situated herself just there and opened her sketch pad to a fresh page. She slipped from between the pages the crude drawing she had made as a nine-year-old girl on the day she had first met Mr. Evans, the paper crinkled and darkened with age, and smiled at the bond they had forged that day. Placing it to the side, she began to sketch.

Martin

The candlelight bounced off of the sapphire in the center of the ring and made the small diamonds surrounding it glitter. Martin's lips pulled up in a self-congratulatory smile and tucked the ring back into the pouch, slipping it into his waistcoat pocket. He'd had the perfect plan for the picnic, but then it was ruined. Of course, that wasn't the end of the world—he would just have to come up with something different.

It was obvious that Kate was growing closer to Peter, but that didn't bother him. All he would have to do is let it slip that

Peter was the brother who had held her down in the forest that day, and she would see him for the bully he really was. How she hadn't seen it up until now was a complete mystery, but Peter's blond hair had darkened to a golden-brown and his monstrous figure likely made it difficult to relate him to the boy he had been ten years prior.

That Peter was growing inordinately fond of Miss Kingston was apparent as well, and only made Martin's relationship with her all the more enjoyable. His brother had made him suffer countless times during his younger years, and it was time to return the favor. Of course, he would never go as far as Peter and Charles had gone, but he would let Peter fall for Miss Kingston. It would make Martin's success that much sweeter.

He sat himself in the chair behind the desk of the study and sorted through his options. He had to come up with a new plan —preferably something that took care of his impediment swiftly, and quietly. If only he had not been so reckless. But, how was he supposed to know Kate would be returning to Split Tree one day? Had he known before Bartholomew Kingston had revealed the news that Kate was returning, Martin never would have trifled with anyone else.

As it was, he'd made quick work of disposing of Bartholomew Kingston once the idiot man had told Martin of his sponging off Kate's inheritance. He wished he'd discovered it sooner.

But he could not change the past. He could only control the future. And with a well-orchestrated plan, it was sure to all work out for his benefit.

Peter

Peter urged Domino forward. He was nearly to the stables of Split Tree Manor, and he would get in, ask questions, and get out before Kate found him. It was imperative or the lady would think he had just used this as an excuse to see her. Naturally, he wouldn't mind seeing her, but he was beginning to fear that he was pushing his company on her too frequently. He enjoyed being around her, of course, but if she was going to marry Martin then he needed to rein in his quickly growing attractions. He'd promised Martin he would respect the man's suit— and he wouldn't go back on his word now.

"Come on, boy," he muttered under his breath. His eye caught a figure perched on a rock beside the road and he didn't know whether to smile or frown. The natural reaction won out and he grinned at Kate as he swung down from his horse. "This is a nice place for a rest," he said, cocking his eyebrow at her. She squinted up to him and her answering smile made his breath catch. Could the woman love his brother when she smiled at *him* in such a warm manner?

"I did have a purpose in sitting here," she gestured to the book in her lap and then to the split tree. He indicated for her to hand him the book and she passed it over before stretching her hands high above her and rolling her shoulders. Peter took in every detail of the sketch, impressed by her skill. He smiled at the bird perched in the top of the tree feeding her babies a worm, and then glanced up to the real tree to see if they were still there.

"There are no birds," Kate said, as if reading his mind. "Call it artistic liberty."

"They add a touch of life. I think it is a wonderful notion." He handed back the sketchbook. He felt uneasy, though he couldn't quite pinpoint why.

"There were birds such as these," Kate said, putting away her charcoals and rising to her feet, "that I saw years ago. It was the day I met your brother for the first time, actually, and not a pleasant one at that." She visibly shuddered, and Peter felt the knot in his stomach grow. Kate's eyes were unfocused, as if she herself was far away. He wanted to reach over and pull her into his embrace, to tell her that he would protect her always, that he was not the same boy that had shot at those birds all those years ago, that he had changed. But he stayed rooted to the spot, his mouth glued shut with fear and apprehension.

"But let us speak of pleasanter things," Kate finally said, back to the present. She gave Peter a smile that he was sure would not be directed at him if she knew the truth. The notion made him sick. Still, he geared himself up to speak. It was the perfect opportunity—practically heaven sent. They were alone, she seemed in a good mood. Perhaps if he told her now, they could come to terms with the situation together.

"What brings you this way?" she said, ending the moment with a quick slice. It was over now.

He let out a long breath, his shoulders relaxing. It had to be the right moment, and this was no longer it. He felt a certain measure of relief at postponing the inevitable. He was intelligent enough to understand that it was, in fact, inevitable. "I was planning to question your stablemen about the accident, to ask if any of them had seen anyone who was not supposed to be there, or someone who had arrived separately from our party."

Kate nodded, her expression turning determined. "I know something is not quite right, but Emily doesn't believe me." She tilted her face up to him and gave him a heart melting smile. "I am glad you do."

His whole body warmed, as if her smile sparked the kindling that burned a fire in his soul. "Kate," he began, guilt eating at him. He couldn't put it off. He needed to tell her, now, before he wasted any more time and she found out some other way— before Martin himself told her. She needed to know Peter was one of the boys that day so she could see that he only had her best interests in mind now.

"Yes?" she prodded. "Do you care to explain your odd behavior at the Smithson's home this morning?"

"Yes," he agreed, all too quickly. Shame nipped at him, but he couldn't do it; he was a coward. He couldn't let her down right this moment, not when she needed good news. "I was questioning their driver and groom that came to the picnic, and they all said they did not see anyone arrive separately from our party. I was disappointed at first, but then one groom pulled me aside later and told me to question your servants. He seemed to think they would be able to tell me more."

"Then let us go!" Kate said eagerly, turning toward Split Tree Manor.

"Just a minute here." Peter pulled on her arm, chuckling at her eagerness. "We don't want to run in waving our guns or we'll give away our hand. We have to do this slowly, thoughtfully."

She looked up at him, her eyebrows pulling together. "I suppose I should trust the man with military experience. I have no idea what I am doing. But I would beg that you keep me informed every step of the way."

"Certainly," Peter agreed. He pulled on Domino and offered his free arm to Kate, escorting her home. She fit beside him perfectly, not so short that he felt he needed to stoop to accompany her, like most women. She fit just right.

"Do you think Miss Smithson is in any further danger in her own home?" she asked. "I would like to think this was a peculiar situation, but my mind will not rest. I had hoped to see her for myself and put my worries at ease, but alas, it was not to be."

"I thought the same thing. The sooner we understand what sort of danger she is in, the better we can know how best to help her."

"At least she is not alone; she has her sister."

"I believe Miss Annie's sentiments are more in line with

Mrs. Nielsen's," Peter said wryly. "She was quick to laugh when Miss Smithson told us that she had been pushed. I don't think Miss Annie believed her."

Kate looked worried. "That is not good. Perhaps I should invite her to stay with me for a while?"

"Under what guise?"

"I do not know," Kate said dejectedly.

"I cannot like you bringing the danger to your own home, either," Peter said, his mind shooting all sorts of uncomfortable directions.

"But if we can bring her here then we can watch her, protect her. No one else is. Especially if her own sister does not believe her."

"It is a noble thought, Kate, but far too dangerous. If someone was willing to shove her down that slope, they were willing to kill her. In fact—" Peter swallowed, unsure if his words would throw Kate into an even worse fit of anxiety. His gaze bored down into hers, his grip tightening on her arm. "They were probably *trying* to. It was a miracle she escaped as unscathed as she did."

"I know," she answered in a small voice. "This is exactly why I want to protect her. I would not be able to live with myself if something happened and I had done nothing."

Peter shut his eyes, racking his brain for a solution that would appease both Kate and himself. His mind kept coming back to the same idea and he shoved it away, conscious of all of the insinuations and things that would become bothersome for him should he suggest it.

But there was nothing else, he would have to do it. He sighed, opening his eyes and smiling down at the worried face which was counting on him.

"I have just the thing," he said.

26

MARTIN

*T*he moon was bright that evening, making for a smooth journey into Larkfield for Martin. A blessing, since he was a lone rider and the hour had dipped past midnight, at least. He slipped into the Blue Boar and located the table in the corner, half-hidden behind a pillar; he was relieved to find it blessedly empty.

Ordering a pint to give him a reason to sit idly, Martin settled his face into a contemplative, broody expression to ward off unwanted visitors and waited.

Peter had explained his idea of holding a week-long house party with the local gentry to break up the monotony of the early summer days and give Miss Kingston the opportunity to get to know her neighbors. He'd been appalled initially—Peter had *no* comprehension of the work that went into preparing for a house party. It was not something one simply threw together at the last minute. But then an idea had formed in Martin's mind and he'd agreed to the scheme, going so far as to assist in the planning of it all.

Little did Peter know, he was presenting Martin with the

opportunity he needed to dispose of his final impediment. And he could do so without the slightest chance of exposure.

He'd gotten away with it with Bartholomew Kingston, hadn't he? It merely required patience and a willing hand. Martin counted himself fortunate for having visited Mr. Kingston that day, well over a year ago, when the man had let slip that he could not authorize the purchase of a horse because the accounts were no longer in his name. His niece, who was the sole owner of both the estate and the fortune tied to it, had come of age and Kingston's power was gone. The man had been desolate but determined to enjoy his spoils as long as he was able.

Of course, Martin had been disgusted and had taken matters into his own hands. He hadn't realized Miss Kingston would one day return—that his guardian angel could, in fact, be *his*. But the moment this realization was set in Martin's mind, he only had one focus, and one purpose. *Her*.

He reached for his mug, moving it to the side and watching the door for his guest. He would normally drink, but at present he needed his wits about him. A quarter-hour later the man arrived, sliding smoothly onto the bench opposite Martin. Drawing himself further back behind the column, Martin held the man's gaze.

"Do you still have access to the plant?" he asked.

The man blinked. For such a cunning creature, he could be oddly dim at times. Martin watched him until his eyes lit with understanding. "Aye," he said. "And I can get more, too."

"Good. There is going to be a house party at Evanslea, and I require your services once more."

The man's eyes narrowed. "That'll be double, gov. I'm not risking my neck for anything less this time."

Martin watched him, sliding his finger around the rim of his untouched mug. "I'll pay the same fee as last time up front, and another ten when the job is done."

"Deal."

Martin tempered his smile. He was well on his way to getting everything his heart desired. Leaning forward, he lowered his voice and began to explain the specifications of the job.

Kate

Kate felt silly packing a trunk to stay at the neighbor's house for a week, but it was worth the trouble. This was the only way they could come up with to keep Miss Smithson safe. When Peter had suggested the house party, she had been so glad she could have flung herself into his arms. She had done so momentarily before remembering herself and hastily backing away.

Peter had probably thought her just as troublesome as Miss Smithson, but she didn't care. He was going out of his way to ensure the woman's safety, and letting Kate be part of it as well. He had been right, anyway, for it would have been foolish to invite trouble to Split Tree when she and Emily lived there alone with no form of protection. She felt much safer under Peter's roof and was glad Miss Smithson had agreed to come as well.

Emily moved aside the carriage's window covering to watch the world pass through it. "I still do not understand why the Evanses are throwing a house party right *now*. There is hardly any society here. If they waited but a month, I am told the society will double, at least."

"Perhaps they are bored," Kate said simply. She stared out the window. She could not force Emily to agree with her about anything but knowing that they so fully disagreed was not easy to bear, either. "Have you heard from Paul?"

"Not in some time," Emily said. "I would like to think it means they are nearing the end. We can only pray it will come speedily."

"I do," Kate said, giving her friend's hand a squeeze.

Their carriage pulled into Evanslea and let them out at the front door. Peter stepped outside with Mr. Evans on his tail, and they welcomed the ladies into their home, explaining that they were the first to arrive.

"I suppose we were just so eager," Kate said, shooting Mr. Evans a smile.

"Yes," Emily agreed. "A house party is just such a splendid notion! We shall get to know the local gentility quickly this way."

The men took them inside, and they all sat to tea. "Would you like to see your rooms before the other guests arrive?" Mr. Evans asked.

"I think we can skip the after-travel repose," Kate said, suppressing a grin. "The drive did not weary me."

They visited for another twenty minutes before the other guests began arriving. Mrs. Gressle and Miss Juniper arrived first, shortly followed by the Smithson family and the Kettlewells. Kate remembered the son, Albert Kettlewell, from the Evanses' last dinner party as being a young gentleman who had appeared easily bored by his fellow dinner mates. Mr. and Mrs. Kettlewell seemed nice enough, though on the quiet side. Mrs. Gressle was their opposite in every way, deeming herself the matron of honor, apparently, since Peter did not have a woman to host. He did not seem to mind, however, and Kate wondered if he expected Mrs. Gressle to step in and take control.

When the guests had assembled after room checks and various post-travel ministrations were complete, Peter stood before the group and cleared his throat. Kate found her gaze traveling to the front door, for Mr. Faile and his uncle,

Mr. Horace had not yet arrived, and neither had Mr. Balham.

"The three remaining guests will not make it until nightfall, I am afraid," Peter said. "So forgive me for the odd number at dinner, but I promise that the remaining company will be worth the wait." He smiled at Miss Annie and Miss Smithson, and Kate felt a tightening in her gut. "Now, for the interim I would like to offer up the gardens for walking, the horses for riding, or the music room for playing. We have also set up gaming tables in the parlor. You are free to spend your time as you wish. We will gather in the drawing room to dine at six o'clock."

The party slowly broke off after this. Mrs. Gressle dragged Miss Juniper and the Kettlewells off to the parlor for card games; the Smithson ladies returned upstairs for a nap; Peter walked away by himself and the remaining gentlemen decided on a ride.

Emily turned to Kate and lowered her voice. "Why did we not bring our horses?"

"I did not think about it," Kate answered with a lift of her shoulder. "Should we walk out to the stables and request that they send for Apple and Josephine? We will be here for a week. I do not think it would be unreasonable."

"Yes, let's." Emily stood and pulled Kate outside. They crossed the lawn some thirty feet behind the men and made it to the stables as they were leaving on their horses. Kate scanned the workers; a good many of them littered the stables and surrounding area, all of their livery an identical blue and silver. Her gaze caught on a familiar set of eyes and she called to the one man not in the Evans livery.

"Mr. Gibson!" The man turned away for a moment before looking over his shoulder. She waved a hand and he handed off the horse he was about to mount before crossing the dirty stable floor to meet her on the outside lawn.

"Miss Kingston."

"How fortuitous that we found you, Mr. Gibson. We were

hoping to dispatch a groom to Split Tree to request that our horses be brought here for the week."

Mr. Gibson nodded, belatedly removing his worn cap. "Tonight, Miss Kingston?"

"I think tomorrow morning would be sufficient. I don't believe we'll have use of them this evening."

"Very good, ma'am," Mr. Gibson said, nodding his head. "I'll see to it."

Emily pulled Kate around the back of the house to the gardens. A tall hedge maze took up a good portion in the center of the garden. Kate could not tell from this angle but assumed it to be circular.

The surrounding gardens were lovely, predominantly roses with some other varieties mixed in. They made their way to a bench on a path facing the back of the house and took a seat, chatting about the possibilities for the house party and whether or not the Evans men were planning on closing it out with an intimate ball.

"Mr. Cruikshank has begun planting the apple trees," Kate said of her new steward. "I hope it is not unseemly of me to ride over in the morning and check on the progress."

"I cannot see Mr. Evans appreciating the immense interest you have in your orchards, no," Emily said. "But that isn't reason to avoid checking on them if you are concerned."

Kate rose, the butterflies swirling around her stomach and filling her with an anxious energy. "I will not give them up, so he may as well see what he would be getting with me."

They peeked into the hedge maze but then continued on the path, neither of them wanting to risk getting lost this close to dinner.

Emily reached out and stopped Kate before they made their way up the stairs to change for dinner. "I do hope you know that while it is bizarre to care so deeply for your land as a woman, it is part of you, and whoever chooses to make you his wife will indeed need to accept it. Do not change yourself to snare a husband, or you will find yourself married to a stranger, for you cannot truly get to know anyone if you are not yourself."

Kate nodded. She gave her friend a smile and squeezed her fingers before moving up the stairs. Little did Emily know, her priorities at present centered on the safety of a certain house-guest. Matrimony was the last thing on her mind. Well, maybe not the last, but certainly not the first.

27

KATE

*T*he female half of the party moved to the drawing room following dinner as the men stayed behind for brandy and port. Kate did her best to watch Miss Smithson covertly during the meal but found nothing noteworthy. The gash on her arm was covered by her long gloves and her demeanor was much the same as it always had been—to Kate's disappointment.

She chose a seat near Miss Smithson in the drawing room and listened to the conversation between her, Mrs. Smithson, and Mrs. Kettlewell about the new milliner's apprentice and her skill with a hat.

"Quite interesting," a voice whispered in Kate's ear, causing her to jump.

"You startled me."

Emily's grin was unrepentant. "Why do you care about the new milliner's apprentice?"

"I was just curious," Kate said honestly, with a slight lift to her shoulder. "How much longer do you think the men will linger in the dining room?"

Right then the door opened to admit Mr. Evans and Albert

Kettlewell. Kate returned the smile delivered to her by the former and glanced behind him to an empty doorway. Her view was interrupted by Mr. Evans and an elegant bow, and she nodded slightly when he gestured to the empty seat on her other side.

"Dinner was superb, Mr. Evans. Though you mustn't let it slip that I said that. I'll have a very jealous cook on my hands if it ever gets back to her."

Mr. Evans smiled condescendingly, much like he would if she was a small child that had said something humorous. "Your secret is safe with me."

Her stomach tightened. She did not mind the loving way Mr. Evans looked at her, but condescension was a step too far.

"Has Sir Peter been detained?" Emily asked.

Kate watched the tick in Mr. Evans's jaw and irritation flashed in his eyes. Much like Peter's, they were currently a stormy color, and she could not tell if they were gray or blue. What could have him so upset with his brother?

"He has received the last of the guests and will be in shortly," Mr. Evans said. He turned to Kate and gave her a searching look. "I would like to take you for a ride this week in my phaeton. I am not sure what Peter has planned for tomorrow, but perhaps we might go in the afternoon?"

"I should like that," Kate said, hoping her face didn't betray her lack of enthusiasm. Her stomach swirled, souring the longer he watched her. How had she imagined this feeling to be the soft fluttering of butterfly wings? There was no mistaking the unease filtering through her, and she felt herself begin to panic.

Mr. Evans was still gazing into her eyes intently, and she smiled, though she could feel the strain of it. Could he sense it, too?

"Are you quite sad to miss your London trip?" Kate asked, desperately trying to force him to speak, to remove his fixated gaze from her person. The way he lingered on her, caressing her lips with his eyes made her want to vomit.

"I don't believe I am missing too much," he responded, with a sigh that said otherwise. "When Peter mentioned these plans of his I immediately wrote my acquaintances in London and begged their forgiveness. Of course, I enjoy spending a little time there every year, but an uninterrupted week with my new neighbors was simply too good of an offer to pass up."

"Guests," an authoritative voice rang out from the doorway, effectively cutting the conversation short and keeping Kate from needing to respond to that pointed remark. She turned to see Peter standing there, his legs planted firmly on the Aubusson carpet and his hands clasped behind him; she could see how he would have easily commanded a company of men in war.

Three men stood off to his side—each of them striking in different ways. The first claimed shaggy brown hair with a gruesome scar that ran through his eyebrow and down the side of his face, standing in much the same position as Peter. Beside him, a blond gentleman leaned languidly against the wall, a look of endless boredom plastered on his otherwise thoroughly handsome face. The third, a tanned gentleman, leaned forward to listen to something the blond man whispered to him. A smile lit his face, revealing a set of even, white teeth—marred only by a chip from his front tooth.

Peter gestured to each man in turn. "Allow me to introduce Lord Marshall, Earl of Marshall, Lord Aniston, Earl of Aniston, and Lord Cohen, Viscount Cohen." The men each bowed as they were introduced, and Kate could not help but notice Lord Cohen's missing hand. He quickly shoved his arm into a pocket following his bow—likely to hide that very thing. His skin was so tan and his hair so dark, she was sure he was not a native Englishman—but his title said otherwise.

Peter continued to introduce the members of the house party and Kate paid enough attention to dip her head in acknowledgement when he reached her. She could not help but feel a little bewildered that their party had grown by three lords, and she suddenly felt childish for asking Peter about things like orchards and stewards or having him teach her to ride a horse when he kept such high company. Good heavens, he had taught her to ride a horse! He must think her such a ninny.

"Shall we begin a game of charades?" Miss Smithson asked, rising to her feet and displaying herself at best advantage.

"I was rather hoping you would delight us with a song," Peter said gallantly.

Miss Smithson blushed becomingly and agreed before turning to consult with her sister.

Kate felt the disconcerting focus of Peter's stare warming her. She kept her gaze on Mr. Evans as he described his favorite opera in London and mentioned, again, how eager he was to watch Kate experience the beauty of the soprano, but distraction from Peter's marked attention held her captive. The candlelight flickered around them, and she looked up, suddenly overcome with shyness.

She caught Emily's eye, who gave her a questioning look, and then glanced away. She could not even explain what she was feeling to herself, so it would be impossible to describe it to Emily.

"Miss Kingston, would you do us the honor of playing?"

"I am sorry," she said, briefly catching Peter's eye before looking back at Mr. Evans. "I am afraid I do not play above adequately."

"Yes," Emily agreed, "but you sing beautifully."

Kate shot Emily a quick look, trying to convey the message that she'd rather not sing, either. Not with three lords in the room.

"And I'd be happy to accompany you, Kate," Emily continued, the innocence in her tone obviously false. Well, obvious to Kate's knowing ears at least.

"You did not tell me that you sang," Mr. Evans said, his tone laced with hurt.

Kate tried to breathe in some patience, and maybe a little strength. "It is not something I do often. I have not been trained by any masters."

Miss Smithson took to the piano and the room quieted. Peter moved back to sit beside his friends, who seemed to enjoy the music.

Miss Annie joined in next, singing a lovely soprano to Miss Smithson's complicated playing. When they switched places, Miss Smithson's voice rang out strong, her sister's playing a little lacking but highlighting her voice all the more. Emily spent a few minutes looking through the available sheet music before showing Kate her selection. They took their places at the vacated piano as the room clapped politely, Emily seated and Kate standing behind her, ready to turn pages. The hush that fell over the room felt louder than before, and Kate kept her gaze on the music as Emily began to play.

Kate sang the song she and Emily had often performed at school functions. Emily's skill on the piano was on par with Miss Smithson's, and Kate's voice was a soft alto; her singing rang pure and clear.

The song spilled from her lips as her eyes darted about the room, unwilling to rest for longer than a moment on any particular guest. They all watched her as she stood poised beside the pianoforte, her hands clasped lightly before her. But Mr. Evans's stare was direct, even severe. She felt it in the core of her stomach, and it drew her gaze to him as though by force. Clear, gray eyes fastened on her, and she nearly stumbled over the familiar words of the song.

Tearing her gaze from his, she searched the rapt faces, landing on the man standing at the back. Peter stood tall and steady, watching her with appreciation. His eyes glittered, flickering in the candlelight, and a smile settled on his lips, elevating her spirits.

They completed the song to a moment of silence before the audience clapped and Mrs. Gressle requested an encore, which was seconded by Mr. Evans and Lord Aniston. Kate watched Emily move aside the sheet music to reveal another underneath, and they performed this one together, Emily singing harmony to Kate's melody. They politely declined a second encore and reclaimed their seats, the musical portion of the evening at a close.

"That was marvelous," Mr. Evans said when Kate returned to his side, his handsome smile radiant. "Absolutely beautiful."

"I cannot help but agree," Lord Aniston said, coming to stand beside Kate. "I have yet to hear such a pure tone tug at my heartstrings so."

"That is very kind, my lord," Kate said, dipping into a curtsy. She could not recall being addressed by a member of nobility in all of her life. Unless Peter counted. Did he? No, not quite. He was a *Sir*, not a lord.

"I hope you plan to grace us with another performance before the week is out," Lord Aniston continued suavely. His fair hair was a golden shade, much lighter than Mr. Evans's, and his face was classically handsome with a tilted nose, not unlike how she'd imagined Adonis to appear.

"Perhaps," was her noncommittal reply.

The group soon after broke up for the night, Mrs. Gressle leading the way with her companion, Miss Juniper, close behind. Kate and Emily bid Mr. Evans goodnight and moved into the corridor close behind Mrs. Gressle. They caught a bit of the conversation between the matron and her companion, and Emily pulled on Kate's arm to hold her back after a particularly spiteful comment.

"You cannot think she means it," Emily whispered harshly.

"The woman is old. And she surely does not have *all* her wits about her."

"No," said Kate, drolly. "Only the ignorant ones."

"Come, do not take offence. Surely she meant that you have gotten to know your neighbors so well because of their proximity."

"Right," Kate said. "I am sure that is *exactly* what she meant when she said, 'that *unseemly* Miss Kingston.'" Kate raised her voice a shrill octave higher, mocking the older woman. "'Taking advantage of those poor Evans boys. And no woman in the house to warn them of her wily ways.'"

"Whoever authored those lies obviously does not know our Miss Kingston, now do they?" a deep voice said behind Kate.

Her eyes drifted closed and she froze, caught out. She drew in a breath before turning to find Peter flanked by Lord Aniston and Lord Cohen.

"Forgive me; I didn't know I had an audience," Kate muttered. She found it difficult to hold Peter's steel gaze and looked to Emily for help.

"Your name is so familiar, my lord," Emily said instead, narrowing her gaze at Lord Aniston.

His surprise was quickly masked with the same bored look he wore earlier.

"Might you have served with the Light Dragoons at some point?"

"I am afraid not," Lord Aniston replied.

"Oh. I thought maybe I had heard your name from my husband," Emily explained.

"Who might that be?" Lord Cohen asked, his voice sounding strained—though he hid it well.

"Captain Paul Nielsen."

A smile lit Lord Aniston's bored eyes and he stepped forward. "I know him well. You must be proud of him. I recently heard he went back when Napoleon escaped from Elba."

"Yes, he did," Emily said with a suspicious sheen to her eyes. "Indeed, I am quite proud."

"His family neighbors mine in Kent," Lord Aniston explained. "We grew up together. Though I've been away, so I haven't had the pleasure of making your acquaintance yet."

Emily nodded again, taking Lord Aniston's arm as he offered to escort her to the stairs.

Peter

"Mrs. Gressle said those words, didn't she?" Peter asked, doing his best to control the anger heating his blood.

"Yes," Kate said softly as she watched her friend walk away, then turned to Peter with determination. "But do not think for one moment that I take her seriously. Cranky old women often feel the need to find faults wherever they can. Even if they create them."

"Well said." Peter glanced to the stairs to find Mrs. Nielsen and Aniston climbing them, as Cohen covertly slipped away. He wondered if Kate noticed, but she seemed distracted. "And I hope you mean those words. You are generous and kind, Kate. The furthest thing from wily in this house."

She glanced up at him, holding his gaze, and he swallowed hard. Kate *was* generous and kind. She was incredible.

But it was late, and Peter did not trust himself if they remained in this darkened corridor much longer. He cleared his throat. "Can I help you with anything before you turn in?"

"No," she said with a self-deprecating smile. She lowered her voice. "I thank you for your kind hospitality, of course. I have only just been thinking that we seem no closer to figuring out who is behind Miss Smithson's fall. I hope this week isn't for naught. It would all feel rather silly, would it not?"

"She is under our watchful eyes," he said reassuringly. "And for all we know, the culprit could be here, too. That is not a waste."

"No, it is not." Letting out a long sigh, Kate turned toward the stairs and took his offered arm.

"Can I interest you in a ride in the morning?"

"I would say yes, but I've already made plans with Emily to ride over and check on Mr. Cruikshank and my trees."

"Has he been working out well then?"

"Oh, yes!" Kate turned to him and the joy on her face was adorable as she squeezed his forearm with both of her hands. "We get on together so well. And he is not condescending to me in the least when I ask for explanations. I cannot thank you enough for the introduction."

"It was my pleasure." Peter smiled down at her, his gaze roaming over her lips. He shocked himself by conjuring an image of leaning down and closing the space between them. An entirely delicious image.

A throat cleared and they both looked up to find Mrs. Nielsen waiting at the top of the stairs beside a smug Aniston.

Kate stepped away quickly, climbing the last few stairs and dipping a curtsy before taking Mrs. Nielsen's hand and scurrying down the corridor. Aniston came to stand beside him and chuckled softly. "It looks like you're smitten, old man."

"Perhaps I am," came Peter's reply. "Is that such a bad thing?"

"No, not as long as she is worthy of you."

They moved down the stairs toward the study where Marsh and Cohen had most likely escaped to. Sure enough they found both men by the fire, glasses of brandy in their hands and a dull silence to the room.

"Our captain here is in love," Aniston said with the bored

tone he had perfected over recent years. He was the youngest of the group by a good margin but the things that he had lived through kept him on par with the rest of them mentally.

"Ah, I had wondered," Cohen said before taking a sip from his glass. "You could have shot arrows from your eyes after we heard what she was saying in the corridor."

Peter shrugged before dropping onto the sofa and stretching his legs out in front of him. "It is pointless. Martin is ready to propose."

Stunned silence took the room.

"But is she ready to accept him?" Marsh asked in his deep, wise voice. The man hardly spoke, but when he did, he did not mince his words.

Peter shrugged again, watching the flames lick the brick of the fireplace and picturing Kate standing beside Martin in the local church. That image made his stomach turn over.

"If there is no understanding between them, then it is not too late," Aniston said with confidence. "Clearly she is not immune to you."

"It is a complicated matter," he said, thinking of the day in the woods so long ago when he had held her down at Charles's bidding, imagining the moment that she connected the dots and the hatred that would surely steal her beautiful features.

A companionable silence fell upon them. If someone would have told Peter that he would be Captain over a viscount and two earls, and this before he had inherited the title of baronet, he would have laughed outright. It came to be, however, that his small company of men was among the highest ranking in their division as well as his closest friends. Though, not one of them had expected the title they had eventually inherited. Peter included.

They went through a particularly trying period together, losing Cohen to England when he had lost his hand and then Marsh, only to be followed shortly by Aniston and Peter himself at the last battle together. They understood one another in a way that others could not, and they supported and cared for each other without hesitation. It was why he had written to them the moment he'd thought of the house party. If anyone was going to help him to discover who was out for Miss Smithson, it was his men.

"Right, Captain," Marsh said gruffly. "Why don't you fill us in on why you've really called us here?"

KATE

"Perhaps we should wait until this afternoon," Emily said, her breath fogging, billowing in a cloud before her.

"No." Kate spoke unapologetically, not pausing her stride. "I am supposed to go driving with Mr. Evans this afternoon. But I do not want to wait until tomorrow to see the trees."

"Very well," Emily muttered, following Kate to the stables. "But I'm not sure how long I'll last. It is so very cold."

Emily requested their horses be saddled, and they waited, glad Mr. Gibson had already brought Apple and Josephine despite the early hour. The sun was rising steadily but had yet to burn off the layer of fog which blanketed the earth, hiding the approaching gentlemen from view until they had nearly reached the stables.

"Good morning," Peter said when he and Lord Cohen came into view. "I thought with certainty I would beat you out here. Have you sent for your horses from Split Tree?"

"We did last night," Emily said. "Kate's stablemaster brought our horses this morning and they are being saddled now."

"Very good." Peter turned away, speaking with a groom before returning to the ladies. "Might we be so bold as to offer our escort this morning?"

Kate held his gaze, warmth filling her chest. "I am afraid it is bound to be a boring ride. I would like to check on my—"

"Trees," Peter finished, his smile revealing a faint dimple on the side of his mouth. How had she never noticed it before now?

"Yes," Kate said softly. Her cheeks grew warm, and she wondered if the reaction stemmed from the comment about the trees or the dimple. She found herself searching for somewhere to look, her gaze continually drawn to that dratted dimple. "Lord Cohen," she said, hearing the strain in her voice. "Have you any interest in agriculture?"

"Quite a bit, actually," he said, coming to her side as Apple and Josephine were brought out to the mounting block. He held Apple's reins as Kate prepared herself to mount and said, "I have recently arrived back from the West Indies where I spent a good deal of time learning the sugar trade. I came home to focus on my family estate here in England, so if you have any helpful knowledge about farming, I would only be too glad to hear it."

Kate chuckled politely, but when the man did not join her, she stopped. "Oh, you are in earnest? Forgive me, I am such a novice myself I could hardly have anything of use to share. But Mr. Balham is a good man to speak to, and he can recommend a great many books—many of which I've found helpful myself."

Lord Cohen nodded, the twinkle in his pale green eyes betraying his amusement. Kate wished the ground might open right then and swallow her whole. Laughing like that at nobility? And she could not even remember his rank. Was this one the viscount? Oh heavens, she *really* hoped he wasn't the earl.

The men mounted their large, powerful horses and Kate averted her eyes when she noticed Lord Cohen holding the reins with one hand, the other arm sitting limply in his lap. It was safe to assume that he had somehow lost his hand in the war, but she also expected that he didn't appreciate stares.

"Shall we?" Peter asked, his reins slack in his hands as he sat in the saddle with relaxed confidence. Kate nodded, and the riders took off in the direction of her property, crossing onto Kingston land in short order.

Lord Cohen pulled his horse beside Apple and began an inquiry, in which Kate filled him in on her progress thus far with the estate, and the ideas and advice Mr. Cruikshank had brought with him. Peter and Emily fell behind them, and Kate caught snatches of a conversation centered around Paul, which did not surprise her in the least.

"Mr. Cruikshank!" Kate called as they neared the rows of infant trees. She understood that they were being transplanted and the possibility of losing some was inevitable, to say nothing for the fact that they would take at least three or four years to yield any fruit. But the sight of rows upon rows of miniature tree stalks was beautiful and made her heart soar. "This looks magnificent!" she said, sliding from her horse.

"The planting went better than I anticipated," Mr. Cruikshank said with a bow, his thin hair blowing in the slight breeze. According to his references, he had worked at an estate similar to Kate's when the owner had passed away unexpectedly and the new owners had brought their own steward with them. He was skilled at his job and would have had no trouble finding a new position, but Kate had applied to him first. Or, rather, Peter had. And she was grateful.

"Should we expect a yield in the autumn, then?" she asked, grinning.

"If you refer to the autumn three or four years from now, certainly," Mr. Cruikshank said with a sad tilt to his brow. "Though, even that will hardly be sufficient for household use. We have years to go yet before we might look beyond our own kitchens."

Kate nodded. She'd heard this before, but she couldn't help hoping it would be different. "Oh, forgive me," she said, directing her attention to her friends, who had all dismounted and were approaching now. "Let me introduce Lord Cohen. Of course, you already know Mrs. Nielsen and Sir Peter." She turned to the rest of the party. "This is Mr. Cruikshank, my productive steward."

The men bowed. "Good to see you again, Sir Peter," Mr. Cruikshank said.

"I must thank you, Sir Peter, for introducing us," Kate added. "I am sure I have already, but I am prodigiously glad."

Peter nodded.

"The pleasure has been all mine," Mr. Cruikshank said.

Peter

Peter wanted to imagine that Mr. Cruikshank was only being kind, but he was not fooled. Kate was an easy woman to fall for. He should know.

"How does your family go on?" Peter inquired, nodding politely as the man answered favorably. He had known Mr. Cruikshank in school years ago and had kept an occasional correspondence with the man. He was ahead of Peter in school by four years, but they'd forged a bond when Peter helped him to avoid Charles's bullying. He shut his eyes to push the memories from his mind. Those were not pleasant years.

"I am not leaning toward trees, no," Cohen was saying. "My brother believes wheat is the answer. I was considering horses, so I imagine it could be a conducive endeavor."

Mr. Cruikshank was nodding, and the men began discussing

the best climates for wheat. Kate had wandered toward the trees and Emily stood shivering, listening politely to the men. Peter left Domino—the obedient horse would stay put—and walked to where Kate was admiring a tiny apple tree.

"They look lovely," he said.

"Oh, don't they?" Kate beamed. "I cannot wait for Alice to get her hands on some of their fruit."

"Alice?"

"My cook," she answered absently. "She's marvelous. You'll see."

Peter had to smile at the indication that she saw him as a regular fixture in her life. Until he realized he *would* be a regular fixture if she was to marry his brother. He swallowed the bitter taste that left in his mouth. "Have you truly made Split Tree your home then?"

Her eyes glazed over before she turned to him. "Yes, I believe I have. Did I tell you that I went into the library?" She chuckled softly and looked down. "I've yet to conquer the study, but that will be next."

"Sometimes we build things up in our mind to be scarier than they are in reality." He swallowed, feeling like a large, uncouth brute, unsure of himself. Well, that was a novel feeling. Peter valued his self-confidence, but Kate had a habit of making him nervous, of giving him reservations which were foreign to him. He cleared his throat, hoping to clear away the awkwardness. Lifting a shoulder, he said, "I can accompany you if you wish."

The moment the words left his mouth he wished them back. What was he thinking? She had Mrs. Nielsen for a companion, and a very capable one at that. She did not need him.

"Oh, would you?" Kate asked, breathless. "I believe I could not be scared of anything if you were by my side." She looked down, smiling wryly. "That makes me sound young and inexperienced, doesn't it?"

"No," Peter said. He was elated by her words but attempted to temper the feelings. It wouldn't do to go and fall in love if she was to become his sister.

"Not to put a damper on the moment, but I am utterly freezing," Mrs. Nielsen said from where she stood with the ladies' horses.

"Yes," Kate called back. "Let us return."

Peter waited for Kate to move on and slipped to Mr. Cruikshank's side. "Any developments?"

"Rumors within the stables," he answered quietly. "Come by later and I'll share what I know."

Peter nodded, clapping the steward on the back before whistling for Domino and mounting in one fluid motion. Placing a trusted man on the estate had been a good move. Originally, he had intended to have Mr. Cruikshank around for an extra watchful eye on the ladies of Split Tree, for they had no male protection of their own. Now that there were nefarious acts going unexplained, he was glad to have a trusted confidant.

He only needed to trust his intuition to lead him to the culprit and he would solve this mystery and return safety to Larkfield once and for all.

Martin

Martin looked in on the women in the drawing room and swallowed frustration at not finding Kate among them. Lord Aniston was leaning toward Miss Smithson and saying something that caused her to giggle. She caught Martin's eye as he was leaning in the doorway and shot him a victorious grin. He dipped his head back, wondering if she had given up on him. Could she be hoping to snag a lord this week?

Why Peter wanted to throw a house party at all was beyond Martin's scope of understanding. He would happily reap the benefits of having Kate under his same roof, though. He was confident that if he proposed she would accept, and he decided that the ball at the end of the week would be the perfect setting. She would say yes, and they could announce it to the entire county at one time.

A smile touched his lips as he continued to watch Miss Smithson. Lord Aniston was just a flirt—that was widely known. But there were also two other lords in the house, both closer to Peter's age and undoubtedly ready to wed. Earldoms needed heirs—and Miss Smithson could very well be carrying one right now, if it was a boy. Not that she would inform any suitor before the wedding took place—but neither could she afford to be picky. Martin had made his position *very* clear.

If Lord Marshall wasn't so withdrawn, he would be a decent catch. Good move inviting him, Peter. He had yet to show his face ever since the initial introduction.

Martin heard laughter in the foyer and clenched his jaw when he recognized it to be Kate's. He watched her walk in on Lord Cohen's good arm and say something that had the rest of their party laughing. Perhaps he should reevaluate his plan. If he claimed her now, then the others would understand that she wasn't available. He watched the gentle sway of her skirts as she moved up the stairs toward her room, undoubtedly to change from her riding habit. He loved the deep green on her and imagined her in all manner of colors.

She was going to make a beautiful bride. And she was going to be his.

29

KATE

$\mathcal{T}$he house party was progressing splendidly. Kate did her best to watch Miss Smithson from a distance, which was not difficult considering how the women were not close friends. She was beginning to feel like maybe she had over-reacted about the whole fall, but then Miss Smithson came down with an illness on the third morning of the house party that forced her to remain bedridden, a fever and occasional incoherence taking hold of her. Kate offered to sit with her for a spell, but her mother was worried about contagion and asked that Miss Smithson not be disturbed until the doctor could see to her first.

Meanwhile, Mr. Evans's attentions increased tenfold. He sought Kate out often, begging to take her for drives, listen to her sing, or even read in companionable silence. She acquiesced for the most part, but occasionally begged to be excused—though she could see that it bothered him when she did.

Her certainty that a proposal loomed on the horizon did nothing but heighten her nerves. He discussed openly the joyful prospect of a future together, persuaded they would be blissfully happy. Yet Kate was equally convinced that she did not love him.

The swirling sensation she felt in her gut when she was around Mr. Evans had only grown in recent days, and Kate suspected it was a mix of anxiety and apprehension, not the pleasant flutter of butterfly wings. Not *love*.

But *why* he made her so nervous went beyond her comprehension, which concerned her a great deal.

Peter had approached her the evening before and had asked to meet her at the stables directly after breakfast—and covertly if at all possible. She was certain he had come closer to solving their riddle.

She skipped breakfast, apprehension chasing her appetite away. Kate was certain something big was coming, and the idea was as scary as it was welcome. She was ready for this to be over. It was exceedingly tiresome being worried for Miss Smithson when it seemed the lady wasn't worried at all for herself. Of course, now that she was in and out of consciousness it seemed too improbable to be a coincidence. Someone *had* to be poisoning her, Kate was sure.

"I was afraid you were not coming," Peter said as she approached. He had Apple prepared and waiting beside Domino.

She could not tell him that she had been looking forward to it since he'd issued the invitation or that would seem too bold.

They rode to Split Tree the back way, cutting through the woods, and left their horses tied to a rear shed that sat on the property line beside the trees. It was a short walk to the stables, and Peter informed her of what he had learned.

"I was told that a member from your stables arrived at the vista after the rest of our party was already seated for the luncheon. He came under the guise of bringing additional desserts from Split Tree's kitchens, but the man who questioned him did not see any parcels on his person."

"Who was it?" Kate asked, her eyebrows screwed together in thought. Nothing had arrived during their luncheon from Alice, nor had the cook mentioned wanting to send anything. Rather, she had seemed happy for an afternoon off, if Kate recalled correctly.

"That's the rub. They had no idea. His information came from a man not acquainted with the members of your staff."

"Who was your source?"

Peter looked down and gave her a smile, saying, "I cannot give away my informant. You understand."

"Yes." She nodded, then shot him a grin. "Though it does not make me less curious."

Peter led her around the side of the stables, pulling Kate to the side so they could approach unseen. "I was hoping we could look around a little."

"And if we are caught?" she whispered, breathless. Peter's large, warm hand encased her own and sent a chill up her arm, which spread over her body.

He glanced over his shoulder, an amused smile turning up his lips and revealing the dimple. "If we are caught, we simply tell them we are looking for an additional lady's saddle for one of the guests."

Kate nodded. She could be stealthy...she hoped. But she was far more eager to watch Peter. He was the one with military training, after all.

He mouthed "follow me" and released her hand before quietly sliding through a side door. The stables were quiet but for the soft neighing of Kate's carriage horses. The workers were likely taking advantage of the break with Kate's absence, which did not bother her, as long as her horses were looked after.

Peter took her hand again and pulled her quietly toward the office where Mr. Gibson conducted his business. A sound within the small room indicated that it was occupied, and Peter paused before pivoting toward the wooden staircase which led to the quarters upstairs. Kate followed him up the steps, impressed by his agility. For a man so large, he was adept at moving unnoticed.

"You begin on this end and I will start over there," he whispered, pointing to the far side of the narrow corridor. Kate nodded and moved to the first bedroom, only to find it empty. She moved to the next and searched the belongings, not quite sure what she was looking for, but confident she would know when she found it. Guilt pricked at her, but she had only to be reminded of Miss Smithson's very real peril and her resolve hardened.

Room upon room came up empty of any valuable clues. Meeting Peter in the center of the corridor, she shook her head and he mimicked the action.

"Drat," she said. "I was hoping we would find something."

"Let us see if the office is no longer occupied."

Nodding, she followed him down the stairs, glad they were away from the bedrooms that would undoubtedly lead to a scandal should they have been found. The door to Mr. Gibson's office was left open and Peter slipped inside, telling her to stay and remain outside the door to keep watch. Her heart sped at the danger of the situation. Should they be found, she was confident she could distract with meaningless questions, the quest for a sidesaddle her fallback. She was relieved when Peter returned, shaking his head, and she was not required to do so.

"Nothing," he said.

It was bittersweet that they had seemed to clear her staff. Of course she did not want a traitor under her roof, but she would have been glad to discover who was trying to hurt Miss Smithson.

"Shall we tackle the study now that we are here?" Peter asked.

It took Kate a moment to understand his meaning. "Now?" she asked.

He nodded, watching her steadily, his gray eyes unyielding. She drew in a deep breath. She had told him she wished to go into the study, and he had offered to stand by her side if she needed support. Gazing up at the man, she realized how deeply she wished for his support—that she'd meant it when she'd said she could do anything if he was by her side.

And now was a perfect time, while her servants believed her to be gone. She would not likely have an audience. "Very well."

They walked quickly toward the house and slipped inside. Her butler was not beside the front door, and Kate was relieved to avoid any spectators. She directed Peter down the corridor, and they stopped at the study door, her hand rising slowly until it stuck, as though glued to the doorknob.

She had entered this room countless times before to take away empty bottles of spirits or tend to the fire. She'd hardly been old enough to put aside fairy tales and young girls' dreams when she'd been brought to her once childhood home and forced to serve.

And all the while, her uncle was merely managing *her* inheritance.

"Would you like me to open it?" Peter asked kindly.

"No," she said on an exhale. Fire burning in her chest, she gripped the knob, the reeded wood digging into her fingers. But hesitancy nipped at her, creating a barrier that prevented her from stepping forward. Kate shut her eyes, shaking her head. "This is silly. I can do it."

Peter's large hand covered hers, pushing her fingers deeper into the ringed wood. She looked up at him, caught by the compassion pulling his eyebrows in, his blue eyes roaming over her as if he could remove her distress by his gaze alone.

"It is not silly to face your demons," he whispered. "It is brave."

She nodded, afraid speaking would unleash a flood of tears. Peter squeezed her hand before letting go, and she turned the knob, pushing the door open.

The creak of the swinging door cut through the quiet house. Kate's gaze swept the room, landing on the oversized mahogany desk. A flash of Uncle Bartholomew sitting behind it assaulted her, bringing to mind his slow perusal of her while she stood in her plain dress for his initial inspection upon her arrival at Split Tree.

The empty room in the dim light looked...pathetic. Kate drifted to the windows and moved aside the heavy drapes, disturbing some of the dust as morning light streamed through the open windows and highlighted swirling particles dancing languidly from their resting places.

Catching Peter's gaze over her shoulder, she smiled. "Thank you."

He dipped his head.

"I was sent to live with a family when my parents died—tenants of my uncle's friend," Kate said, unsure of why she was telling Peter this, but feeling the need to speak. She was faintly aware of him closing the door behind himself and she moved to the desk to look within its drawers. "My uncle probably had me go because he did not wish to deal with me. But then he sent for me when I was nine and forced me to return to Split Tree." She turned, holding Peter's gaze. "I did not realize until years later that he likely only did so to gain access to my money— money I did not even know I had until a few months ago."

Peter shook his head. "I knew he was ruthless in business. But this? I had no idea. What an awful man."

"Yes, he was." She smiled at Peter before opening the top drawer of the monstrous desk. "He was awful. I was a servant he did not have to pay. And when he did not have a use for me, he kept me locked in the school room with a horrible woman until he sent me away to school. I was glad to go. I found a home within the school, with the teachers and the other girls."

"You never went outside while you were here?" Peter asked, an odd emotion in his voice. She glanced up, but he seemed at ease, his arms crossed casually over his chest as he watched her with interest.

She shook her head, rummaging through the quills and ink bottles. She stopped suddenly and looked up at him. "Oh, I suppose I did once. But it wasn't a very pleasant experience. And the switching I got on returning convinced me not to try it again."

Peter looked arrested.

"What is it?" she asked.

"I..." he started. He cleared his throat and came around the desk, resolve hardening his features. "I'm afraid there is something—"

The door swung open to reveal Mr. Cruikshank, eyes wide as he halted midstep. "Forgive me, I didn't realize..." He looked between the two of them, unsure of what to do.

"Do not mind us," Kate said, shutting the drawer and taking a step back. "We were just finishing up here. Please, Mr. Cruik-shank, feel free to use this room as you see fit. I plan on instructing Mrs. McKinley to keep this room cleaned and open for use. I do not imagine I'll be using it myself, but that doesn't mean it must remain closed up."

"Very good, Miss Kingston." He cleared his throat awkwardly and glanced away.

"Is there something you wish to say?" Kate asked, mildly defensive.

"Only, I have been coming in here on occasion to access the bookshelf that is kept in here. And I found a small stash of ladies' belongings. I was unsure of what to do with them."

"Oh? Perhaps I may see them." Kate was unprepared for the pile Mr. Cruikshank led her to. Underneath the massive desk in the cavity where knees would hide was a small pile of items, including the missing slippers, jade earring and riding glove, along with a few ribbons, a worn pocket watch, and green thread that perfectly matched the horse blankets kept in the stables.

"I've seen the cat come and go," Mr. Cruikshank explained. "I wondered if that was our culprit."

Kate chuckled as she leaned down and picked up her earring. "That explains it. I have been slowly losing halves of a pair ever since we moved in."

Peter reached for the watch. He looked at it, his stony face failing to reveal anything. "I believe this belongs to my brother. He must have dropped it during one of his visits."

A silence settled between them that was broken by Mr. Cruikshank's toe scuffing the carpet.

"Shall we?" she asked Peter. He was gazing at her intently and she was eager to be alone again. She wanted to know what he had started to say before they were interrupted.

He followed her from the room, and she paused. "Might I just meet you by the horses? I'd like to check in with my cook while we are here."

"I will go with you," he said instead. "I have a mind to formally meet this famous woman."

Smiling dryly, she recalled their first meeting when Peter had stopped her carriage like a highwayman. She turned for the servants' stairs and took them down to the kitchen, where she found Alice humming over a soup pot.

"Alice," she said, "I hope we are not interrupting."

The cook looked up to see the large man standing beside Kate and her young eyes widened. "Oh, nonsense, Miss Kingston. You know I'm always happy to have you in my kitchen."

"Does everything go on well here?" Kate asked. She hoped Alice understood that she meant the entire household and not just the kitchen.

"Well, I suppose so. But there was an odd thing last night." Alice screwed up her face in thought. "That man from the stables was snooping around my kitchen. I don't know why—I suppose he wanted a late-night snack. But when I found him, I was surprised by his quick escape. I even offered to cook him up something right quick."

"Which man was it, Alice?"

She glanced to Peter and leaned in closer to Kate. "You know I'm no good with names, miss. But this one had those beautiful eyes. You know the one I mean? A girl can get lost in them, she can."

"Yes," Kate said, extremely aware of Peter standing just behind her. "I know precisely whom you mean."

"And you found him in the kitchen?" Peter asked.

"Well, the still room. But it's just right there," Alice said, flinging her soup spoon in the direction of the still room. Kate stepped out of the way just in time to miss a string of onion. "I made some blackberry jam yesterday, so I thought that's maybe what he was looking for."

"Alice, that sounds delicious. I can hardly wait until we get back home to try it."

Alice set down the spoon and scurried into the still room, bringing back a jar of the dark, sweet substance and held it to Peter before hooking a stray curl behind her ear. "Take it. We've got quite a bit stacked up in there."

"Thank you," Peter said, sounding touched. "I have heard great things about your work."

Alice blushed. A compliment from a handsome gentleman would do that to a girl.

"Thank you, Alice. I hope you are enjoying your break this week."

She nodded and went back to her soup, most likely thinking that cooking for the army of servants really wasn't much of a break at all.

They barely made it outside when Peter rounded on Kate. "Who's the man she caught in her kitchen?"

"Oh!" Kate said, taken off guard. She tottered backward and fell onto the grass, so taken aback by Peter's enthusiasm.

He helped her up with a quick apology but did not let the question drop, his free hand resting on her shoulder.

"That would be Mr. Gibson," Kate said warily, warm from his touch. "He runs the stables."

He dropped his hold and she found herself able to breathe normally again. "And he is also the man you ran into at my stables at the start of the week, yes?"

"Yes, that would be him." Kate began walking toward the shed where they had left their horses. They'd already spent a good deal of time at Split Tree and needed to get back before the guests of the house party began noting their absences.

"Why was he there?"

Confused, Kate stopped. "I beg your pardon?"

Peter ran a hand agitatedly through his hair. "Did he tell you why he was in my stables when your carriage had already delivered you and he had not brought your horses?"

She felt silly. "No, I hadn't thought to ask."

Peter beamed—the exact opposite reaction than she had anticipated. "I think we have found the first piece to our puzzle."

"Mr. Gibson? He is kind. And helpful." She scurried to catch up to Peter, his long stride carrying him toward the horses quickly. "He was the only servant who stayed after my uncle died."

Peter came to a stop. "What was that?"

Kate was breathing heavily. "I was just commending his loyalty."

"No." Peter shook his head. "Did you say he was the only servant who remained? Kate, he did not work here when your uncle was alive."

She looked at him warily, wondering how well he'd known Uncle Bartholomew or his servants.

"Trust me," Peter said. "I spent a good deal of time with the stablemaster at the end there, Mr. Farley. Bartholomew and

Farley were dabbling in horse breeding, and I went in on the investment since a friend of mine has hopes of breeding himself."

"Lord Cohen."

"Yes," Peter said, looking a tad surprised but recovering quickly. "Why did you think your uncle had willed me the stock of his stables? I owned half of them already. And I stole his stablemaster at the end there, too. After Bartholomew died, of course."

"I had no idea," she said with an unladylike shrug.

Peter gawked at her for a moment. "You didn't think to find out? What if the old man had just given away all of the horses on your estate and they were, by rights, yours?"

"He had a good solicitor. I figured if I had any claim to them, he would have told me."

Peter laughed. "That was very trusting of you."

A smile spread over her lips, aware of the naivety of her own actions. "I have not been steered wrong yet."

"Except," Peter said with a raise of one eyebrow. "By your Mr. Gibson."

"Oh, right." Frustration rolled through her. Had she really been taken in so easily? And if he had malicious intentions toward Miss Smithson, why would he set up at Split Tree?

Peter rubbed a hand over his face. "I cannot figure out the connection between Miss Smithson and Split Tree."

She smiled to herself. They reached the horses and Peter untied them, saying, "Perhaps we can check in on her when we get back. I have a feeling she does not suffer from a typical illness."

"I had the same thought," Kate agreed. "If only I could understand who might have something against her. She seems harmless."

Peter placed his hands around her waist, pulling her thoughts away from Miss Smithson entirely.

"Can I help you into the saddle?" he asked, his voice lowering considerably as his slate eyes darkened to a deeper gray.

She nodded, quite sure that if she opened her mouth, she would accomplish nothing beyond a croak.

Peter gazed at her and she wondered for a moment if he would lean down and kiss her, but he seemed frozen in place. His hands tightened a fraction and his thumbs began drawing circles where they rested just under her ribs. She could feel her breath quicken and realized that the pleasant swirling within her was what butterflies were supposed to feel like.

Suddenly the air left her lungs as Peter threw her up into the saddle. She scrambled to get her legs into position and arrange her skirts. He was beside her seconds later, his face a tight smile but his eyes stormy. No doubt he had gotten carried away in the moment. Her own smile felt strained and she was glad when he turned to lead the way. The quicker she could get out of his presence the better; she needed to get her wits about her.

She was not entirely certain, but it seemed possible that she could very well be falling in love with Sir Peter Evans.

30

KATE

"How is Miss Smithson?" Kate questioned Emily after she had changed out of her riding habit and into a gown of dark mauve with burgundy trim. Her wardrobe was growing exceedingly more enjoyable with the new gowns.

"The same, I gather. The doctor came and left, and he believes it to be influenza."

"Oh dear, I do hope no one else catches it," Kate said. She was nearly positive no one else would catch the illness, for she was almost certain Miss Smithson was being poisoned somehow. But Emily didn't believe her anyway, so she'd rather not discuss it with her friend. "I should like to check on her," she said instead.

"Mrs. Smithson is guarding her room like a French gargoyle." Emily rolled her eyes, plopping herself onto the edge of Kate's bed and watching her fix her hair in the looking glass. "She will not admit anyone to the room who is not essential."

"Well, I suppose that is a kindness to those of us who do not wish to be ill."

"Poppycock," Emily said. "She is just controlling."

"What makes you say that?" Kate turned on the chair, half of her hair still falling down her back.

"Have you not watched her? She approves or denies Miss Smithson's every move. It is not nearly so bad with Annie, as far as I have seen. But with Miss Smithson, the mother is clearly in charge."

Kate mulled over Mrs. Smithson's control. The woman seemed to hover constantly over her daughters, it was true, sharing her opinions whether they were desired or not. It did not appear in any way related unless Mrs. Smithson was the one poisoning her daughter, but that seemed altogether ridiculous.

She finished putting up her hair and followed Emily down to the drawing room where the guests had gathered for games. Peter was already seated at a table for whist with Miss Annie, Lord Cohen and Lord Aniston; Miss Annie appeared delighted. Mr. Evans approached Kate and requested a game of draughts, which she graciously granted.

Kate needed to determine a way to extricate herself from Mr. Evans's expectations. But it could wait. It would not do to be rude to one's host.

She caught Peter's eye as she sat down to draughts, but he turned quickly back to his hand of cards, laughing at something Miss Annie had said. Of course, he laughed a little too loudly, but Kate was certain the others hadn't noticed. She felt disappointment that he did not acknowledge her further, but then again, if the way he threw her up into the saddle to put space between them was any indication, he was not interested in her. Or if he was, he felt strongly that he shouldn't be.

"How was your ride this morning?" Mr. Evans asked.

Kate was startled and wondered how much he knew of her morning. "It was enlightening," she said. "Did I tell you I am planting an orchard?"

"I heard as much." Mr. Evans gazed at her intently before moving a piece on the board.

"The trees are in," she explained, hoping the change of subject would seem natural. "I am quite excited for their development."

"Right," Mr. Evans said, giving her an odd look. "Did my brother enjoy looking at your trees as well?"

There was an insinuation in his tone that caused the hair on the back of her neck to stand up. She needed to tread carefully, for this was how rumors began. "He and Lord Cohen, as well as Emily were all happy to see the orchard." She spoke down to the board as she made her move. Raising her face, she offered him a tight smile. "I would love to show you as well, Mr. Evans."

He picked up a black piece and spun it in his fingers. She was watching to see where he'd move it and instead felt his gaze boring into her. Mr. Evans placed the piece on the board with a snap and leaned back in his chair, his demeanor softening to a breezy, carefree attitude that she was fairly sure she could see through. There was something more at stake here, though she did not know what it was.

"Have you thought back on that day often, Miss Kingston? I hope I am not bringing up a sore subject, but I cannot let another day pass without mentioning it. What you did for me when we were children was the kindest thing anyone had ever done for me at that point in my life. I have never forgotten it, and I need you to know you were a sensitive and sympathetic influence in my life. A lasting influence."

Kate swallowed, uncomfortable by the level tone of his voice and his hard eyes—as though he was doing his utmost to retain control of his emotion. She wondered if anyone else in the busy room noticed the shift in their conversation but doubted it. The rest of the party was occupied by card games and conversation.

"I have thought about it many times," she said. "Though if I am being completely honest, it was a very disagreeable day for me, and I long to forget it."

"I understand," Mr. Evans said plainly. "I commend your innate kindness, Kate."

She was startled at his use of her given name but tried not to show it. It felt like he was building up for something, and she had the sudden panic-inducing thought that he was about to propose.

Sighing, he continued. "It could not have been easy to choose to protect me then, and it certainly cannot be easy now. I have noticed that you are on reasonably friendly terms with Peter, and I applaud your capacity for forgiveness."

She hesitated, noting the shift in Mr. Evans's demeanor. A warning tightened her chest, and she swallowed. "I am afraid I do not follow."

The look of innocence was so strong on his face that Kate found herself focusing on that instead of what he was saying. "Of course, a man can change a lot in over ten years, but after the experience we shared in the woods so long ago, it is amazing to me that you were able to so easily overlook Peter's character and the way he treated you."

Kate's body went cold and she found herself unable to move. The blood drained from her face, her mouth dry. *The way he had treated her?* That could only mean one thing. *Peter* was one of the savage boys—the one who'd held her back. A flash of memory flicked through her mind of the boys running away in search of Martin and the minion's sorrowful, blue-gray gaze holding hers before he'd followed Charles.

She sought Peter out, finding his gaze trained firmly on her, his steel-blue eyes unyielding, brows drawn together in concern. Her heart rebelled against his anxious expression.

Swallowing a sandy lump, she stood, surprised her feet could hold her up. "If you would excuse me," she muttered, certain Mr. Evans had no idea what she had said before she fled from the room.

Peter

Peter muttered a curse under his breath and tossed his cards on the table. He'd watched Kate and Martin the entire time they sat together, positive that Martin was brewing something. The look in his sharp eye was one he often got before pulling some sort of prank. Charles and Peter had often picked on Martin as children, but Martin got them back every time. It was never in the same brute manner the older brothers relied on, but Martin was intelligent and clever, and he had found ways to go around them and use their father to get even. Of course, according to Father, Charles could do no wrong, so Peter had ended up enduring the bulk of the punishment.

"Excuse me," Peter said as he jumped up and walked swiftly out the door, hoping to avoid Martin's line of vision. He saw dark skirts swish at the top of the stairs, and some level of relief hit him that Kate had chosen to retreat to her room within Evanslea instead of leaving completely. He had the feeling that if she would have gone back home, well and truly left him, there would be nothing he could say to her. As it stood now, she could not have given up entirely.

It was with a small grain of hope that he took the stairs two at a time and caught up to her just before she reached her own door.

"Kate!" he called. He could tell she recognized his voice from the way her body stilled, her hand pausing just before it reached the doorknob. "Please." He was unsure what he was asking for, but he knew he needed to beg.

She did not face him, but she dropped her hand. He would

take anything he could get. "Please tell me what Martin said that bothered you so much."

"I have a feeling you already know." Her voice was flat, void of emotion. That was not a good sign.

He'd done it. Blast Martin—why did he have to tell Kate before Peter could? He regarded her closely, wishing she could see into his heart, could see the depth of his remorse.

"Then can you understand why I feared telling you myself?"

She turned her head slightly toward him, and his heart quickened at the pain in her profile.

He implored her with his gaze. "I did not realize you were *that* girl until after we had become acquainted."

She squeezed her eyes closed. Was it in frustration or to block tears? His heart ached at the possibility. "It is what you were trying to tell me this morning, was it not? In my uncle's study."

"In *your* study, yes." Somehow the distinction mattered. "I have been waiting for the right time."

She turned, and he held his breath.

"Did you not think that perhaps ten years had eased the memory of that day?" Kate asked. "That an apology from your lips would earn you forgiveness immediately?"

"Even after I admitted to being the foolish boy who chased you down, gave you that scar" —his fingertips grazed the faint line that ran through her eyebrow, causing a shiver to shake her shoulders— "and held you back while my brother threatened you?"

She nodded, and he felt more the fool. His shame mounted as his gaze raked her face, drinking in the strength of character and compassion. But he had remained quiet for too long, had held the secret too close to his heart. He opened his mouth but found himself at a loss for words, panicking as Kate's eyes grew hard.

"Do not worry, Sir Peter. I forgave that boy long ago. But this man" —she gestured to him— "ought to have come clean, ought to have realized I would not hold youthful follies against you." She went to leave but then stopped, her voice lowering. "You know, perhaps we were on to something earlier. I suppose I really am a terrible judge of character after all."

With this parting shot, and unmistakable pain lacing her eyes, Kate turned from him and quietly let herself into her room. He was positive she would release her pent-up emotions, and he wanted to be by her side, holding her and wiping away her tears. But he had ruined everything. There was a time for pursuing and a time for retreat, and Peter realized that for now, he needed to withdraw.

31

KATE

*K*ate's eyes were red and sore by the time Emily came to find her an hour later. She had cried a good deal of sorrow and felt deflated and empty by the end.

"Goodness me!" Emily screeched, shutting the door behind her and running to Kate's side. "Whatever has happened?"

Kate let out a hiccup and then sighed. "I am overreacting, naturally. I cannot help but feel embarrassed and angry."

Emily searched her face and Kate screwed her eyes closed again as a warm tear rolled down her cheek.

"I met Mr. Evans a long, long time ago when I lived here as a girl. I did not realize until today that I had also met Sir Peter." She paused and ran a finger down her faint scar. "Of course, now I feel foolish for not making the connection earlier. *Of course* he was the bully from that day. And Sir Peter even told me of his older brother's passing. Still, I did not realize."

"Perhaps you did not want to," Emily supplied gently. "Was it so very bad?"

Kate looked into her friend's compassionate eyes and nodded. "For a nine-year-old girl, it was traumatizing. I forgave him long ago, for Mrs. Presley helped me to see that by holding on to my hatred I was only hurting myself. But that does not change—"

"No, it doesn't. Sir Peter had many opportunities to tell you," Emily said reasonably.

"But he did not."

"Undoubtedly," Emily agreed. "Though, if you had acted badly as a child and met the person you had wronged a decade later, would you not want to get to know them as you are now, and not with the tainted memory of the past?"

This was not what Kate wanted to hear. She wanted Emily to be as outraged as she, to rant and rail against Peter's character and poor choices. She did not want to admit that there was a great deal of truth to Emily's words. Rubbing her eyes with the heels of her hands, Kate sat up and looked Emily in the eye. "But that does not mean I have to be happy about it."

"No one would expect you to be. How did you find out, anyhow?"

"Mr. Evans spoke about it. He acted as if he assumed that I already knew, but there was something not quite right about his demeanor. I have a feeling he enjoyed revealing the information."

Emily muttered something under her breath. Kate raised an eyebrow, and Emily cast her eyes to the ceiling. "You really aren't very bright sometimes, are you?"

Kate would be offended had it come from anyone else, but she knew Emily to be teasing. "Just spell it out for me."

"Mr. Evans was probably feeling threatened by Sir Peter. It is quite obvious that they are both taken with you."

Kate shook her head. "Mr. Evans has been trying to court me. Sir Peter is only my friend."

"Perhaps you are more than that to him, though."

Kate stood and leaned against the window, sapped of energy and motivation. The day had turned stormy, reflecting her mood.

"Are you going to forgive him?" Emily asked.

"I already have," Kate said softly. She took a long, shuddering breath. "But that does not mean I have to run out there and be in charity with him. I am a woman; it is my divine right to hold this against him as long as I want to." She tried to smile, realizing she was being irrational, but finding she did not care.

"Perhaps," Emily conceded. "But take it from someone who learned the hard way through the last few years of marriage, you also have it in your power to relieve *his* suffering. And which course of action do you think will make you feel better?"

Duly chastised, Kate sighed. "Either way, it can wait until after tea. I am sure we are late as it is."

"Indeed, that was the reason I was sent to fetch you."

They arrived last to the drawing room, and Kate was disappointed to find Peter and his friends all absent. She supposed she had brought that upon herself. Of course he wouldn't wish to share her table after she had said such a hurtful thing. She was suddenly overcome with a wave of regret. She caught Mr. Evans's eye and he gave her a commiserating smile. She wanted to grin and show him that his words had not affected her. But that would not be true.

Instead, she turned to Miss Annie, who sat on the other side of Mr. Kettlewell. "Do forgive my rudeness for speaking over you, Mr. Kettlewell, but I was hoping to hear good news about Miss Smithson."

Miss Annie wiped her mouth with a napkin and shook her head. "I am afraid she is very much the same."

Kate nodded and went back to her tea. She didn't think she was unpleasant to be around, exactly, but she *was* introspective, and the other guests seemed to sense it and left her largely to her own musings. The rest of the day passed slowly, and it was not until that evening following dinner that Mrs. Gressle asked Mr. Evans about the lords' absence.

"I am afraid they had some business to take care of. Or that was the excuse I received." He shrugged. "I am not sure when to expect them back."

Mrs. Gressle took this as a personal affront and bid the group goodnight, dragging poor Miss Juniper upstairs with her. It wasn't until she overheard the Kettlewells discussing the probable cancellation of the ball due to Miss Smithson's illness that Miss Annie stood to leave as well. Kate bid the group a quick goodnight and followed her into the corridor, hailing her on the stairs.

"I was hoping to inquire about Miss Smithson," she explained. "Earlier was the wrong time to ask for you could hardly go into any detail surrounded by all the guests."

"I am afraid there isn't much to say. Dr. Styles came again today. He thinks it must be influenza for how long it has lasted. The symptoms do not indicate anything else."

"Who is caring for her?"

"Our maid. And my mother sits in with her almost always." Miss Annie sighed, and Kate thought of Emily's comments about their controlling mother.

"Any strange visitors?" Kate asked as they reached the top of the stairs. This question earned her an odd look, and she said, "I'm just curious who else has been exposed."

"Well, there's the kitchen maid and sometimes the footman who brings her meals. But everyone else is kept out of the room. Even me."

"That is wise," Kate said. "You do not want to catch her illness."

Miss Annie shrugged and walked the opposite way to her bedroom. Kate waited until she had disappeared inside to go back downstairs. She did not stop there, however, but kept going down to the kitchens. A soft glow lit the fireplace and a round woman sat at the long table, sipping a cup of tea. She moved to stand when she noticed Kate, but then stopped at Kate's upraised hands.

"I only came down here to ask after the cook."

"'Tis I," the woman said warily.

"I was wondering if you could tell me what is being done for Miss Smithson?"

"Not much to do." The woman shrugged. "She isn't keeping much down. I send up toast and tea, various broths and jellies. But for now we just wait and pray."

"And do you prepare everything for her?"

The woman cackled. "Mercy, no! I've got enough to do without fixing tea for one sick guest. That's why I've got a kitchen staff, you see."

"Right, of course," Kate said. "I was only wondering if perhaps Miss Smithson suffers an aversion to something that is keeping her sick. The doctor seems to think that her illness is rather dragged out."

The cook pursed her lips in thought. "We haven't made her any tea that's different from what every Englishman drinks every day of his life. As for beef broth, I don't know what she can have an aversion to in that."

"Thank you for your time. I must pay my compliments. The meals I've enjoyed here have been wonderful."

The cook smiled proudly and continued sipping her tea as Kate slipped away. She was frustrated to the point of boiling over and she was ready to receive some answers. She was dangerously close to barging into Miss Smithson's room and demanding information from her mother. Did the woman even understand the danger her daughter was in? Did anyone?

Kate swallowed down her frustration at Mrs. Smithson and Miss Smithson for not being forthcoming with *any* information; at Peter and his friends for abandoning them; at Mr. Evans for his pointed attentions that were no longer reciprocated; and at the rest of the party members for being so clueless when all of this was going on right under their noses.

She found herself knocking on Miss Annie's door and stepped inside when the girl answered it herself.

"I need to ask you some things, and I need you to answer me without argument."

Miss Annie's face was bewildered. She hadn't pulled a wrapper on and stood there in her thin night rail.

"But please put on a dressing gown or a blanket or something first," Kate amended.

"What is going on?" Miss Annie asked, sliding her arms into a silk dressing gown and tying the sash.

"A great deal. Or nothing, perhaps. I don't know. Is there anyone that has been upset with your sister recently? Or someone who may have reason to be upset with her?"

"Well, yes," Miss Annie said as if this was common knowledge. "She can be rather...trying sometimes. Most of the women that live around here aren't very fond of her. The unmarried ones, at least."

Kate understood this sentiment. She recalled the day Miss Smithson had snubbed her in the Larkins' shop and then approached Sir Peter with the brightest of smiles. "Anyone in particular? Is there anyone that would have reason to try and hurt her?"

The younger girl reared back as if she'd been slapped. "What are you saying? You don't believe that she was pushed too, do you?"

"I do not know," Kate answered honestly. "But I would rather be safe and believe her than be sorry I did nothing."

Slumping down on the edge of her bed, Miss Annie rubbed her eyes. "I do not know. I just do not know."

Kate sat on the feather mattress, sliding an arm around the weary girl. "Would you tell me if anything comes to you? I am not entirely sure there is anything to figure out, but if there is someone trying to hurt your sister then we must be very cautious."

"Of course."

She went to leave when Miss Annie's arm shot out and stopped her. "There is one thing. I'm not sure there's any merit to it. In fact, I feel rather silly even bringing it up."

"What is it?" Kate asked. She could feel a humming through her body, anticipation that she was about to discover a key piece to the puzzle.

The guilt in Miss Annie's face had Kate holding her breath. "If I tell you this then you must promise not to be upset with either of them—and not tell a soul. You *must not* tell a soul."

"I won't be upset," Kate said quietly.

"My sister is betrothed, though it is a secret. She only told me because I discovered them in an intimate embrace in our gardens." Annie looked as though she had deflated, as though it was a relief to unburden herself by sharing this secret.

Kate felt the breath leave her body. She whispered, "Who is the man?"

"Martin Evans."

32

KATE

*K*ate's body went cold. She assured Miss Annie once again that she was not upset with either Miss Smithson or Mr. Evans and left the room before she gave away her distress. If only Peter was around and she could tell him this development. Surely it had to mean something. Leaning against the closed door in the dim corridor, she nearly jumped out of her skin when a deep voice came to her from the shadows.

"Is everything all right?" Mr. Evans asked, stepping from the darkness toward her.

She swallowed and offered him a strained smile. "Yes, of course. I was only wishing Annie a good night. I hope she does not catch her sister's illness."

"That would be a shame," he said, stepping closer.

"I find myself very weary now. I must bid you goodnight."

His arm shot out and grabbed her by the elbow. "I'll escort you."

Kate had no other option but to accept and let Mr. Evans lead her down the corridor to her own room. When he halted and didn't let go, she sent a pleading prayer that Emily would come to her and avoided Mr. Evans's gaze.

"I feel a connection to you, Kate." His voice was low, and she feared he was going to ask for her hand now. But how could he? He was already betrothed to another.

He continued, "I did not believe my luck when you happened upon me that day in the woods, when my brothers were searching for me." He seemed contemplative for a moment but didn't let her go. "I was afraid they would force me to be a moving target for their arrows. Of course, it was fate that brought you back into my life now, before—" He paused. "Well, you must see that."

His lips were upon hers before she realized what was happening. Something within her revolted even as her mind was taken back to Miss Annie's words about finding him in an intimate embrace with Miss Smithson. He backed away a moment later and smiled down at her affectionately. She wanted to gag, but she swallowed the sour taste in her mouth and slipped into her room the moment he released her, bolting the lock behind her.

Rinsing out her mouth with clean water from the pitcher on her washstand, Kate took a rag and washed her face, neck, and hands, clearing away the vile remnants that clung to her from Mr. Evans's touch. She wrestled off her gown and scrubbed the areas on her arm where he'd possessively taken hold of her.

She felt violated. Her skin crawled, a bitter taste filling her mouth.

She was completely certain now that Mr. Evans had something to do with Miss Smithson's unfortunate circumstances. What he had to do with it exactly was still a mystery. But it could not be a coincidence that he was secretly engaged to her while outwardly courting Kate. Besides, that kiss was as dominating as it was possessive. He had been staking his claim.

Kate crawled into bed and pulled the blankets up to her chin, but she was positive that sleep was a long way off. Instead, she wondered exactly what Peter was doing at that very moment.

***

Peter

"Another round?" Cohen asked, his grin wide, proving how amused he was at his own joke. He was a far cry from Lord Aniston's slumped shoulders and heavy snore.

"We aren't drinking anymore," Peter reminded him. "This is reconnaissance." He picked up his full mug again, then set it back on the table. He wasn't interested in drinking. He needed information.

They had ridden over to Split Tree and talked with Mr. Cruikshank before Cohen had distracted Mr. Gibson while the other three thoroughly searched his office. They had found a few papers with cryptic messages, and Peter had taken them to compare handwriting. He found nothing within the office that matched it, but they all stated the same meeting place: The Blue Boar.

Peter raised his head to take in the blue painted boar on the wall as Mr. Sims asked the group if they wanted anything else. He ordered dinner for the table to give them a reason to stay and Marsh shook Aniston awake once the food arrived.

"This was much more exciting on the Peninsula," he said in a sleepy voice.

"Then, it was a matter of life or death," Cohen supplied around a bite of roast beef.

"And it isn't now?" Marsh said in his deep voice. The group was silent as each of them seemed to think over the implications.

"Do you think they'll meet here tonight?" Aniston asked Peter, who shrugged in response.

"I doubt it, but I don't know what else to do."

The men nodded in understanding and went back to their food. Another two hours of eavesdropping on conversations and wasting their time in the inn's taproom and Peter called their mission to a halt. "We may as well get some sleep and reevaluate in the morning," he explained, receiving no complaints from his men. They returned to a very dark Evanslea and a weary groom rubbed his eyes as he took their horses.

They were halfway across the lawn when Marsh came to a halt, throwing up his fingers in a sign they had developed to indicate silence. The men didn't ask questions, they simply obeyed. Marsh was not the captain, but he had seen something and the rest of them trusted him implicitly. He motioned to the kitchen door, and Peter nodded, signaling for Aniston to go with him while Marsh and Cohen went around the back.

Peter moved toward the kitchen door, a faint flickering inside revealing the single candle someone was holding. He crept up to the window as a dark form rushed past him in the opposite direction. Motioning for Aniston to chase the escapee, Peter dashed into the kitchen, eager to find who the shadowed man had met up with. He came upon a dark, empty room and moved about as quickly as he could. When he located a candle on a shelf by the stairs, he lit it with embers from the fireplace and glanced around to find the kitchen bare. He checked the pantry, larder, and still room, but all of them were empty. It was when he was leaving the last of these rooms that he heard the door at the top of the stairs close abruptly.

Panting sounded behind him, and he found Aniston in the doorway, shaking his head with his hands on his knees, his breath coming ragged.

Leaving Aniston in complete darkness, Peter took the candle up the stairs two at a time and went after whomever was escaping. He banged the door open—and hit someone with it if the sounding "oof" was any indication.

"What the devil?" exclaimed Martin in a dressing gown.

"Which way did he go?" Peter asked.

"What are you talking about?" Martin said, bewildered. He searched the floor for his candle and found it, holding it up to Peter's to light it. "I was just coming down to the kitchen for tea."

Peter stepped around his brother and ran down the corridor, cupping a hand around the candle flame to keep it from going out. He checked all of the downstairs rooms and headed back toward the kitchen to question the other men.

Martin remained by the top of the stairs, gaping at Peter. "Are you mad? You'll wake the whole house."

"No," Peter said, walking past his brother and swiftly down the stairs. Cohen and Marsh had arrived, and Aniston had located another candle. Peter set his down on the worktable before leaning both of his hands on the surface. "Anything?" he asked his men. Well, his friends now.

"Nothing," Marsh said, and Cohen just shook his head.

"I chased him to the woods, but he had a horse ready to go and took off quicker than I could catch him," Aniston said. "I wish I had the foresight to go for a horse myself."

"Which direction did he go?"

"Toward town." Aniston nodded his head in the direction of Larkfield.

Peter let out a frustrated breath. "That doesn't narrow it down much."

The men quieted when Martin stepped into the kitchen. He lifted a teapot from the counter, poured a measure of water into it from the pitcher and lit the stove, all the while being watched by four pairs of intent eyes.

"Couldn't sleep?" Marsh asked gruffly, causing Martin to startle.

"Correct. This usually helps." Martin pulled down the tea box from a cupboard just to the left of the sink and prepared his cup.

It was easy to believe that Martin regularly came down for tea given his ease in the kitchen and how well he knew where everything was. Peter watched his brother move the kettle and put out the fire in the stove, before Martin took his cup of tea to the stairs. Martin turned and saluted the men around the table before walking up slowly and shutting the door behind him.

"Do you think?" Aniston asked Marsh. They communicated silently and Marsh nodded once.

"Someone needs to tell him," Cohen said, his head flicking toward Peter.

"Go ahead." Aniston threw his hands in the air in surrender.

Marsh rolled his eyes, then faced Peter head on. "It's your brother."

"What is?"

"The man we've been looking for. It's obvious."

Peter glanced at each of his friends. They all had the same sober look. "But I just ran into him at the top of the stairs. You all saw that he was coming down for tea. Do you think most men know how to boil a pot of tea in the middle of the night?"

"Only those who need to use it as a cover."

"Oh, be reasonable," Peter said. He looked into the eyes of the three men he trusted most in the world and they each looked back at him with intent. They were serious. "But what would he have against Miss Smithson? For mercy's sake, he's the one who has been visiting her over the past year."

Marsh raised an eyebrow and leaned back in his chair. Cohen moved to where Martin had left the kettle and began brewing himself a cup. Aniston lifted a finger and Cohen pulled down a second cup.

"I think the motive is irrelevant at this point." Marsh said. "We have found our man and we need to move fast. If it is in fact Martin, then Miss Smithson is in more danger than she knows."

Peter wanted to continue arguing but saw that it was fruitless. They made valid points, but he'd known Martin his entire life. Martin might have a penchant for revenge against his *brothers*, but he would not hurt a woman.

"I think we've found what we've been looking for," Cohen said after storing the tea away in the cupboard. He reached on his toes and pulled a dried plant out of the same shelf, turning to place it on the center of the table. "This, my friends, is foxglove."

33

KATE

A soft knock sounded at the door and pulled Kate out of her distressing dream. She had been on edge ever since the events of the evening before and had shifted those anxieties and fears into her sleep. The knock sounded again, and she panicked momentarily. It was completely dark in her room, not even the barest hint of light coming through the drapes. It had to be sometime in the middle of the night.

She feared it could be Mr. Evans and jumped out of bed, moving to the door to confirm it was locked before responding. "Yes?"

"I'm sorry. It's me," came the reply.

"Peter?" she asked to be certain. She knew his voice, but it was quiet and muffled through the door.

"Yes."

She unlocked the door and opened it enough to peek outside. "What has happened?"

He was standing close, his face lit by a small candle. His hair was in disarray and his clothes looked like he had slept in them. Given the time of night, perhaps he had. He dragged a hand down his face. "Quite a bit has happened. No one is in immediate danger, but I felt it was important to fill you in. The cover of night may be an advantage, too."

"Or a danger to our reputations. What if you are seen?"

"There is no one awake except for my friends. And I trust them implicitly."

"But may I?" she asked softly.

He looked into her eyes intently. "Yes."

"Give me a moment." Kate closed the door and immediately was swallowed by darkness. She opened it again and reached for his candle. "May I borrow this?"

A smile tilted one half of his lips, and he handed over the candle, their fingers brushing in the process. She mumbled her thanks and used the light to quickly pull on her dressing gown and slippers. Her hair was braided, the end tied with a ribbon, and she pulled it over her shoulder. It would have to do. She was not going to put it up.

Kate cracked the door open and Peter came in, closing the door behind himself. She led him to the only chair in the room, but he pulled over the vanity seat and sat a good distance from her, for which she was grateful.

"I need to apologize first," Kate said. To her dismay, Peter said nothing. He looked to be struggling within himself, so she forged ahead. "I do not doubt your character, Peter. And I only said I did because I was angry, and I wanted to hurt you."

"It does not change what I did."

"No, it doesn't," she agreed. Standing, she moved to his side and held his hand in her own. "But you are not that same boy. We all make mistakes and I forgave you long ago when someone helped me to see that holding onto that anger only hurt *me*. If you are still grieving over your actions, then it is time you forgive yourself."

Peter stared into her eyes, his own expression indecipherable. She lifted his hand and placed a chaste kiss on the back of it before releasing him and moving back to her chair. "Now what have you come to tell me?"

Peter's gaze flicked away, pain on his face. She wondered if it was because of what she had just said or what he was about to tell her.

"Martin is behind everything."

Peter

Peter searched her face, but he did not detect any surprise. "You already know?"

"I may have figured it out this evening." She shrugged. "I spoke with Annie and she told me that your brother and Miss Smithson are secretly engaged. When I saw him after that, he made it abundantly clear that I am the object of his affections."

"How so?" Peter asked, stiffening. Never mind that he had just learned Martin's motive. He would consider a secret engagement later, for this was far more pressing. If his brother had taken advantage of Kate, he'd go find the man right now and put him out of commission. That could solve both of their problems.

"He made it clear," Kate said in a voice that brooked no argument. "How did you know?"

"We arrived home to someone sneaking into the kitchen," Peter said. He explained how he had sat in the taproom of the Blue Boar after finding the notes in Mr. Gibson's office, and then bumped into Martin by the kitchen entrance. "Whether he was hiding the poisonous plants there until he could safely transport them or leaving them hidden for whatever maid or footman he has adding the foxglove to her tea, we do not know. But it is clear she is being poisoned; there are too many signs for it to be a coincidence. Our only dilemma is considering what to do with this information. I hoped you could give me some insight."

Kate nodded, her look contemplative. "We must get Miss Smithson out of here posthaste. It would be too much work to ensure that she is not being given any more of the foxglove, and in her own home she could recover quickly."

Peter nodded. He had had the same thought. "But will we be tipping our hand?"

"Not if we make it Mrs. Smithson's idea."

Peter grinned, glad he had bothered Kate with this. *Of course* he had to make it Mrs. Smithson's idea. He felt a little dumb for not having thought of it himself. The woman made all of the decisions for her family and it would be quick work to use Aniston to make her feel like the best place for Miss Smithson to heal would be her own home. The man was so charming he could convince the woman in a trice.

"But what do we do about everything else? Are you positive that Martin is behind her fall? He was with me that entire day."

Peter felt the familiar jealousy and tried to push through it. "If not him, it could have been someone under his direction. Mr. Gibson, perhaps? I am hopeful we can get Martin to confess. Trust me—he likes to be acknowledged for his devious plans."

She gave him the startled look that he expected to see earlier, and he rose from his chair. "I must let you get some sleep. Please do not feel like you must rise early tomorrow."

She nodded at him, and he bowed quickly before retreating. The image of Kate with her plait falling over her shoulder and the dressing gown wrapped tightly around her waist would be one that he never forgot. It had taken all of his self-control to remain in his seat as they spoke. When she kissed his hand, he had wanted to pull her onto his lap and show her precisely how he felt about her. But it would be wrong to act so ungentlemanly, particularly after she had praised his character.

His room was quiet, and he placed the candle on his bedside table before removing his coat and loosening his cravat. He had his waistcoat unbuttoned when a creaking floorboard pulled him from his thoughts of Kate crawling back into her bed, and he turned around. The last thing he saw was a large brass object coming straight for him.

And then he blacked out.

PETER

*P*eter felt the banging in his head even before he opened his eyes. Light streamed over his face and he screwed his eyes closed, for trying to peek just pierced his skull even more. A bustling sound came from the side of the room. "Who is there?"

A reply came from his valet and he eased back on the pillows, turning his face away from the sunlight. Covering his eyes, he began to open them when he realized he was in his bed and he sat straight up.

The resulting pang in his head was horrific; he would have cried out if he had not been using all of his strength to stay upright. But how did he get in bed in the first place? He squeezed his eyes shut. Thinking was far too painful.

"Can I fetch you anything, sir? Tea, perhaps?"

Peter decidedly did not want tea. "What time is it?"

"Just after eleven," came the reply.

Stunned for a moment, Peter found his voice again. "Send for Lords Cohen, Marshall and Aniston, at once."

He lifted his fingers and gently touched the lump on his temple, recoiling from the pain the pressure caused. There was no sticky substance, which was good. But what a ghastly headache.

It was only ten minutes or so later that his friends arrived.

Aniston's eyebrows lifted and he sucked in a sharp intake of breath. "That's quite a lump, old man."

"We thought you were just tired from last night," Cohen said, guilt stealing his features. "I should have thought to check on you."

"No, I only spoke with Kate for a few minutes, briefing her on the developments. And…" Fear snaked through his body and he bolted from his bed. Running past the bewildered men, he raced down the corridor, his head pulsing with each footstep and stopped short of throwing Kate's door open. He knocked, resting his hand on the wall to still the dizzying sensation. The sound of the knob turning sent relief coursing through him.

Until the door opened to reveal Mrs. Nielsen.

Peter cleared his throat, uncomfortably aware of his current dishevelment. Whoever had knocked him on the head and thrown him in bed had not bothered to remove any of his clothing. A blessing and a curse in this moment.

"Might I ask what I can do for you?" she asked.

Peter cleared his throat awkwardly. "Is Miss Kingston in?"

"No," came the reply, a hint of panic reflected in her eyes. "Actually, I have not seen her all day. But Apple is missing from the stables, so I just thought to check her wardrobe for her riding habit."

"Is it there?" he asked, pushing the door open and walking past her.

"No," Mrs. Nielsen said. "I was about to go out and look myself. She is still so new at riding and could easily be unseated." She looked from him to his three friends that had followed him down the corridor at a more sedate pace.

He didn't feel like disagreeing with a lady, particularly in front of all of these men, but he had more faith in Kate's riding

A FORGIVING HEART

than Mrs. Nielsen did. A fact that was not exactly a comfort in this moment.

"Is Martin here?" Peter asked, holding himself taut. He was so afraid of the answer.

"No," Mrs. Nielsen replied. "He left this morning for London. Apparently, there was an event he could not miss."

"I'd say," Marsh muttered under his breath. Mrs. Nielsen shot him a confused glance, but Peter hardly noted it as he looked to his friends. They each nodded and within a moment, the four of them were racing for their own rooms.

"Wait!" Mrs. Nielsen called. "Where are you going?"

"We are going to find Kate," Peter called back over his shoulder.

They rode hard, each of them having only taken a few minutes to pack a bag. Peter had changed his clothes and sent his valet down to the kitchens for food supplies. He would have raced straight for Domino and been off after speaking with Mrs. Nielsen, but years at war had taught him the correct way to launch a campaign. And proper preparation went a long way.

Cohen possessed the fastest horse and rode over to Split Tree before meeting up with them on the road to London. He'd spoken with Mr. Cruikshank briefly about the recent developments, warning him and asking him to find a way to covertly send the Smithsons back home and away from Evanslea. Peter wondered how he would accomplish it but knew him to be a clever man. He could handle it.

The countryside raced by in his peripherals, but all he could think was that he needed to get to Kate. It was undeniable that Martin had decided it was time to cut his losses and steal her away. Whether he was planning on an elopement to Gretna Green or a special license in London was anyone's guess. Peter

275

originally wondered if Martin had announced his leaving for London to throw them off, but his gut told him that Town was where he needed to go. His intuition had never let him down.

They slowed their animals to give them a reprieve on an uphill, and Marsh called from his own horse, "What's the plan, Captain?"

Peter looked to his friend, hoping the helpless feeling within was not showing on his face. "I think I know where he would take her."

Marsh nodded. It was good enough for him.

But not good enough for Aniston, apparently. "Where is that?"

"We have an aunt who has a small townhouse in Cheapside. She is traveling overseas, so her house has been locked up these last few years. It must be completely empty."

Aniston nodded and Peter dug his knees into Domino's side as he crested the hill. He could just now see the haze of London's coal fire smoke on the horizon, the mass of buildings just touching the skyline, and anxiety rippled through him. He just hoped he wasn't too late.

3 5

KATE

𝒦ate's wrists ached from the twine holding them together. Her back was bent at an odd angle on the sofa, and she longed to stand up and walk around. Or away. The house Mr. Evans had taken her to was dark and drafty, and she imagined it had remained unused for some time. That was not a good sign.

The sun had made its full descent, and aside from a flimsy candelabra on the table in the corner, the room was cast in shadows. Mr. Evans had left some time ago, and it was with great relief that she had heard the door close behind him. Of course, it was also impossible for her to escape. She could not untie the twine around her wrists without getting up, and her feet had long since fallen asleep, as tight as they were tied together.

Glancing around as well as she could with her neck leaning against the arm of the sofa, Kate decided that she had been placed in an outdated and seldom-used parlor. It was on the smaller side with a minimum of windows, and she wondered if it was part of a small house, or just one in a set of rooms. She hoped for the latter, for if Mr. Evans had rented rooms, that meant there were other lodgers nearby and she could find help.

The idea grew within her, and she was about to yell for help when the door creaked open, and heavy boots tread inside. Her heart leapt momentarily until she caught sight of Mr. Evans's pale hair.

"We're all set for the morning, my love," he said as he came to sit on the edge of her sofa. She watched him with apprehension as he lifted the papers in his hand. "Special license," he explained.

Kate swallowed, the fear rising within her. "I will not marry you," she said with conviction.

A frown marred his forehead. He looked at her for quite some time, his gaze sweeping her every feature before he said quietly and clearly, "You need not consent. Now get some sleep." With this, he swept from the room, taking the candelabra with him and leaving her in darkness. She squeezed her eyes closed to stem the warm tears that were gathering and leaned her head back on the sofa, sending up a prayer. If ever there was a time for a miracle in her life, it was now.

Mr. Evans's boots could be heard moving about the room adjoining hers. Faint sounds drifted through the window of horses trotting or people walking by. She knew from the view through the carriage windows that he had taken her to London, but as he had wrapped her in a blanket to carry her in the house —a gag in her mouth that prevented her screaming—that was the extent of her knowledge. She listened to Mr. Evans move about the other room and continued searching her mind for any possible way of escape. If they were all set to be married in the morning, that meant she had hours left to devise a plan. A lot could happen in the course of one night.

Peter

Peter slammed his fist into the wall, causing Mr. Fleming, his London butler, to jump. Aniston, Marsh and Cohen had not, for they were all used to his temper on some level or another. Not that they were relaxed in any way themselves, for all of the men were vastly disappointed at finding both the townhouse belonging to Peter's aunt and the Evans's townhouse void of Martin or Kate.

"Can I get you something to eat or drink?" Mr. Fleming asked, wearing the mask of a placid butler, though his eyes told a different story of concern.

"No," Peter snapped. He faintly recognized the sting of his knuckles as he paced the corridor and shook out his hand. He'd rather smash in Martin's face, but that wouldn't be possible until he located the man.

"What about Doctors' Commons?" Aniston said, perking up. "He'd have to go there if he wanted to obtain a special license."

"This late? They wouldn't be there," Cohen said.

"No," Marsh agreed. "But we might still be able to retrieve some information."

Peter looked at Marsh and was briefly taken back to Spain, when the giant man had obtained his scar. Peter never wanted to be on Marsh's bad side when he was in need of information. But it was a blessing to have him there helping Peter.

The men took off at once, and Peter was glad he had paid a street urchin to hold his horse for him. He arrived at his destination not ten minutes later and tossed Domino's reins to another boy, briefly wondering if the children ever went home. Or if they even had a home to go to.

"I'll take the back," Cohen said, nodding to Marsh. The two took off around the side and Aniston walked the street with Peter. He wasn't sure precisely what he was looking for, as the streets were mostly empty, save for a few beggars. Aniston began questioning a few of the people in the street to no avail, and Peter went as far as asking the woman seated in a doorway across the street if she had seen a man fitting Martin's description that day. When the woman replied with the best recipe to season a joint of beef, Peter walked away.

"Nothing," he said when he came back to Aniston.

"Same," Aniston said, his eyes full of compassion.

Marsh and Cohen returned, their gazes sorrowful. Peter couldn't stand the pity he saw there. He just needed to find her.

When they returned to their horses, Marsh halted. "You there," he said to the trembling boy holding his horse's reins in his most authoritative voice. "Have you seen any blond gents coming in for a license?"

The boy's mouth went slack.

"You'll be rewarded for what you tell," Marsh said, lessening his intensity a fraction. The boy started to slowly shake his head when a small voice peeped up from behind them.

"I saw him."

Peter turned around and took in a young girl, her dress in rags, and a coat that must have belonged to a man at some point hanging over her slender frame. "My brother don't see nothing out here by the street, but I saw a gent couple hours back that don't come here regular. He had papers when he left."

"What did he look like?" Peter asked, anticipation making him antsy.

"Light hair. Angry eyes. He was a gentl'man, he was."

Peter would have chuckled at the description if he wasn't feeling so desperate. "Do you know where he went?"

The girl shrugged. "Jumped in a big fancy carriage and took off that way," she said, pointing down the street. That direction could lead many places, but Martin had taken Kate somewhere he did not think he'd be found. And there was no better place to become lost in London than the infamous rookery.

"The East End?" Marsh asked with a raised eyebrow.

"You read my mind," Peter said as he tossed the girl a few coins and jumped into the saddle. Her grin was worth every penny, so he tossed her a couple more.

They rode down the street, the buildings and tenements becoming more foul smelling and dilapidated the further they went. They searched street by street, methodically looking for the Evans crest and the sleek blue carriage. He would spend all night looking if he had to, and as the hours passed, he was nearly positive that that was exactly what he was going to do.

Aniston and Cohen dismounted and searched in pubs and inns as Marsh and Peter scanned the stables and carriage houses. The expanse they had remaining to search was seeming more and more impossible, and Peter was wondering when his trusty intuition was going to kick in. He realized he hadn't prayed in a while and found himself fervently begging God to lead him to Kate.

"We've got it!" Aniston shouted, running from the Black Knight's taproom and flagging Peter down. "A man in there saw Martin's carriage three streets south turning toward an inn he called the One-Eyed Sailor."

"Let's move," Peter commanded, turning Domino around and pressing him forward at full speed. He recognized a voice behind him reminding him to be cautious, and he reined in slightly, but not enough to stop him from running square into a hackney that pulled into the street right at that very moment. Peter flew from Domino's back, his head smacking on the ground as his bad arm smashed against the cobblestone street. He moved to stand and fell again at the pain that shot up his arm.

"Captain!" Aniston called, jumping from his horse and kneeling at Peter's side. He helped him to stand and led him back to his horse. "Let's walk. We are nearly there."

Peter shook his head, the action causing him excessive pain. He grabbed Domino's saddle with his good hand and tried to pull himself up with one arm the way he had seen Cohen do many times. It took a few tries, but he was finally seated and moving again toward the inn, this time at a much more cautious pace.

Flanked by his men, he approached the rundown One-Eyed Sailor and slid from Domino's back.

"What's our plan, Captain?" Cohen asked, coming to stand beside him.

"We rescue her," Peter said simply, gazing up at the multiple stories of the inn and the possible rooms she could be kept in. He waited until Marsh and Aniston flanked him before taking a deep breath.

"All right men, let's move."

Kate

Dawn was peeking through the window of the parlor when Kate came fully awake. A fitful night's sleep in between cries for help and unsuccessful escape plans had left her exhausted. It was on the second yell for help that Mr. Evans had come in the room and slapped her hard across the face. She could still taste blood on the cut near her mouth.

His menacing eyes took her back to the moment in the woods that she had seen his oldest brother Charles for the first time, and it terrified her. She should have noticed the resemblance earlier. As for Peter, she was ashamed for ever thinking him as evil as either of his brothers. It was obvious now that he regretted the way he used to follow his older brother's ways, and even clearer that Martin had never forgiven either of them for it. The innocent boy she had saved that day long ago was gone, replaced by a soul so full of anger and resentment that he was heavy and dark, unable to move on.

The fresh light of morning brought a clearer picture of the room she was in. The sofa was battered and old, the carpet threadbare. Through the thin drapes, she could see a sign for the inn across the street: The One-Eyed Sailor.

Kate searched the room until her gaze stopped at the cold fireplace. There beside the mantel sat a poker, and she kicked herself for not thinking of checking for one the night before. In her defense, of course, there had been no way to know if the room even held a fireplace, for the thin tallow candles had hardly lit the corner of the room they'd sat in.

Swinging her legs over the side of the sofa, she gave herself a minute for her head to stop spinning and then fell, as gently as she could, onto the floor. The soft thud was louder than she had anticipated, and she closed her eyes and counted to twenty, waiting to hear movement in the next room. When all remained quiet, she scooted herself to lie in the proper direction. She felt a bit ridiculous, but the only way to get from where she was to the mantel would be to roll, so roll she did.

Boots sounded on the stairs, and she heard another door swing open so loudly it hit a wall. She began rolling quicker when footsteps sounded in the room beside hers; the noise had awoken Mr. Evans. Anxiety raced through her blood and she nearly made it to the mantel when another door banged open and hit its wall. Someone was getting closer.

She panicked, getting off course before righting herself and rolling again when her own door flung open and Mr. Evans ran into the room. In his shirtsleeves and trousers, he looked disheveled, unprepared. His gaze searched the room before locating her and he closed the door behind himself, sliding the lock into place.

Dread gripped her, and Kate shrunk back. Mr. Evans's steel

eyes were hard and unyielding. He looked crazed, calculating, and she feared for her safety.

"I don't know how he did it," he said, shaking his head. "Somehow, the idiot found us."

Found us? Hope broke through her fear. If Peter was here, she wanted him to know exactly where she was. Kate drew in a breath to scream. Mr. Evans seemed to sense what her intentions were and lunged for her when a pounding on the door startled him and he jumped back.

"Peter!" she screamed.

The door pounded again, and Mr. Evans looked from it to Kate, his mind working through the dilemma if the scheming expression he wore was any clue.

The door banged again, as though someone was doing their best to force it open, and Mr. Evans flinched. He crouched, sliding his hands under her and lifting her, despite her wiggling to get away.

"A weapon," he said under his breath, glancing about the room. Dropping Kate on the sofa, he patted down his shirt, and Kate was glad he seemed not to notice the poker near the hearth.

The door slammed open and Marsh stepped inside, Peter on his heels. Peter swept the room, his gaze flicking to Kate before landing on Mr. Evans, and hardening. She'd never seen such anger pulsing through him before, and the raw energy he exuded was alarming and comforting, all in the same breath.

He crossed the floor in three large steps, reared back his fist, and delivered a swift uppercut to his brother's jaw. Mr. Evans flew to the floor, lying in a heap.

"Marsh!" Peter bellowed, his chest heaving, causing Kate to wince at the volume. He flicked his head toward his prone brother and Lord Marshall moved into action.

Kate lay her head back as relief poured through her veins, her body relaxing into the sofa cushions. She was saved.

Peter dropped to his knees beside Kate, pulling a knife from his pocket and slicing through the twine that bound her hands and feet. She gasped at the pain from the blood rushing back into her feet, and tears came to her eyes unbidden.

"Oh, dear Kate," Peter breathed, gathering her into his arms. She didn't miss the wince as he lifted her or the large lump on his temple. He tucked her into his shoulder and rocked her gently.

Lord Marshall lifted Mr. Evans onto his shoulder and Kate lifted her head in that direction, noting the line of blood trickling from Mr. Evans's swollen lip. Peter softly urged her head to his shoulder, soothing her.

"Do not worry," he said gently. "He cannot hurt you anymore."

36

KATE

*E*mily was a mess by the time Kate returned to Split Tree Manor. The house party had been disbanded by the cunning Mr. Cruikshank, who had mentioned to the stable boys of Evanslea that he had heard that scarlet fever was making its way around the big house and wanted to know if there was any validity to the rumor. Before long the stable hands had spread the rumor to the housemaids, and from there it moved about the house like wildfire, the tale growing with each new person. By the time the guests were hearing it from their personal servants, they were told that Miss Smithson was on death's doorstep with scarlet fever and they best be leaving soon if they wanted to be safe from catching the illness as well.

The Smithsons departed shortly after the rest of the guests, though Miss Smithson was feeling miraculously healed by the time they had left Evanslea not two days after Peter had gone after Kate. Emily had returned to Split Tree, growing increasingly nervous with each day her friend had remained missing. It was all Kate could do to console her well enough to learn of all that had transpired in her absence as well as fill Emily in on her own adventures.

Peter had immediately taken Kate to his London townhouse the morning that he had found her and insisted she be seen by a doctor. He had needed one as well and they had spent the day and night resting before leaving the following morning to go back to Larkfield. Peter had hired two coaches to transport them back. The first had transported Kate, the maid they had borrowed from his townhouse for propriety's sake, Lord Aniston, and himself. The second coach had conveyed Mr. Evans, with Lord Marshall and Lord Cohen acting as guards.

Kate had been anxious sleeping in Peter's house in London knowing that Mr. Evans was under the same roof, however irrational that was. She had seen Peter burn the special license herself and had known that Mr. Evans was locked in a room with a rotating guard posted outside of his door. A guard of lords, no less. Peter had not taken any chances.

Eventually her exhaustion had won out, and she'd enjoyed a night of solid sleep.

The carriages had parted ways at the turnoff to Evanslea, and Kate had finally let out a breath of pent up energy. Peter had sent her a kind smile, and soon after she had been helped down from the carriage and brought here, to her tearful reunion with Emily.

"Oh I have never worried so much in my life!" Emily cried, tears rolling freely down her face. Finally noticing Kate's borrowed gown of coarse, brown wool, Emily's eyes widened fractionally. "I can scarce imagine all you've been through."

"It's a long story," Kate replied with a strained smile. She lowered her voice. "And I find myself in great need of a proper bath."

Emily nodded, no doubt glad she had been given a chore she could easily accomplish. "Come, I'll send for one straight away."

Peter remained by the coach, and Kate turned, confused at why he wasn't following her inside until she realized that he most likely wanted to go to his own home and deal with his brother. She pulled her arm from Emily's grasp and turned back to him.

"Thank you," she said simply.

He nodded. Their gazes were linked momentarily in a heavy connection. She was both saddened and anxious at the thought of being separated from him; she could not be certain, but she sensed he felt much the same way. He stood there with a beaten expression and she knew that he was about to go and do a very hard thing.

"Kate?" Emily nudged, pulling them both out of the moment.

"Right, then." Peter bowed and climbed into his carriage, and Kate watched him pull away before Emily took her arm and led her inside.

"What was that about?" Emily asked when they reached the safety of Kate's room.

She sat on the bed, feeling overwhelmed and fatigued. A maid carried in a tin bath and another followed with two pails of water.

Kate watched the steam curling off of the water and felt her eyes drooping. The madness of the last few days had caught up to her, and she watched the maids come and go with boiling water until the bath was prepared. She went through the motions of bathing then dressed in a nightgown though it was only midafternoon, and crawled into bed. Emily quit asking questions after her first few went unanswered, and Kate was glad for the reprieve when her friend slipped away. She would explain everything eventually, but for now she needed to sleep.

Peter

Peter paced back and forth in his study. The path was clear, but he didn't want to follow it. A large part of him was torn between the love he carried for his deranged brother and the need to let the justice system do its job.

Cohen had come up with a good solution, but Peter did not know if taking his friend's advice would be going against King and Country, which he had a strong inclination to do. His mind kept flashing back to the image of Kate tied up on the floor, and he wanted to strangle Martin. But he also knew Martin held a sort of hero worship for Kate after she'd saved him from his mean older brothers.

Peter could not help the wry smile that fit on his lips. Of course, it had all been Charles's idea. It always had been. But Peter hadn't helped much. It wasn't until he was older and away at school that he had grown enough of a backbone to step away when things had gotten out of hand. It was no surprise to Peter that Charles had died in a reckless race, however hard it had been to cope with at the time.

"Have you come to a decision?" Cohen asked from the doorway. He was leaning back with his arms in his pockets, a common pose the man used to hide his missing hand.

Peter sighed and dragged a hand over his face. "Yes, but is it the right one?"

Cohen shrugged. "That is for you to decide. I will support you either way."

Peter sat down before the fire and rested his head in his hands. When he heard Cohen come and sit beside him, he voiced the question that plagued his mind. "Do you think Kate will take it as a personal offence if I take you up on your offer?"

There was a long stretch of silence, and Peter glanced up. The look in Cohen's eye was all he needed. He nodded once and stood, finally decided on the matter. "Well," he said. "I suppose it is time to go and tell Martin."

"Would you like me to come?"

Peter clapped his friend on the back with his good hand and squeezed his shoulder. "I better do this on my own."

Martin

Martin sat in the parlor, the oaf, Lord Marshall, watching him from a plush, wingback chair on the other side of the room. As if he needed such close supervision. He was no child.

Sighing, he crossed his foot over the other ankle, fingering the ends of the thin rope that bound his wrists. He'd tried to pull on the loose end, but it seemed to only tighten the knot. If only he'd gone to Gretna Green instead, he'd be a married man now, with naught anyone could do about it. Least of all, Peter.

Lord Marshall looked on with a shrewd, narrowed gaze, and Martin had to admit that the man was quite intimidating when he chose to be. Not that Martin would ever give him the satisfaction of admitting so aloud. Instead, he remained still, composed in the face of this uncertainty.

The door opened and Peter stepped inside, creating a deep, hard knot in Martin's stomach. Peter nodded to Lord Marshall, who immediately rose and stepped out of the room, closing the door behind him. It was disgusting how devoted these men were to Peter, how he bossed them around with no thought for their opinions or cares.

Peter stood at the end of the rug, five paces from where Martin sat. He raked his gaze over Martin as though attempting to puzzle him out. "I won't mince words. If the magistrate gets his hands on you, it's gaol at the very least, hanging at worst."

Martin went cold, the blood draining from his face. Hanging? Death? He wanted to shrink, to beg—but he couldn't, so frozen he felt. Everything had been so meticulously planned, from the foxglove in Bartholomew Kingston's tea, to extricating himself from the bounds Miss Smithson had tried to shackle him to. Gibson had slipped in and out of the outing to the vista perfectly unseen, he'd shoved Miss Smithson from the edge of the lookout undetected, and *still* she remained with child. But Martin had planned so thoroughly, been so flexible when things hadn't gone his way. Up until London. He screwed his eyes shut. He'd been *so close* to having Kate as his own. Where had he gone wrong?

Peter cleared his throat. "I have an alternative, but the choice is yours."

Silence stretched as Martin refused to speak, to give Peter the satisfaction of seeing him grovel.

"Cohen is willing to escort you to Antigua and teach you the sugar trade," Peter said. "You'll be out of England's reach and have the opportunity to build a life for yourself there, but you will not be able to return. Ever."

Martin clenched his teeth. He didn't want to go to a barbaric, lowborn island and *work*. He was too smart for such a menial life, and he deserved far better than that. He regretted now, more than ever, not directing the carriage to Gretna Green. But failing to secure a marriage was all Martin regretted. Nothing else. "And what if I refuse?"

Peter

"Then I'll take you to the magistrate, and it will be out of my hands."

Peter hated this. Martin sat slumped and angry, a shriveled

man destroyed by bitterness. But he had made his choices; no one had forced him to do any of it.

"Can I ask why you did it?" Peter asked.

"I love her."

Well, that was misguided. At least according to Peter. "But why hurt Harriet Smithson? Surely it would be far better to break a betrothal than take her life?"

"I wasn't trying to take her life," Martin said, his voice cold. "My purpose was to remove the child."

Peter's heart clenched, disgust souring his stomach. He'd seen the depths of Martin's derangement in recent days, but this was too much. He was tempted to leave, to call on the magistrate at once.

"But it was foolish of me. I can see my error now." He scrubbed a hand over his face. "I'll do it. I'll go to Antigua."

Peter didn't know if Martin referred to the error of his ways, or his errors in failing. He cleared his throat. "Cohen will manage you closely. It will not be easy."

"My penance?"

"I hope so."

37

PETER

*P*eter stood on the front portico of his vast home and watched the hired coach carry his brother away for the last time. He was glad his brother had chosen Cohen's offer, and was equally relieved it was Cohen escorting Martin away, and not himself; he did not think he could leave Kate again right now, even if he had to. He was already in his riding attire, and the morning air was crisp and clean, the sun burning off the last of the frost that dusted the earth.

When he came around the corner and Split Tree came into view, he scanned the area for Kate before moving toward the stables. A groom informed him that she was out at her orchard; he was equally excited and nervous to see her again.

When she came into view, his heart skipped a beat. Mrs. Nielsen was beside her, their horses tied to a nearby elm.

"Sir Peter," Mrs. Nielsen said, her voice laced with surprise. Kate's head shot up and the shock in her widened eyes momentarily worried him. Was she not happy to see him?

"Good morning, ladies. I was out for my ride and thought to come bid you a good day." He could hear the strain in his own voice and wondered what Kate made of it. He gazed at her intently, the height from his horse adding to the distance between them. He slid down to be on more level terrain with her.

Mrs. Nielsen cleared her throat and turned to Kate. "I will go ask Mr. Cruikshank that question we had about...the, um...the plum tree. Should you need me."

And like a good chaperone, she slipped away quietly.

Kate

Kate did not know whether to run into his arms or sit down and cry. She was anxious, alternating between feeling a decided fondness for the man—more than fondness, if she was being honest—and wondering if he reciprocated her feelings. She stood where she was, stiff and taut.

The way he'd saved her, held her, cradled her head with such tenderness had led her to believe the man felt more for her than that bound by the confines of friendship, but after leaving London he had kept a decided distance from her.

His eyes in the morning light were a clear blue, and his hair shone more gold than brown. Purple marred his forehead, the faint bruise beginning to yellow at the edges. He shuffled his feet and looked away briefly before clearing his own throat. "Are you well?"

"Yes," she answered.

Silence hung between them as he nodded. She traced the bruise on his temple and the smaller one on his opposite cheek with her gaze, wondering if they pained him much.

He watched her intently. "Martin left this morning."

"Oh?" she replied. She felt foolish for her benign answers.

Where was the easy banter between them? The comfortable conversation?

"This is ridiculous," he muttered, running a hand through his hair.

"Agreed." She drew in the sweet morning air and blew the breath out between her teeth.

"Can we walk?" Peter asked.

"Certainly." She took his arm, and they began walking down the first row of apple trees. They were so young they hardly peeked over Peter's riding boots, but she still loved the feeling of being surrounded by the beautiful trees—the new, fresh life.

"Mr. Gibson has yet to be found," Peter said. "If that was indeed his real name. He appears to have vanished from Larkfield entirely."

Kate shook her head. "I am sure he is miles away now. Though, I do not find that worrisome. He was merely Martin's pawn, was he not?"

Peter nodded. Clearing his throat, he said, "Cohen offered Martin a position at his sugar plantation in Antigua, and Martin took it. There were stipulations, of course, but he agreed to every one of them. It was either that or turning him over to the magistrate, and I think he found Antigua to be the lesser sentence. According to Cohen, he is in for a world of hurt. It is not an easy climate or culture to acclimate to."

"Right. He would know."

Peter stopped. They were halfway through the aisle of trees, and he turned to face her. "Does this bother you?"

Her eyebrows pulled together in confusion. But Peter looked so concerned, his eyes darting about, raking her face as though searching for something. But Martin was going to be an ocean away—why would that bother her? "No, I think it is a fine solution."

Peter let out the pent-up breath he must have been holding in for ages. His entire body relaxed, and she could see, now that the lines of his face were serene, just how troubled he had been before.

"Did you worry that I would be upset?" she asked. "I do not wish him ill, Peter."

He looked dubious, and she placed a hand on his arm.

"Your brother may frighten me, and I can truthfully admit I do not want to ever see him again, but I cannot wish harm against him. He was a foolish man who made irrational, alarming decisions, but what good would it do *me* to hold onto anger?" She softened her voice, squeezing his arm. "What kind of person would I be if I preached forgiveness to you and then held hatred in my heart for Martin?"

Peter's eyes shone, the beautiful blue-gray stunning in the sunlight.

She smiled sadly. "I have a feeling that getting him out of the country before Miss Smithson catches wind of what he did was a very smart move."

"Actually, it turns out that Miss Smithson's situation is far more complicated than I'd imagined." He rubbed his temples. "She's with child."

Kate's mouth dropped open, stunned. That certainly explained why Martin would be so concerned. "Will she go to Antigua?"

"I'm not sure it's safe. No, I think I will have to make certain she's cared for, that she finds a comfortable situation. I thought to offer her the dower house behind Evanslea. It's been closed up for some time but would be a fine home with some heavy cleaning and possibly a few upgrades. I owe it to her after what Martin did."

Kate nodded. "I will do what I can to help."

He gazed at her with adoration, and her heart skipped a beat. This was the expression she'd seen when he'd found her tied up. This was the man she believed might care for her.

Her pulse raced, and she lowered her gaze. It would be best

to calm her heart, but she did not know how. Clearing her throat, Kate did her best to remain composed. "Can I ask what the stipulations are on his return?"

"I thought he should never return, but we shall see. He cannot come back before seven years have passed, and he must have it approved from me in writing."

"That is reasonable."

Peter nodded. "I hope seven years of hard work will teach him a thing or two. Cohen knows of a man thinking of selling his plantation in a year or so, and it happens to neighbor his. I would consider buying it and hiring Martin to manage it if he has proven himself by that point. But we will have to wait and see."

Kate smiled proudly up at him, gratified to see the compassion and kindness he showed to his brother despite the terrible choices Martin had made.

"Meanwhile," Peter said, gazing into her eyes with a sudden fierceness that thrilled and scared her at the same time. "There is another joint venture I would like to propose to you."

"Yes?" she asked, breathless. He was probably going to ask her about trees or something, but she just could not pull herself away from his handsome smile and the dimple that appeared next to his lips.

"How would you feel about combining our resources and sharing a life together?"

The world felt as though it ceased moving. Birds became silent, Emily and Mr. Cruikshank disappeared, even the wind quit howling softly in her ear. Kate searched Peter's kind eyes and found joy shining within them, mirroring the happiness erupting within her soul. She stepped toward him as if his very smile was pulling her closer. "I think I should enjoy that very much."

"Then what do you say to becoming my wife?" he asked,

snaking his arm around her waist and resting the other palm on her neck, his fingers getting lost in her hair.

She wanted to close her eyes against the feel of his fingers on her, but she could not tear her gaze from him. This was comfortable. This was the easy banter she'd been missing. Peter had begun as a confidant, a friend. Now, he was far more dear. "I say yes."

Peter gave her a decidedly boyish grin before closing the gap between them and bringing his lips to hers.

An explosion of warmth moved through Kate's body in his comforting embrace, his arms tightening as if he could not get close enough. She rested her hands on his chest and relished the quick beat of his heart under her palm as he made her feel loved and cherished. He pulled back a minute later—all too soon in her opinion—and gazed into her eyes. "Should we post the banns this Sunday?" he asked.

Kate couldn't help but laugh loudly, Peter joining in with a chuckle that rumbled under her fingertips. "If you wish," she said when her tears dried. "Though I must meet with Mr. Cruikshank and Mr. Balham together before any plans are finalized."

"Whatever for?" Peter asked, taking her hand and leading her back to where they left their horses, his thumb rubbing lightly over her knuckles.

"Well, if I am going to move into Evanslea, I must find a way to keep my orchard."

He paused midstride. "We cannot sell Split Tree," Peter said, affronted.

She gazed up at the beast of a man with a tender heart. "Why? We will have Evanslea, and we do not need two estates."

"We can rent it out for a time, perhaps," he conceded. "But what if we have more than one son? I should think you'd like to pass on some of your own legacy."

Kate smiled at the thoughtful man. She imagined him sitting beside a cozy fire with his arm around her and a golden-headed baby nuzzled in her arms. It was absurd thinking back on the past few months that she had considered herself well suited to Martin, when she and Peter were so clearly meant to be. Perhaps Emily had been right all along, and the best way to go into marriage was with a strong foundation of friendship.

"Very well," she agreed. "But one last condition."

Peter raised an eyebrow to her, and she sighed dramatically. "We must find a gentle way to break the news to Mrs. Gressle that she is being booted out of her honorary role as Evanslea's mistress."

"That will be tough," he agreed. "She's taken on the role for a good decade, at least."

"I think we'll manage to come up with something," Kate said, stepping up on her toes to kiss him once more.

"I have a feeling," Peter said, his fingers splaying over her back, "that I am going to find a life with you to be both wonderful and full of surprises."

"Well, naturally. It would be so boring any other way."

He chuckled and pulled her closer. She sent up a prayer of gratitude for the things that surrounded her; a man that cared for her, new land she had a hand in developing, and most importantly, a home within this new adventure that would be full of love, compassion, and forgiveness.

EPILOGUE

"*F*retting will not bring us to London any faster, Emily," Kate said, reaching across the carriage seat to pull her friend's gloved hand into her own.

Emily tipped her head back, resting it on the squab and closing her eyes. "But what shall I do if he is very much changed?" she asked quietly, her voice hardly above a whisper.

Kate shot a look to Peter, sitting directly across from her, and he nodded once, his eyebrows drawn together in compassion.

"No man returns from war unscathed, Mrs. Nielsen," he said gently. "And from what I have heard about Waterloo thus far, your husband will indeed be much changed."

Emily squeezed Kate's hand harder, her eyes pinching in accordance with her fingers.

Shooting a wide-eyed look at Peter, Kate wondered at his motives. He merely shook his head, however, and continued, his voice low and warm. "What you can do for him, Mrs. Nielsen, is give him your unceasing love and support. He will undoubtedly need time to heal from his wounds, both physical and mental."

Emily sat up, regarding Peter warily. "Mental? Surely you are not suggesting—"

He lifted a staying hand. "Trust me, and you shall be able to help him far better. He will need understanding, even if he believes you to be incapable of offering it. And he will need support. It is not unheard of for soldiers to have terrible dreams after returning home, recounting their time on the battlefields, or even recalling those horrid moments in the middle of the day. Some men wish to discuss everything, to unburden their souls, and some men cannot bear to speak one word of it."

Pregnant silence fell upon the carriage occupants as they rolled forward, jostling from the pocks in the road.

"But," he said, his voice unwavering, "whatever you do, never cease loving him."

Silent tears rolled down Emily's cheeks as she shook her head. "I never could."

Sliding an arm around her friend's back, Kate pulled her into an embrace, rubbing Emily's shoulders as her friend cried concerned tears.

They had received the news of Wellington's triumph at Waterloo just a month prior, and the entire households of both Split Tree Manor and Evanslea had waited with bated breath for a missive from Paul. When one finally arrived, Emily had ripped it open, devouring the contents before throwing herself onto the sofa in a fit of sobs and tossing the letter at Kate for her to read.

Paul was returning to England, but he was not whole. A bayonet had slashed him near the ribs, and while he was expected to make a full recovery, he was not yet fully healed.

Right away, Peter had set to securing a swift transport to London and offered his townhouse to the Nielsens for the duration of Paul's infirmity.

They had planned to arrive in London prior to Paul but had received word that the soldier was ahead of schedule, and Emily had been a frantic nest of nerves ever since.

Peter reached across the carriage and took Kate's fingers in his own, squeezing them softly while he shot her the smile she loved so dearly. Their wedding had been set for the end of the summer, and she found that time seemed to crawl while she waited for that blessed day to arrive.

"We are nearly there," Peter said softly.

Emily pulled away from her friend and wiped at her eyes with her sodden handkerchief. Kate pulled her own from her sleeve and offered it to her friend as the carriage rolled to a stop.

Releasing a shuddering breath, Emily held tightly to her handkerchief. Resolve fell over her face.

"Are you ready?" Kate asked.

Emily nodded, and Peter opened the carriage door, letting down the step before helping Emily to alight. The woman climbed the stairs, immediately stepping inside and speaking to the butler before Kate had so much as placed both feet on the paving stones.

Kate followed Peter up the steps and into the foyer. The last time she had stood in his townhouse was shortly after wondering if she would be forced to marry his deranged brother. Her gaze resting on the handsome, giant man who had saved her, she was overwhelmed with gratitude and relief. Martin was far, far away, and Peter loved her enough to wish to become her husband.

"Mrs. Nielsen has gone upstairs, sir," the butler said to Peter.

"Thank you, Farley."

Peter directed Kate upstairs and they followed the stifled cry they had heard the entire way to London until coming upon a chamber with an open door. The scene arrested Kate. Paul lay on the bed, stroking Emily's head. She had thrown herself across the mattress, her hands buried in Paul's chest as he continued to stroke her, his eyes closed and a contented expression on his face.

Closing the door quietly, Kate stepped away from the

chamber and leaned against the wall. "I am so glad he has returned to us."

"I'm certain he feels the same way," Peter whispered, stepping closer.

"And I am more delighted that they've accepted our offer to rent Split Tree and manage the house. It is my dearest wish to have Emily and Paul for neighbors."

"Only a fortnight left until the wedding, and then Split Tree is all theirs."

His hands came down to rest on her waist and Kate placed her fingers on his arms. "Thank you for preparing Emily."

Peter shook his head. "Perhaps Paul will not be so badly distressed. I only hope he can recover quickly, in every sense of the word."

Tugging on Peter's sleeves, Kate drew him closer before coming up on tiptoe to place a kiss on his lips. She flattened her feet once more, but Peter bent down, continuing the kiss with fervor, his hands leaving her waist to cup the back of her neck. Warmth filled her heart as Peter drove her against the wall, his fingertips pressing into the skin behind her ears.

Drawing back, he held her gaze, his chest heaving quietly. "I love you, Kate."

She smiled, displaying her uneven teeth to completion. But with Peter's love, she did not care. She was not concerned with delivering the perfect smile for the man who loved her wholly, unabashedly.

"I love you, too."

SEASONS OF CHANGE

*Stand-alone books that can be read in any order

ACKNOWLEDGMENTS

I will never be able to thank all of the people who made this novel possible, but I'll do my best.

Thank you Jon, my husband, for being my biggest support. For doing all the dishes, keeping the kids fed, and making it possible for me to pursue my dream.

Thank you to my kids, my little cheerleaders who still think I'm cool and make me feel like a celebrity. I'll enjoy this as long as it lasts.

Thank you to my incredible editor, Jenny Proctor, who helps me develop my stories and polishes them into something readable. I could not publish without you.

Thank you Ashtyn for creating a beautiful cover. I have such talented friends.

Thank you to my incredible critique group for helping me improve each step of the way, Martha, Jess, Emily, and Evelyn, your input and support is invaluable. Thank you to my beta readers, you are so instrumental in this process and I am so grateful for you! Martha, Deborah, Emily F, Grace, Kandice, Emily S, and Nic, thank you for your feedback!

And thank you to each woman participating in the Seasons

of Change series, I feel so fortunate to have found such a fantastic group of authors and grateful they were willing to include me. To the SRR admins: you ladies are such a wonderful support group and I'm so glad my author career has led me to you!

And finally, thank you readers for being willing to step into this world I've created and giving my book another life.

ABOUT THE AUTHOR

Kasey Stockton is a staunch lover of all things romantic. She doesn't discriminate between genres and enjoys a wide variety of happily ever afters. Drawn to the Regency period at a young age when gifted a copy of *Sense and Sensibility* by her grandmother, Kasey initially began writing Regency romances. She has since written in a variety of genres, but all of her titles fall under sweet romance. A native of northern California, she now resides in Texas with her own prince charming and their three children. When not reading, writing, or binge-watching chick flicks, she enjoys running, cutting hair, and anything chocolate.

Made in the USA
Coppell, TX
16 November 2021

65871116R00187